NOTORIETY C

'Ned, something quite momentous has happened. Something which will put the name of Knockpeddar on the lips of the whole artistic world – something that will bring down tourists by the thousands, industries by the hundreds and vested interests by the score. Something which will make every one of us stinking rich if we play our cards right.'

'Eh?' said Ned uncomprehendingly. At nine a.m. and after only one swig of his curer, Edward's was not the sharpest brain in the district.

'Remember Pat Brodie's brother that went to America and got married out there to some lassie from West Cork? Well, they have a son – Jim Brodie. Did quite well for himself by all accounts – he has an important job in a big hotel in Hollywood and seems to know all the film stars and all that. Well, he sent a letter to his uncle Pat to say that some producer out there is coming here to make a film in Knockpeddar. There now, what do you think of that?'

Knockpeddar and the Sweet Life

DOLORES ROCKETT

SPHERE BOOKS LIMITED
30–32 Gray's Inn Road, London WC1X 8JL

First published in Great Britain by
Sphere Books Ltd 1984

Reprinted 1984

This novel is a work of fiction. Any resemblance to actual events, locales or persons, living or dead, is purely coincidental.

TRADE
MARK

Set in Times

Printed and bound in Great Britain by
Cox & Wyman Ltd, Reading

Chapter One

In the peaceful village of Knockpeddar, a very minor gem in the heart of the Irish tourist crown, the day started like any other day. It rained.

The cluster of houses was a dirty white under the downpour and in the local hostelry, of which the village boasted but one, the proprietor Mr Edward Clancy, familiarly known to one and all as Ned the Head, surveyed with loathing the debris of glasses from the night before.

Again he told himself, how much wiser it was to clear up after closing time, until his head reminded him that he had really been in no condition to do more than pull down the blinds, take off his tie and his boots and retire to his unsalubrious couch – he was a bachelor as the cream of Irish manhood is.

Reluctantly he filled the basin under the bar with hot water and dumped in the glasses. Almost absentmindedly, he dried one and poured himself a curer. He had hardly put the first hair of the dog into his protesting stomach when there was a thunderous knock on the door of the pub.

'For God's sake!' he moaned, staggering painfully over to the entrance, and unfastening the large and old fashioned lock which ensured his nightly safety from disgruntled imbibers after hours. 'Do you want to burst the head off me entirely?'

He opened the door to admit the lean and hungry looking figure of Miss Margaret Mary Dunphy, Knockpeddar's post-mistress, who was in a state of wild excitement.

She had not even taken time to put on the black pudding bowl-shaped hat without which she was rarely seen even behind her post office counter, so that one never knew whether she was going or coming. In fact, there were some who said that judging by the way the office was run, the postal authorities were not so sure either.

Miss Dunphy led an uneventful life among her stamps and pension forms. She had, however, a fascinating and sometimes informatively profitable hobby – she steamed open every mortal bit of mail that came stuck down or otherwise secured – with the exception of course, of registered jobs, since she had not yet discovered a foolproof method of lifting the seals. Now, it was obvious that something outstanding had been steamed open. She was even clutching the envelope in one bony hand to prove it.

'Ned!' she said dramatically – Miss Dunphy was an ardent member of the Knockpeddar Amateur Drama group and had never quite recovered from the excitement of being honourably mentioned at one of the Southern drama festivals ten years back.

'Ned, something quite momentous has happened. Something which will put the name of Knockpeddar on the lips of the whole artistic world – something that will bring down tourists by the thousands, industries by the hundreds and vested interests by the score. Something which will make every one of us stinking rich if we play our cards right.'

'Eh?' said Ned uncomprehendingly. At nine o'clock and after only one swig of his curer, Edward's was not the sharpest brain in the district.

'Of course, we must make plans – many plans. Everything must be done to perfection – yes, to perfection.' She clasped her hands before her. 'I only hope the dear Canon won't disapprove. After all, these people may well learn much from the humility and piety of our people and when they return home, they may go with a deep appreciation of the worship of God rather than Mammon. Anyway, the church collections are bound to treble themselves, and that should keep himself as happy as a bird on a bush.'

'Look Maggie Dunphy, will you give over tryin' to do St Joan and tell me what in hell you're talkin' about,' cut in Ned irritably. His head was banging like a Lambeg drum on the Twelfth and he yearned with only a hungover Irishman's yearning, to get back to his waiting glass with its comforting amber liquid.

'Amn't I telling you if you weren't too drunk to take it in – and don't call me Maggie; I keep telling you I was called Margaret after my mother's sister who went to Australia and was the first ever who took her pile with her when she died, the stingy oul' faggot – and they added Mary after my father's eldest sister, who was the most cultured and beautiful woman that ever drew breath.'

'A pity then that she didn't pass on a bit of that culture an' good looks along with her name,' said Ned sourly, heading back behind the bar, and grasping his life-giving shot in a large and trembling fist.

'Politeness is the mark of kings and I'll have a small port, thank you,' rejoined Miss Dunphy, happily chalking up a mental victory to herself, since Ned was as ready to give a free drink as a mink is to part with its skin. Glumly he poured the port.

'Now, will you start all over again and tell me what all the excitement is about?'

Miss Dunphy took a dainty sip from her glass and laid it back on the counter. With a fine sense of drama she withdrew the letter from its envelope, now slightly the worse for wear from the steam of her kettle and the driving rain of the Irish day.

'This!' she said, unfolding the letter with a flourish.

'Remember Pat Brodie's brother that went to America and got married out there to some lassie from West Cork? Well, they have a son – Jim Brodie. Did quite well for himself by all accounts – he has an important job in a big hotel in Hollywood and seems to know all the film stars and all that. I believe he actually met Bing Crosby.'

'Will you for the love of God get on with it?' said Ned in exasperation. Left alone, Miss Dunphy was likely to develop the theme so well that her original reason for coming in would get smothered in an avalanche of family history.

'Oh yes, now where was I. Well, this lad of the Brodies sent a letter to his Uncle Pat to say that some producer out there in Hollywood is coming here to make a film in Knockpeddar. There now, what do you think of that?' She lifted her glass again with a triumphant gesture.

'So what?' said Ned sourly, feeling about the show case for an aspirin.

'Ned Clancy, have you pickled your brains entirely in liquor?' Miss Dunphy stamped her foot. 'Don't you see what this is going to mean for all of us? Hundreds of big nobs looking for somewhere to stay. Yanks dropping in all day long for beers and whiskies. Doughnuts and sandwiches by the thousand to be sold and parts in the picture for the lot of us. Where else are they going to find all the extras they use and not a Christian living within forty miles of Knockpeddar other than the residents here themselves. And you ask me, so what. It's easy to see you're not a business man. You've no imagination at all, at all!'

Ned suddenly began to feel a lot better. The music in his ears was not from the aspirin but from the future tune on his cash register. He did mad mental arithmetic – a hundred people drinking six bottles of beer a day at a minimum, for didn't everyone know that a film took a power of people to make it?

He looked around the bar with glistening eyes, visualising them all standing four deep at the counter. Then he stopped. Four deep – good God, the pub wouldn't be half big enough to hold them all. Now, here was a dilemma. For a moment his spirits dropped, but another swig from his glass revived them. Something would turn up. Devoutly he hoped that a miracle such as was about to happen would be covered from every angle by a beneficent Providence. Yes indeed, something would be bound to turn up that would keep those hundreds of bottles moving regularly up and down his counter en route to the wealthy American gullets waiting to receive them. 'Gimmee a look at that,' he said, leaning across the bar counter.

'It's private property and I as a public servant am not at liberty to show personal mail to outsiders,' said Miss Dunphy primly, whipping the letter out of reach.

Ned sniggered and she gave him a piercing look.

'Have another,' he said hastily and Miss Dunphy choked on the mouthful she had just taken. A second free drink from Ned Clancy was an event worthy of being recorded in the annals of local history.

'Now tell me, what else did it say?' said Ned, pouring her no less than a double port.

Opening her coat collar, Miss Dunphy perched herself on the bar stool and with a slightly rakish gesture, knocked back half her port, reflecting that one would have to get used to drinking early and often, when one became a film star.

Chapter Two

In that mighty land of free white Americans, one red-headed James Brodie was filling in the time between his college degree and his co-option to any board of directors as a junior vice-president, by operating the elevator in the plush Hotel Etoile in Hollywood. A splendid figure of second generation Irish in his pearl grey and blue uniform which distinguished the staff of the Etoile from the anonymity of the clients, in Ireland James would have been snapped up by the officials for the promotion of Irish tourism, for he was one of the loudest and most inspired carollers of the beauties of the Irish scene.

The unimportant fact that he had never, as yet, planted a sneaker-shod foot on the land of his father's birth, had little bearing on his expertise in Irish lore. For Papa Brodie was one of the most ardently vocal patriots who ever shook the dust of Irish soil from his brogues and then spent the rest of his life from his safe American financial vantage point, lauding the charm of caubeens and cabins.

Not for James then, the beat, the pop scene, the world of rhythm, blues or Dixieland. To this once removed son of Erin, the scene was made in the ballads of the Gael, old and new. His eager heart delighted in the stirring roundelays penned in Denmark Street and in small offices on his native city's East side. As a small boy, his main object in life was to save up his weekly ten cents until he had enough to close the deal on Killarney, and indeed, he took it as a personal affront when someone beat him to the post. However, his savings were well spent on paperbacked collections of authentic Irish ballads, most of which he learned, and with a selection of which he whiled away the monotonous rise and fall of his day in the elevator. Fortunately for the hotel customers, he had a pleasing light tenor voice which they could put up with for the duration of the ride, even to the forty-second floor, and complaints to the management were few and far between other than from a jaundiced few who wanted to concentrate on taking their stomachs with them as they descended – James was a bit heavy on the button pushing at times.

This particular morning he was feeling exceptionally at peace with the world. His local movie house had run a travelogue on the Ring of Kerry the night before, and he had been fortunate enough to have been ensconced in the back row with his dearly beloved, the irreplaceable right hand woman of Hollywood's Most Adventurous Producer (We're Not Frightened of Life or Love) Mr Oscar Lipperstein. Miss Susan King, that delightful dark haired queen of the dictaphone, the written and the shouted word, who had a highly developed sixth sense concerning the requirements of Mr Lipperstein, most of which she attended to, a few of which she martyred at birth before he had a chance to put life into them.

Now, as he sat waiting by the lift for passengers, she came tripping into the hotel en route to Oscar's penthouse and James got the customary dash of adrenalin into the veins as he watched her progress across the terrazzo floor.

'Hi,' said Susan cheerfully. 'What new song have we to listen to this morning?'

James gazed at her with that slightly pie-eyed look which the first three months of courtship temporarily develops in warm-blooded young men. 'There's no song which could correctly describe your eternal beauty and charm, my adored one,' he said gallantly. 'But if I were asked to suggest an appropriate lay, then I would certainly decide on "My Love is the Joy of my Irish morning".'

'Very neat indeed,' rejoined Miss King demurely, 'except that your bump of locality is not working very well – this is America, my boy, and not your old man's beloved Knockpeddar.'

'Ah,' declared James, punching the lift button with a flourish, 'if only I could bring you to that quiet and gentle little village, where life moves as slowly as the easy flowing river; where white thatched cottages nestle against the bosom of the protecting soft green Irish hills; where you can find the real people – simple, uncomplicated, untouched by the vain struggle for riches which are so fleeting – at least, that's what my father always told me. Not,' he said by way of diversion, 'that I couldn't do with a few extra greenbacks right now – preferably the ones with the four figures in the top right-hand corner.'

'For what?' asked Susan sympathetically.

'My father's brother keeps writing to know when I'm going to brighten his life with a visit to Knockpeddar,' said James broodingly. 'He thinks I own this kip, so I'll have to go in style – if and when I ever raise the fare. And there's the important fact that he has no one to leave his farm to except me, and if I don't go over soon and stake my claim, he's likely to kick off without making a will.'

'There's no doubt about it but there's a lot of your mother's Cork blood in your veins, calculating like that and planning to sucker the poor man into willing you the old sod,' said Susan disapprovingly as the elevator slowed to a halt.

'Don't be daft – that's the practical Kerry man in me – who else is more entitled to it than his family? Do you want the Irish government to take it over and me to stay an elevator man all my life?' James called after her as she disappeared into Mr Lipperstein's suite.

As he brought the elevator down to the ground level again, James tried to picture Susan in snowy white apron feeding grain to equally snowy white hens. Somehow, even coloured by his romantic feelings, she just didn't seem to fit into the pastoral scene. However, he considered, maybe they could turn the farm into a guest house, where her undoubted business talents could be better utilised.

In Mr Lipperstein's suite – the most palatial in the hotel, naturally – a conference was about to begin. Mr Lipperstein was due to commence planning another epic which would keep the censors working overtime. Surrounded by his menials, he was a gruesome sight so early in the morning. He was, regrettably, one of those people whose stomach dimensions had expanded with his notoriety, while his stature remained at its original five feet three inches. Neither the perfumes of Arabia nor the chlorophyll tablets his pharmicist provided could sweeten the odour of garlic to which he was profoundly addicted; his breath and the smell of extra strong cigars which he chewed unlit meant that even Mr Lipperstein's devoted mother would have found it no easy task to come close enough to smooth his curly head.

The Most Adventurous Producer was seated at the head of the table, while his assistants parked themselves at a safe distance further down the sides. Susan had her own unobtrusive way of staying out of range of the garlic-laden aura surrounding her employer – she had her chair placed slightly behind him and, except when the door was opened, which was seldom since Oscar ordered a 'Do Not Disturb' sign for the outside when he held a story conference, Susan was spared a fate worse than seduction, that of being blasted to death by garlic and Corona fumes.

Oscar's temper was on the boil. He was under pressure from his top star, the scintillating knock-em-cold girl, Miss Dawn O'Day, originally named Loulie Bell, until Oscar discovered her shaking her hips in a strip joint, and saw enormous profit in their potential. Watered down enough to make it only slightly immoral, her pelvic gymnastics had been incorporated by Oscar's astute publicity team into Loulie's star build up, and she was now billed as 'Dawn "The Frivvle" O'Day', famed on screen and off for her libidinous undulation, vainly emulated by every would-be femme fatale who followed her career with avid longing.

Miss O'Day had Oscar well sewn up contractwise. Unless he turned up an epic in which she could appear, collect fifty per cent of the gross and her flat fifty thousand as well, Dawn could opt out and take her 'Frivvle' to another studio. And Oscar was well aware that at least three other competitors were breathing down her decolletage to get her to sign an even juicier contract than the one she already had with him. She was due at midday at the penthouse to vet the new story, and as yet, Oscar hadn't even the smell of anything which he felt she might go for.

'Whaddya got, Script?' he bellowed to the worried looking bespectacled writer on his left. Mr Klatch, who had long ago given up reminding Oscar that his name was actually Stanley, blinked nervously and swallowed.

'What about a nice South Seas picture, Chief?' he asked placatingly. 'I roughed out a little something last night . . .' and he shuffled through a tome of manuscript.

'Crap – you know that O'Day is allergic to mosquitoes and she wouldn't hear of humpin' herself off to the sunshine in case her goddammed nose might peel,' said Oscar, glowering at the company.

'What about takin' her to the North Pole and doin' a saga of the Black North? She'd look good in those fur outfits,' suggested the Assistant Director helpfully.

'Oh God! What a bunch of bums I got workin' for me,' mourned Oscar, mangling his cigar in the ashtray. 'Them fur robes are cut that loose that no one would see her hip shimmy and without it O'Day would be acted off the screen by them huskies!'

'And it would certainly destroy her image if she had to crack her whip and shout "Mush you bastards",' murmured Miss King with a grin. To Susan, Miss O'Day was a large dose of castor oil, and in Miss King's opinion, good for neither man nor beast.

Oscar ignored the comment, contenting himself with jamming another cigar into his mouth and giving threatening looks around the table. 'Someone had better come up with somethin' good pronto or I'm gettin' me a new team,' he rumbled.

'Well, how's about a lush harem job – the minimum covering the maximum, you know,' said the Publicity Chief after deep thought.

Oscar's face swelled up to awful proportions. 'I oughta fire you for that crack,' he bellowed. 'You should know by now that O'Day is very sensitive about anythin' that smacks of her old burlesque background. An' in my book, an Eastern harem is only a step removed from the "gettem-off-ya" routine.'

The Publicity Chief subsided. 'I only thought of the sort of stills and teaser photographs we could get out, Chief,' he muttered.

'Well forget it, and get your dumb brain to work on a new nugget. O'Day will be frivvelin' in here at noon and if I don't have somethin' on the table, there'll be hell.'

Susan who had lost interest after the North Pole had been knocked over, was thinking pleasant thoughts of her red-haired swain. Suddenly her eyes brightened. A perfectly brilliant idea had popped like a champagne bubble to the surface of her mind as it lingered on the ambitions of her ballad-carolling broth of a boy. Play this one cool, my girl, she told herself as she moved over to Oscar's chair, garlic fumes notwithstanding.

'Oscar, I've got an idea,' she said.

'Ya have?' rumbled Oscar, somewhat sceptical that even his treasured Girl Friday could come up with something which would fish them all out of the soup.

'Oscar, this country is made up of Irish back to the sixth generation, right?'

'Right,' agreed Oscar, hanging on to her every word.

'So, every time you get a picture with an Irish background,

what happens? The box office makes a packet, every mother's son who has a vein's worth of Gaelic blood queues up to see it. You have to keep it clean so that you don't wreck the legend of the place being full of saints and scholars, so the censor's office hardly runs it through, they're in such a hurry to mark it for family viewing. And Oscar, those Irish costumes, short red skirts, petticoats to swing around, sexy shawls and bare feet – they're a cinch for the bachelors' peep merchants in the audiences!'

'Well?' breathed Oscar, his mind running blissfully around the mental vision of Dawn O'Day frivelling her way about in a red flannel petticoat.

'So let's take the movie to Ireland and make it there with O'Day as a sweet innocent Irish colleen, God forgive us all. You get unspoiled scenery, no mosquitoes, no competition from huskies, no dance of the Seven Veils – just a nice simple, wholesome Irish romantic movie.' Susan stopped and looked around the table. Everyone was sitting motionless watching for Oscar's reaction to the idea.

'Don't you see Oscar, it'll be the Most Adventurous thing you've done yet – giving Dawn a chance to try and act. She's been moaning that her inner self as an actress is unsatisfied – mind you, I think she eats too many oysters, but that's not the point. She'll go for it hook line and sinker and you might even get her to renew her contract if she thinks you're going to treat her like she was a serious actress!'

Oscar removed the cigar from between his lips. 'I like it,' he pronounced, giving Susan a gold-tipped grimace which was the best he could do in the way of a smile. 'Yeah, I like it a lot. I guess it has plenty of possibilities and she can still frivvle as usual in between kidding herself she's a second Garbo.'

Everyone relaxed.

Susan geared herself for the next move. Knowing Oscar, she could anticipate what was to come, and she settled back with a secret smile.

'Right,' said Oscar. 'Now, what do youse guys know about Ireland?'

There was a deafening silence.

'Why Oscar,' Susan said sweetly, 'we've got an expert on Ireland right here in the hotel – a Mr James Brodie, the elevator man. He knows the country like the back of his hand!'

'An elevator bum?' said Oscar in disbelief. 'What in hell would a guy like that know from nothin''?'

Susan bristled. 'He's a college man, if you must know,' she said. 'He's on his way up and being an elevator operator is purely temporary until he finds someone interested enough to make full use of his talents.'

'An' you think I'm goin' to be de guy?' asked Oscar loudly.

'If you want to do this movie you'd better be,' said Susan, fighting hard. 'And in fact, if you don't hire him, you don't get me to go along either, and who's going to carry the can for you then?'

Oscar reviewed the situation in silence. Such an ultimatum from his right-hand woman was not to be lightly ignored. He made his decision. 'OK, let's have de guy in an' see what he knows.'

Chapter Three

The third Sunday of each month was quite an occasion in Knockpeddar.

His Reverence, Canon Finbarr Hackett, an understanding man who believed that the pleasures of the flesh and the demands of religion should be separated as far as possible, organised all the monthly church meetings on the third Sunday, so that over the years his congregation had accepted that day as being one entirely devoted to saving their souls, and they were happy to divide the day into church service, the Pioneer Total Abstinence Meeting (somewhat sparsely attended it is true), the monthly meetings of the Altar Society, the St Vincent de Paul and the Parish Committee, concluded by an evening service. The other Sunday evenings were their own which they could devote to keeping Ned Clancy in business and hangovers, or to the quaint rural pastimes peculiar to the Irish, which ranged from poteen making in the outlying hill country to more innocuous pursuits of lamp-shooting, poaching, ceilidh dancing, seduction and cockfighting.

The third Sunday then was obviously the best date for the big meeting to organise Knockpeddar's resources for the American invasion, Miss Dunphy decided, after consultation with Ned.

'It's the only day we'll get them all sober enough to make a definite decision on anything,' she said firmly.

'Are you suggestin' that I serve drink to customers already well under the influence?' bristled Ned, realising seconds too late that he had given the redoubtable Miss Dunphy an opening too good to be missed.

'Not at all,' she answered sweetly. 'I'm only saying that it does seem odd that it takes them four days a week to get over the effects of the rot-gut you pass out for branded liquor. If you had any competition here in Knockpeddar, you'd be able to drink yourself to death in half the time it's taking you as it is, because you wouldn't have a Christian in the place for the seven days of the week.'

Being a betting man, Ned knew he would be on a loser if he tried to win a conversational round over Miss Dunphy, so he didn't bother to sharpen his wit. Instead, he turned to the important matters of the moment. 'Who's going to talk the Canon into agreeing to holding the meeting in the Parochial Hall next Sunday?' he asked.

'You are,' said Miss Dunphy smartly.

Ned was horrified. 'Not me,' he protested. 'You know yourself that him and me don't see eye to eye.'

'Hmm, nor face to face either, Ned Clancy, from what I know about you,' replied Miss Dunphy drily. 'You don't exactly beat a path to the church door or to the confessional either.'

'My God,' said Ned bitterly, 'neither fuck nor fart is a man's own business in this bloody village. If you women were that busy saving your own souls ye wouldn't have the time to check up on the rest of us.'

'Be that as it may,' said Miss Dunphy somewhat disapprovingly, since she did not approve of questionable language. 'Maybe you are right about approaching the Canon. After all, he'd know right well that unless it was going to line your pockets, you'd never go near the presbytery to begin with, and he'd be sure to put a spoke in the whole thing. Perhaps I'd better do the job myself.'

'Ay, you do that,' said Ned with considerable relief.

'After all,' continued Miss Dunphy, 'I'm one of his hardest workers in the Parish and besides, no one bakes a soda bread as good as I do. You know the Canon loves a bit of soda bread. Particularly my recipe. I think it's the little drop of whiskey I always put into it when I bake a soda cake for him.'

'A soda cake to win him over with?' said Ned in disbelief. 'Are you mad? Shure nothin' less than a good donation for the St Vincent de Paul Society is called for at this time?'

'Now that's where you'd be very wrong,' replied Miss Dunphy. 'That would look like a bribe.' And she gave a most un-Dunphyish wink.

Canon Hackett was relaxing in his study after a particularly good dinner of roast pheasant, generously donated by one of his parishioners – just whom the Canon was not quite sure, and indeed, was not over-anxious to be told, since the only productive shoot was owned by Knockpeddar's only bit of real gentry, the Earl of Grange Peddar. Since the Earl was as much in the financial red as the rest of the village, he was more likely to flog the bag to Shannon Airport catering department, than present a bird to the Parochial House. The Canon's conscience dimly told him that his gastronomic gain was the Earl's financial loss. He was contentedly rounding off the meal with an excellently drawing pipe, when Miss Dunphy was announced. The Canon sighed a little when his housekeeper mentioned his caller's name. A worthy woman, Miss Dunphy, he reflected, but over-given to uncharitable comment on others and on the manner in which his Reverence conducted the parish affairs, especially the drama group. He hoped most earnestly that he was not to be subjected to a list of shortcomings tonight. It played hell with his digestion.

'Ah, do come in Miss Dunphy,' he said, making a gallant effort to look pleased. 'And what can I do for you?'

Miss Dunphy was well aware of his feelings and set out to be at her most charming. 'Thank you Canon,' she answered brightly, 'I won't delay you. Really, I came around to leave you a little bit of soda bread that I just took out of the oven. I know your appetite is not the best –' throwing a covert glance at the carcass of the pheasant still on the table – 'and I thought you might fancy a little cake.'

The Canon was delighted. He fussed around, finding her a comfortable armchair, removed her coat and the soda cake in one dexterous movement and poured her a cup of tea from the silver pot.

They chatted a while and then Miss Dunphy decided it was time to forget the courtesies. 'I have a little bit of news for you Canon,' she began tentatively.

'You have?' The Canon moved his chair towards her – one of Miss Dunphy's more valuable assets was the fact she kept him well informed on everything happening in Knockpeddar, so that he was forearmed with the right lecture when the erring came to get him to pull their particular chestnuts out of the fire. 'If you're going to tell me about the Heffernan girl, I already know. The mother came in to see me yesterday.'

'Mmm...' said Miss Dunphy tartly. 'It's not who she thinks it is, let me tell you. The fellow responsible for Mary Heffernan being in the family way is a transient from Galway, and he took himself back there to his wife over a week ago.'

'Oh dear,' said the Canon in dismay, 'and I did so hope we would get Mary fixed up at last and put that Maloney fellow out of circulation at the same time. He's such an undesirable influence on the young girls of the parish.'

Miss Dunphy sniffed. 'If you want to scuttle him, you'd better remove the distributor cap from his car. His operational area depends on his transport at the moment,' she said. 'He's exhausted the talent within a fifteen mile radius, and if you're not careful, in twenty years' time, you'll run the danger of intermarriage.'

The Canon sighed. 'Well, at any rate the Heffernan girl blames him and maybe he'll do the right thing by her.' He brightened. 'Ah well, the Lord will provide . . .'

It'll take more than the Lord's provision to get that ram up the aisle with the Heffernan girl or any other one, thought Miss Dunphy, but as she did not wish to shock the Canon's sensitivities she stayed silent.

'But I interrupted you,' said the Canon courteously, pushing Mary Heffernan and her growing problem to the back of his mind.

'Canon, what do we need most in Knockpeddar?' Miss Dunphy asked, leaning towards him until her eyes caught him with an almost hypnotic gleam.

The Canon was about to remark facetiously, 'a transient from Galway,' until he realised she was serious.

'Employment for our people, that's what we need,' Miss Dunphy rushed on before he got time to mention the new roof on the Parochial House.

The Canon nodded his head sagely. 'Too true Miss Dunphy, too true. We are sadly lacking in sources of employment. More occupation, less time for the vices of the flesh,' he said wistfully, his mind still on that quick-footed transient and the slow-witted Mary Heffernan.

'Canon, everyone knows how hard you and Mr O'Malley, our very respected Dail representative have worked to get industrial development for Knockpeddar without much success,' said Miss

Dunphy, raising her eyes upwards with commendable dramatic planning. 'Don't we all know how anxious you are to see our people prospering through an honest week's work, and haven't you always said how much you'd like to see Knockpeddar progress in the right direction?'

The Canon nodded in agreement. Encouraged that she had struck the right introduction, Miss Dunphy continued delicately. 'Even the tourist department in Dublin has ignored us – and here we are with one of the prettiest villages in the whole of Ireland. Why, there are beauty spots well worth mentioning around Knockpeddar that the Tourist Board could well include in their brochures if they knew about them.' Miss Dunphy hoped that the Canon was unacquainted with the lushest of Knockpeddar's beauty spots – the old Friars' Walk at the rear of the Earl's stately mansion, where most of Knockpeddar's shot-gun weddings got their target practice.

'Canon, opportunity comes but once, and one must take Time by the forelock, remembering that the Moving Finger writes,' said Miss Dunphy, frantically digging up half remembered passages from her literary readings. 'We will shortly have a unique opportunity to establish our village as an ideal tourist mecca and perhaps as an industrial centre for American big business, and that's what I came to see you about.'

The Canon gazed at her in fascination. A bead of perspiration was travelling relentlessly down the bridge of Miss Dunphy's nose to its tip with the effort of her declaration. His bemused attention was entirely taken up with the final potential destination. He calculated on the possibilities of its eventual arrival on her upper lip, but to his disappointment, as she paused for breath, she threw back her head and displaced the bead irretrievably. 'Dear Miss Dunphy, I am not quite with you,' he said mildly, dragging his mind away from its time and motion study with something of an effort.

'Canon, an American film company is about to come and make a film about Knockpeddar.'

The Canon immediately looked disapproving. Films, he thought, Sex, Orgies, Built-up bosomed blondes wandering down Knockpeddar's main street, cultivating even worse thoughts among his male parishioners than he already had to lecture about in the confessional. The few fifteen-year-old virgins left around the village in dire danger of yielding for a film part what they would undoubtedly lose happily for vague matrimonial promises in another year or so.

Miss Dunphy had a clear picture of what was passing through the Canon's mind. 'Canon, if we handle things properly this film could put Knockpeddar on the tourist map and even arouse the interest of some American magnate to come and build a factory here.'

The Canon still looked unconvinced.

'You know, you've often said that the village needs new blood and this would mean more marriages, more family life and more new people into the district. Indeed Canon, thinking it over, I wonder if the present church would hold all those people or if the school we have will be big enough at all. And certainly a couple of curates would take some of the work off your poor shoulders. Sure, we all know you're killed as it is.'

For a moment Miss Dunphy thought she might have overdone it, but she quickly saw she'd lost the Canon after the suggestion of a new church. For years, he had fought a losing battle with the termites, the woodworm, the ground damp and the rising damp, and the thought of a firm, soundly roofed and well heated place of worship was almost too much for him.

'This is quite a surprise,' he said, surfacing from the mental image of himself in a gilt ornamented hand-carved pulpit delivering a brilliant sermon to a massed congregation. 'And how did they decide on Knockpeddar as being a suitable choice?'

Miss Dunphy explained, carefully omitting the source of her knowledge. After all, she didn't tell the Canon absolutely everything.

'And what do you want me to do then?' asked his Reverence helpfully.

'I think this calls for a public meeting next Sunday after the devotions, to discuss the whole matter. Our people need to be advised on procedure and things like that, so that these people will not take advantage of them. You have shown them the value of their dignity, Canon, and it must be upheld. We don't want to look like a crowd of bog trotters, now do we?' Miss Dunphy smiled winningly.

The Canon looked a little less happy. To tell the truth, he was anything but keen to sit for yet another couple of hours in the freezing environs of the Parish Hall, after a whole Sunday of meetings. He had a monthly date with the Earl of Grange Peddar to play chess and he looked forward with an almost childish anticipation to the game and also to the exceptionally fine brandy the Earl still had in his cellar.

'Such a pity you cannot take the chair for the meeting, Canon,' Miss Dunphy rushed on hastily. 'But I know how much the Earl looks forward to your regular visit and the poor man has little enough in life since his wife passed away. It would be a shame to disappoint him, wouldn't it?'

With what she had in mind, Miss Dunphy was determined that the Canon would be anywhere but in the Parish Hall for her meeting, and to her relief, he nodded his head in agreement, his heart almost warming to the postmistress for her unexpected concern for the Earl's solitude.

Without much persuasion, he donated the Parish Hall for the meeting, lent his name in absentia to the Chairmanship, and, his duty done, he could betake himself with a clear conscience to the Grange and a decent supper.

Chapter Four

Her meeting with the Canon having been a resounding success, Miss Dunphy decided that this was her night for getting things done in the way she wanted them. So her next port of call was to the home of the politician that the people of Knockpeddar had been sentimental enough to return as their representative, despite a singular lack of success where their affairs were concerned on his part.

Mr Fonsie O'Malley was a fortunate man in many ways – he had gained his initial political seat, as indeed is common Irish practice, by virtue of the fact that his father had held it before him, thanks to having fortuitously chosen the right side during Ireland's uncivil war. And though he was the backest backbencher the Irish seat of government possessed, that is, when he was in the House at all, the general feeling in Knockpeddar when Fonsie's re-election came up was that he had his uses which had little to do with his ability to represent them. He was usually good for a donation to something or other, he could fix minor summonses for poteen making, provided he got a sample of the produce from the still, and he was always prepared to pull a string or two if one needed a job, a County Council grant, or a fast removal to the building sites of Britain.

Fonsie, an overweight bull-necked man who believed that fifteen minutes relax and stretch before his open window each morning made up for a tendency to eat enough for three other men, owned a contracting business which, he assured his voters, had gone to rack and ruin since his onerous political duties took him away from it. Strangely enough, as most of the leading Irish hotels could confirm, Fonsie was not exactly lacking in scratch. But then, Fonsie definitely had his uses – even if they could come a bit pricey at times.

He was in his study, checking his financial situation when Miss Dunphy approached the house. There were a couple of items . . . Fonsie shook his head dolefully and reflected on woman's inhumanity to man. As Miss Dunphy entered, however, he pushed the bank statements and account books aside. He didn't really like Miss Dunphy – she scared him considerably. Still, she was a voter, and a politician's first duty, he told himself righteously, was to interest himself in the concerns of his constituents.

Miss Dunphy wasted no pleasantries on Fonsie. After all, his operations, both business and personal, were more of an open envelope, as one might say, to her than they were to the rest of Knockpeddar. She removed her black woollen gloves and got right to the point. 'Fonsie, you've got to fix a council grant for me,' she announced without preamble.

Fonsie felt a vague irritation over what he considered Miss Dunphy's lack of proper respect towards a government official, not to speak of her complete lack of subtle delicacy in the approach she was making for what might well be one of the more valued favours that Fonsie could obtain for his constituents. He was about to adopt his favourite Dail expression of wounded dignity until he caught a peculiar look in Miss Dunphy's sharp eyes and he wisely forgot the whole thing. 'But surely the post office is government property and as such is maintained by them?' he queried in surprise.

'This is not post office business,' said Miss Dunphy.

'How much does the job involve?' asked Fonsie. As a building contractor, he naturally had his eye on the main chance.

'Not so much, really,' said Miss Dunphy airily. 'It's just for a little redecoration around the village. I'd say a few thousand would cover what has to be done.'

Fonsie swallowed. 'To cover what?' he croaked.

'A face lift for Knockpeddar, for one thing. A new lounge bar extension for Ned Clancy, a car park somewhere, big enough to take about thirty cars, a conversion job on one of the shops into a restaurant snack bar, and a few bits and pieces like that.'

She sat back and smiled at him.

Fonsie began to sweat. He looked around his study for a suitable weapon to defend himself with, should Miss Dunphy suddenly launch herself at him. It didn't seem possible that she could be working on all cylinders and, Fonsie reminded himself, one never knew what these nut cases would do.

'Relax Fonsie, I'm not out of my head,' said Miss Dunphy

calmly. 'There could be plenty of business in store for you, not only if you get the grant, but later on too. But we've got to get the grant in a hurry.'

She thereupon related to Fonsie the events which were about to rocket Knockpeddar to world fame and even though Fonsie could see the potential, he was definitely against pulling the particular strings which would bring in the loan from the Council.

'I can't do it,' he announced firmly. 'If I got a single job out of it, I'd be in dead trouble and anyway, I fixed a couple of loans lately for a few clients of my own. The pitcher can go too often to the well, you know.'

Miss Dunphy glanced around the comfortable room. 'What a lucky man you are to be sure, Fonsie,' she said gently. 'A fine home, and a healthy family – five children isn't it now? And you have a right good wife, stern perhaps, but firm in her religion and upright in her character – very upright. Ah, yes, Fonsie, many would envy you – sure haven't you everything that could make a man happy and contented?'

Fonsie nodded a little uncertainly. He hadn't quite caught up with the sudden change of topic.

'Of course, raising a family today is an expensive business,' Miss Dunphy continued, still gazing into the middle distance. 'That must take a fair share of money, what with your two boys at the University and your youngest girl at that hoity-toity boarding school . . . and I see you've been working on your accounts before I came in. Times get tougher financially for all of us, all the time. Tell me now, are flats dearer in Dublin these days than they are in Cork city? I hear that clothes are costing the girls a fierce price up in Dublin too . . .' She smiled at him again and Fonsie's jaw dropped. Miss Dunphy ignored it.

'You know Fonsie, I've been thinking that one of the things you ought to raise in the Dail is a way to have more careful censorship of the imported newspapers – really the reports of violence and scandal are getting quite beyond the boundaries of good taste. And the damage those scandal stories must do to the home lives of the people involved. Sure, what the public don't know about, the family can't grieve over!'

Fonsie was beaten. Even as he agreed to fix the loan for her, he swore he'd fix Miss Dunphy as well, but when she left him he realised only too well that he had little hope of achieving his newest ambition. No one, he told himself hopelessly, but no one was smart enough to call Miss Dunphy's tune, and he would be only one among many who had tried and failed over the years. It said little for the efficacy of the prayers of Knockpeddar's leading citizen that Miss Dunphy arrived safely outside her own front door and woke up next morning, refreshed and ready for action.

One of the greatest amenities since the arrival of the frying pan in the opinion of the people of Knockpeddar, was the advent of the Irish national television service. The village joyfully seized upon this piece of national ineptitude with the same eager delight as a customs official intercepting a suitcase of gold watches. For a full month after the village skyline was aerialised the flickering boxes were an exquisite diversion in the tedium of country existence.

Only Ned Clancy failed to throw his headgear in the air at the arrival of the world of commercials. Except for the village's acknowledged alcoholics, who would not have forsaken his pub even if Ireland was announced to be back in her former thirty-two county glory, Ned's business was suffering badly from a dearth of customers. However, on the grounds that when he couldn't lick it, he'd join it, Ned installed a television in the smaller snug at the back of the general bar, and business picked up to its old pace. In fact Ned's television snug was worth its weight in gold to all – Ned put a penny extra on the drinks to cover the cost of viewing and the male population quickly discovered an ideal refuge from their womenfolk, since the language got so blue on occasions that no self-respecting female could possibly join the company.

Passing the word of the Sunday meeting then presented few problems since Ned got a hundred per cent male attendance in his goggle room, while Miss Dunphy spread the word in the Post Office as she paid over the child allowances and the pensions.

Not that either of them related the full story – it was sufficient to whisper the words, 'there's money in it,' to guarantee that man, woman and child, the village would be in the Parish Hall on Sunday.

Chapter Five

Only his deep involvement in affairs of the moment could induce Ned to close up shop on the third Sunday, but shut the doors he did, much to the puzzlement of Mr Brenno O'Mahoney, whose doubtful honour it was to be entitled, with considerable justification, the village's leading imbiber. What time Brenno could spare from his corner seat in Ned Clancy's pub, and that was remarkably little since he had long devoted his career to maintaining his feat of drinking thirty pints at a sitting, if not to breaking his own record, Brenno spent on his ramshackle farm teaching his pet billy-goat as many tricks as it could master.

Admittedly, the goat was low in assimilation if reasonably willing in intent, and to date had only made two achievements, that of drinking stout from a milk can, and the ability to charge at full pelt when anyone enticed him with the pertinent words of command. However Brenno was greatly attached to his somewhat cumbersome pet, and would have been happy to bring it with him to Clancy's pub seven nights a week, had not the other customers objected so vociferously that he had to make the choice between leaving the goat at home or taking the pledge, since Ned refused to serve him if his odoriferous playmate was also included in the round. Still, drunk or sober, Brenno was always careful to bring his pet a nightcap of a can of stout when he returned from Clancy's, which they both shared in perfect unanimity, belching contentedly together, without the ridiculous notions about hygiene which were responsible for keeping Beauty, as Brenno had rather surprisingly christened his goat, tethered in the haybarn, instead of sitting like a respectable drinker in Clancy's.

When Brenno arrived at the pub he was astounded to find it in darkness, and even an investigation round the back, to see if Ned was knocking back the profits on the quiet, produced only firmer evidence that the place was closed to custom.

Brenno looked blearily down the street. At the far end the Parish Hall was still illuminated and he could see people hurrying in. Surely, he thought mistily, it's out they should be coming at this hour – unless there's a hooley on. Now here was fresh food for thought – in Brenno's book, an hooley meant refreshments of a liquid kind with a delicate cream spumy collar. At the back of his mind there trembled a thought that most of the Parish Hall entertainments were of the concert variety at which nothing stronger than committee tea was available, unless one counted the two back rows where a surreptitious bottle made continuous traffic back and forth until empty, by which time the occupants of the seats were usually ejected anyway to continue the session outside.

Well, it was worth trying at any rate, Brenno told himself, so he made his way down the street and sidled into a vacant seat in the back row.

The stage curtains were drawn back to reveal a table and three chairs which were as yet unoccupied.

'When's it start?' Brenno whispered to his neighbour. 'Is it a hooley, and when's the bottle comin' round because I'm fallin' with the drought, and that's for sure.'

'It's a meetin',' replied his neighbour, adding with a grin, 'Alcoholics Anonymous, Brenno – they're out to get you!'

Brenno half rose – he took a hunted look at the door but his avenue of escape had now been blocked by an overflow of patrons and it was impossible for him to get out again. With a moan he slid down in his chair, convinced that before the end of the night he would breathe his last in the Parish Hall and that the inquest which would certainly be held would reveal that he died of de-liquoration.

Miss Dunphy swept on to the stage with an aplomb which would have satisfied Sara Bernhardt. Her entrance was however, somewhat marred by that of Mr Edward Clancy to whom the limelight was an acute embarrassment without a glass in his hand. As he knocked over his chair before sitting down with a thump, Miss Dunphy frowned. Ned was going to mess up the dignity of the occasion unless she was careful, she told herself. Ned was followed by a perspiring Fonsie O'Malley, whom Miss Dunphy had also pressurised into coming along. She stepped forward to the edge of the stage and waited until the shuffles and the coughs had died down, before she began to speak.

'Mr Clancy and I have called this meeting because we have

important news for you, news which will prove remunerative for all of us.'

She paused, seeing puzzlement on the faces in the first two rows. 'We're on the way to making a power of money in the near future,' she explained tersely, and immediately there was a visible stir of interest among her audience – the first two rows sat forward intently.

'An American film company is going to make a picture here in Knockpeddar. We'll have to give them beds, feed them, probably act in the picture if I'm any judge, and between everything, there's going to be plenty of pickings for all of us if we do things right. That's why I got you all in here tonight because we want to discuss the whole thing and see how we can get the best deal that's going.'

Miss Dunphy paused again to observe the reaction of her audience. If she had just announced that the Goverment was doubling the amount of the child allowances, she could not have hoped for greater applause. She bowed with enormous dignity at the wave of clapping and held up a skinny hand to stem the flood.

'Now these Yanks are used to comfort and everything streamlined. And what have we got in Knockpeddar? Nearly half of you own privies instead of flush lavatories; everyone apart from his Reverence and his Lordship the Earl swabs down in a tin bath when they manage to get around to bathing at all, and there's hardly a tiled roof to be seen.

'Now, thatched cottages may look fine on picture postcards, but Yanks are used to everything done by push buttons and they're not going to settle for this little lot.'

There was a buzz of conversation and she held up a restraining hand once more.

'It stands to reason that if we have no ordinary amenities they may well go somewhere which does provide them, and then you can kiss your profits goodbye. So, we've got to give Knockpeddar a face-lift. Ned's going to do over his pub and install a decent lounge bar with proper stools and no spittoons. We've got to find somewhere we can turn into a restaurant so that we make sure they will eat in the village. And they'll need somewhere to park their cars, so we've got to provide a car park in some convenient spot. The more we can keep in the village, the more money we'll get out of them – that's the long and the short of it.'

By now the first two rows, composed of the farmers whose broad-striped Sunday blue suits belied the fact that the on-the-level tax returns of their incomes would probably clear the National Debt, were getting uneasy. They began to look round for the exits before they were asked for the inevitable donation to the face-lift fund. But Miss Dunphy pressed on rapidly before they had a chance to break up the meeting.

'I know you will be wondering where we're going to find the money for all this, but I'm happy to tell you that our respected government representative, Mr O'Malley, who is just as anxious as we all are for the village to make some real money, has agreed to put forward his recommendation to a County Council grant to meet the cost of all improvements.'

She bowed charmingly to Fonsie, who threw a slightly haunted smile at his constituents and ran a finger around his collarband. Miss Dunphy stemmed the wave of applause for Fonsie, led with great relief by the farmers in the front row – no use in letting him think he had a major part to play in this venture, she thought. Before one knew what was happening, Fonsie would be using the film in his next election campaign and vowing that it was his influence that brought the unit, the prosperity and the notoriety to Knockpeddar.

'Now there are a few facts we ought to get straight,' she resumed, giving a slightly steely glance around the hall. 'Americans are well-off and known to be fairly open-handed when it comes to paying for things. They love to stand drinks and look the big fellows in any party. They don't understand the value of the Irish coinage. They go overboard for anything connected with leprechauns, shillelaghs, Irish jigs, come-all-ye songs and rameishy stories that no sensible Irishman would ever believe. The Yankees are convinced they know it all, so it will not be necessary for us to try and educate them. This is all to the good and we might as well get what we can out of it.'

She looked around and dropped her voice a little. 'There's only one thing I must mention – our dear Canon is a simple man, the ways of big business opportunities are beyond his saintly brain, so we would be wise to keep the commercial side of this away from him. After all, this does not involve politics.'

A low murmur indicated that Knockpeddar had got her

message loud and clear, and Miss Dunphy was satisfied. One thing, she reflected, where finance was concerned, you never had to spell it out for Knockpeddarites.

'Now to begin with,' she said briskly, 'I propose that we organise a ballad group – that will provide the typically Irish entertainment our visitors will expect, just as long as no one decides to include such unsavoury numbers in the repertoire as "The Bedding of Molly O'Shea", the "Good Ship Venus" or any of the other disgusting innovations that appear to lighten the road of Saturday night drinkers, Fair Day boozing parties and wedding celebrations in this village. And do remember that an electric guitar is not the national instrument of this country, even if our national television authorities seem to support the illusion. One of you young women will have to learn to strum a harp, or else someone must find out how to handle a melodeon.'

Again, she fastened her audience with a steely eye. 'Remember, if you want to make money, no fee, no ballad singing. And I would ask you not to accept payment entirely in glasses of Guinness – it will set such a bad precedent for the rest of us who like our rewards in hard cash.'

In swift rotation, Miss Dunphy initiated the natives into Big Business – a load of leprechauns, Irish cottages, shamrock pen wipers, ashtrays and such like, stamped with the magic words 'Made in Japan' and now conveniently translated by the astute little yellow men into inaccurate Gaelic script, could be bought from a plump and highly prosperous Dublin agent with commendably patriotic ambitions to increase the Irish/Japanese trade until it infiltrated even the farthest reaches of West Cork. A quick conversion on the Irish side stabilised the Knockpeddar pound to stand at an exchange rate of four dollars – after all, it wouldn't do to be too greedy. All prices could take a twenty per cent rise to visitors, and Irish hospitality in Knockpeddar could not be denigrated by any sum less than eighty pounds a week, half board of course. It was not necessary, naturally, to advise Mr Clancy about his drink prices – indeed, Miss Dunphy reminded herself that a strong word of advice about marksmanship on Ned's part, when he had the golden geese between his sights, was definitely essential.

'Seems to me it's goin' to cost a power of money before we see a ha'penny back for it,' grumbled a voice from the centre of the hall. 'Flush toilets, interior sprung beds, bathrooms – how can we clean up from them if they think we're all livin' in the lap of luxury with all these codologies?'

'Look,' said Miss Dunphy patiently, 'you'll get the lot back in the first week with the rates we'll be charging them. The Americans may love quaint Irish customs, but they'll certainly hate our quaint Irish conveniences – they're the "Cleanliness is next to Godliness" kind, and they'll be too busy laundering themselves in your nice new bathrooms to have time to calculate what it's going to cost them in other ways. I know what I'm doing.'

The questioner subsided, and suddenly to his own surprise, Brenno, who had been only vaguely listening to the proceedings got his brilliant idea. It was so magnificent that it stunned him. He struggled to his feet, almost sober with the inspiration which had illuminated his mind. 'Ma'am,' he stammered. 'Did you say that somewan is goin' to make a fillum picture in Knockpeddar?'

Miss Dunphy stiffened for a moment, but when she peered into the dim recesses of the hall and recognised Brenno, she merely threw up her eyes and patiently explained that this was indeed the case.

'An' you say they're goin' to make the picture about Knockpeddar, an' everyone 'll get a part in it?' questioned Brenno. Miss Dunphy nodded. 'Ma'am,' said Brenno in a rush. 'Ye'll put in the word then for me goat. Shure, he'd have a good part once they'd take a look at his cleverality!'

'You'll keep that revolting animal out of sight, Brenno O'Mahoney, or you'll find it missing some night,' shrilled Miss Dunphy angrily. 'Bad we may be, but I guarantee that if your goat were brought within two miles of the producer, the whole thing would fizzle out and we'd be left without as much as an inch of wire to show these Yanks were ever in Knockpeddar. Remember now, I'm warning you – keep that goat out of the village!'

'That goat is as clever as any dog, and twice as human,' protested Brenno without much hope of convincing his audience. 'I'm teachin' him plenty of good tricks – they'll be lookin' for him, you'll see Maggie Dunphy.'

'Not,' said Miss Dunphy majestically, 'if I have anything to do with it they won't. And *I* expect to have a fair say in what goes on when the film people come.'

Brenno was outraged. 'Let me tell you, Beauty is more like to get a part in the fillum than you will – ya oul' bag. At least my Beauty has his looks!' With which remark, Brenno stalked out of the hall, dropping his cap as he did so, for which he was too indignant to return. He was mortally insulted at the rejection of his pet and later, as he rubbed its bony nose and told it the night's happenings, Brenno promised himself that somehow Beauty would have his chance of film fame.

'They'll be bookin' ye for the Late Show up on the Dublin television yet, me dandy,' he whispered as his four-legged companion licked out the last of the stout from the milk can. Just how he was going to arrange it, Brenno hadn't a clue, but with native optimism he felt something would surely turn up to assist his ambitions.

Chapter Six

Three weeks later, with considerable dignity as befitted the new Technical Adviser to Stupendo Films Incorporated, Mr James Brodie descended from his New York plane onto the unquiet land of Erin, and got his first ever look at the land of his forefathers.

Taking it all round, his illusions were a little shattered already. Where were the thatched cottages, the creel-laden donkeys, the untrodden Gaelic roads winding playfully without benefit of asphalt; where were the lilting Irish colleens whose musical native language and shy maidenly blushes were so legendary? So far, all he could see were Americanised factories, sleek fast moving automobiles; could only smell the drifting odours of curried prawns and floral air purifier, while the dulcet voices he listened to bore a definite resemblance to the dulcet vocal tones he had left behind in New York. And not an Irish cottage had he seen so far.

He collected his self-drive car and took off for Knockpeddar. A mile from the airport he was overtaken by a motor-cycled guardian of the law.

'Just got off the plane have you, sir?'

'That's right officer,' said James a little nervously.

'Ah,' nodded the minion of the law sagely. 'We drive on the left-hand side here, you know. Makes it less complicated like, if everyone follows the rule. You wouldn't want to do yourself a mischief on your first day here, now would you?'

James nodded co-operatively and the policeman leaned companionably against the door of the car.

'Will you be staying long in Ireland?' he asked, pushing back his scooter helmet.

'I expect I'll be here for a couple of months anyhow,' replied James. 'I am Technical Advisor to a film company which is planning to make a movie in County Kerry.'

'Do you tell me?' said the policeman with interest. 'That's a powerful job you must have to be sure. And where are they going to make the picture?'

'Knockpeddar,' said James. 'Do you know the village?'

The policeman burst into the kind of laughter one hears when a man with thirteen children is asked what he does for a hobby. James recoiled, a dreadful premonition gathering in his eager bosom.

'Knockpeddar is it?' sniggered the policeman. 'The village of spoiled virgins – I'm tellin' you there's more bastards to the mile down there than there are stone walls in Connemara. Your boys will want to come with plenty of American dollars – the women in Knockpeddar have a fierce firm way with the paternity allowance. There's little else for anyone to do down there, you see,' he added somewhat sympathetically.

'Is it a real simple unspoilt Irish village then?' enquired James with new hope.

'Oh it's that all right, if you don't count the virgins!' the policeman said, remounting his motor-cycle. 'However, if you keep the traffic lights in mind – you know, Caution, Stop and Go – you'll probably stay out of the courts!' He guffawed again and zoomed away leaving James still working it out.

James transferred his vehicle across the road and continued, thinking frantically of the demands of his new job. He had two weeks to get things organised and to familiarise himself with the ways of the land on which he was supposed to be the number one expert. Suddenly he wished he had concentrated less on O'Casey and rather more on Brendan Behan.

The country was overloaded with architectural monstrosities, stiletto-heeled women and greasily coiffured humans of indeterminate sex which he took to be the male of the Irish species. Every town he passed through looked like the previous one, a jungle of ugly council built matchboxes backed by equally ugly cigarette box-sized gardens dwarfed by clotheslines laden with diapers in varying shades of grey. Hotels and restaurants assailed his unwilling ears with juke box specials, piped all over the interiors, so that even in the Mens' Room he did not escape the screaming guitars and echo-chambered nasalities of the singers. And every one of the hotels had absolutely lousy coffee.

By the time he reached Knockpeddar James was somewhat chastened. He pulled up outside the local hostelry, observed with considerable interest by Miss Dunphy from the window of her post office.

'That's young Brodie,' she said jubilantly to herself. 'Good looking young fellow, good suit, nice quality luggage. I'd better get over to Ned's before that fool starts gabbling too much.'

She pulled down the window blind and slipped the lock on the door, calmly ignoring old Mrs Murphy who was about to step inside to draw her pension. 'Can't stop now Mrs Murphy – urgent business. Come back tomorrow.' And she hastened down the street to Clancy's.

James was seated in the corner, gazing mournfully into his drink. He was a beaten man. Without consultation, he'd been served a double bourbon, handed a pack of Chesterfields and been relieved of five dollars. As he looked around the bar, he saw a juke box still in its wrappings, a pile of chromium high stools in one corner, and one wall of the room was half papered in a bilious-looking black and yellow striped wallpaper with every indication of the entire area about to be similarly desecrated. For in the previous three weeks Knockpeddar had been busy. Even now, a distant hammering from further down the street proved that someone's thatched roof was being removed to make way for a tiled job, and the rash of television aerials he had passed on the way into the village told him its own sad progressional story.

Miss Dunphy nodded to Ned and raised her eyebrows in James' direction. Ned shook his head and without being told actually set up a round of drinks. Miss Dunphy took them over to the table and seated herself beside the depressed Mr Brodie.

'We're delighted to welcome you to Knockpeddar dear boy,' she said sweetly. 'Your uncle has told us a great deal about you – we feel we know you very well indeed.' Ned coughed loudly and Miss Dunphy threw him a dirty look.

'Happy to meet you ma'am,' responded James sadly.

'You are – ah – over about the film I believe,' commenced Miss Dunphy, probing delicately. 'I'm sure you'll find that Knockpeddar is moving with the modern trend. Your company will find us very up to date in everything. Why, by the time your company people get here, we'll have a modern snack bar, a car park and it'll be America at home!'

'That's just the point,' said James in despair. 'They don't want it to be just like home. They want a quiet unsophisticated village, absolutely in the backwater, without the pressures of modern ways of life, where the simple innocent world of real Ireland is moving along just as it did a hundred years ago. Where simple pleasures are still enjoyed and people are content with the simple things of life. My God, from what I've seen on my way down here, the whole thing is a complete myth – it never existed. I sold the producer the idea of an unworldly Irish village in which he could make a simple Irish picture, and look what I've landed him with!' He gestured to the jukebox and the wallpaper and buried his head in his hands.

'You mean you don't want bathrooms, lounge bars and car parks?' asked Miss Dunphy in amazement.

'No!' said James unhappily. 'We want flannel petticoats, pigs in the parlour, dancing on the village green, a real Irish shebeen of a pub with poteen on the side, hens round the half-door and cow dung in the front yard. That's what the movie is all about, don't you see?'

'Oh,' Miss Dunphy reflected in silence. 'Well,' she said after a moment or so, 'If that's what your company wants, that's what they'll get. Knockpeddar will be the simplest Irish village you've ever seen or heard of by the time we've finished with it. What do you want us to do?'

James felt his heart lift again. 'For a start, those television aerials will have to go,' he declared. 'You'll have to get your girls into flannel petticoats and shawls and this pub must go back to its old look – I can see you've been redecorating.' He shuddered slightly. 'Get rid of that damn juke box and get a few spittoons for the place.'

Ned looked horrified. He could see his extra source of revenue on its way back to the rental company within hours. 'The people will never agree to goin' without their telly,' he said positively. 'It's the big thing here ever since the station started.'

'What they want is plenty of money in their pockets and if it means going without their precious weekly serials, then they must make the sacrifice,' snapped Miss Dunphy.

'Another thing ma'am,' cut in James, who had been looking out of the pub window in the meantime. 'Can't you organise a few thatched cottages for me? I know the Producer will certainly expect them.'

Ned was delighted – it was adding years to his life to see Miss

Dunphy and her theories put on the spot. 'Well, it's this way Mr Brodie,' he said with a smirk, 'we had quite a share of thatched cottages round the street up to a week ago when we got talked into strippin' them. Still, I'm sure Miss Dunphy here can organise for you whatever you want. She's a great little organiser.'

Miss Dunphy glared at him with such a virulent scowl that Ned regretted his desire for revenge and placatingly poured the postmistress a double port in a hurry.

'You'll get your thatched houses,' promised Miss Dunphy and excused herself rapidly, speeding down the street to halt any further tiling operations, which later proved of considerable discomfort to the two householders when the nightly downpour of rain started and they were soaked to the skin in their beds.

With such a reversal of her improvement plans it was necessary to call another meeting, and Miss Dunphy again approached the Canon for the loan of the Parish Hall.

His Reverence showed a surprising reluctance to agree, much to her surprise, and Miss Dunphy had strong suspicions that the clerical ear had been closer to the ground than she would have liked.

'I feel the commercial side of this undertaking is rather leading our people into materialism,' remarked the Canon gently. 'So much alteration in their way of living within the past three weeks that I am beginning to wonder if it will not prove more detrimental to their ultimate well-being than advantageous. Really there are people who haven't been able to pay their Church dues for two years back, who are now installing flush water closets.'

Miss Dunphy coughed reprovingly and mustered her new information to do battle. James had been boarding at the post office since his arrival.

'Why Canon, this film is going to represent all that is best in our Irish way of life,' she explained quickly. 'The Producer disapproves of television sets, short skirts, ballroom dancing and such modern vices. He has especially requested that national costume be worn and is most interested in the preservation of our thatched cottages and all our ancient ways. This is what I have been told by James Brodie, who, as you know, is the Technical Advisor to the film, and of course, one of Our Own. He is anxious to make this clear to the village and this is why I am asking for the Hall.' She paused for a moment and delicately laid a cheque on the arm of the Canon's chair. 'I almost forgot to say that Mr Brodie hopes this will help pay for the Hall. Very independent young man, Mr Brodie, and most considerate about the financial difficulties of the parish.'

The Canon took a surreptitious look at the amount on the cheque and swallowed. He folded it up almost negligently and continued his conversation without pausing. Miss Dunphy politely ignored the transfer, and finally rose to go.

'Tell Mr Brodie that he has my permission to use the Hall. I expect I will look in myself,' the Canon said, and as she went down the Parochial House pathway, Miss Dunphy had the distinct feeling that she had been warned.

Chapter Seven

James surveyed his packed audience with considerable nervousness. His public speaking training which had stood him in such excellent stead at college seemed to have deserted him, its flight aided by the recollection of the rundown given to him by Miss Dunphy on the trend of Knockpeddar thinking, both lay and clerical. He was now about to tread a pussyfoot path between the iniquity of Mammon and the rectitude of Righteousness, and with the gleam of the Canon's clerical collar visible from the opposite side of the stage and the glare of avarice in the eyes of the patrons out front, James grew more and more doubtful of his verbal agility.

However with the family maxim of the Brodies 'Leap in and damn the splash' to the fore of his mind, James began to sell the village its New Image.

The Canon nodded approvingly when James delicately pointed out the Producer's need for thatched cottages, turf fires and blackthorn sticks. He was quite relieved to hear that the local Saturday night jive session would have to give place to ceilidh dancing for the duration of the film – at least, the Canon told himself, he would be saved the uncomfortable task of doing the rounds of the snugs in the ditches to rout the courting couples who forsook the excruciations of 'Jem and His Jumpers' to make beautiful music of their own in the seclusion of the greenery. Open air ceilidh dancing was at least a public affair, the Canon reflected, and would make its own difficulties for those with illicitly amorous intent. Or so he hoped.

The village was content to go along with James up to this. It was only when he got around to the television question that he felt a wave of dissension, and the low murmur which gathered in volume told him he was losing popularity even faster than a French politician.

'I'm sorry,' he said unhappily, 'but that's how it must be. If the Producer sees you're so modern that you have television, then there's no way he'll buy the idea that the village is untouched by progress, so he'll just call the whole thing off. He just does not expect to find that it has reached this village and if we want to make Knockpeddar into a household name, then the television will have to go.'

A burly man stood up at the back of the hall, mercifully out of sight of the Canon. 'What in hell do you think we're goin' to do at night if you get rid of the television?' he asked loudly.

'Anything, as long as it's not what you did before we got it,' commented another voice, 'otherwise, we'll have to start locking up the women at night again!'

The Canon shushed the unknown speakers reprovingly, making a mental note that next Sunday's homily would definitely deal with charity of tongue and the control of the baser urges of man, and Ned, who had been giving the subject considerable thought over the past few days, now got to his feet with a new assurance. He was a contented man at that moment. For Ned was about to do a deal which would, naturally, be profitable to Ned Clancy.

'I propose that we leave the television I have in my snug, and I am prepared to offer free viewing to patrons if this is done. The aerial can be hid up the tree at the back of the premises where it won't be seen.'

There was a general nudging among the males to whom this proposal sounded like an ideal move – too many of them were being routed out of Ned's at night by irate spouses, just at the exciting part of the horse operas with which Uncle Sam's vested interests continued to assail the Irish small screens, with the considerable financial approval of the Irish television authorities. With only a minimum of home-produced material in hand to fill the hours of transmission, the national television organisation had been successfully lumbered by smarter operators than themselves, with atrocities that were old when movie cameras were cranked by hand. However, the Irish sense of humour being what it is, viewers' continued enjoyment was basically assured by the nightly confirmation of their opinion that the whole television authority was a complete shower of idiots to have paid good money for such rubbish. This meant nightly compulsive viewing so that the ratings kept the selectors secure in their misconception that they really knew what suited the Irish viewing population.

The public ballot on a community viewing in surroundings that only fell short of an Irish Shangri-La in its décor, was one which was dead sure of the vote of the male fraternity of Knockpeddar.

The women on the other hand were not at all as enthusiastic. Apart from the obvious factor which sprang to their minds – a dire reduction in the weekly pay packet and a continual absence of husbandly communion for what it was worth – there was the little matter of their own viewing rights to be considered.

'Ladies,' pronounced Ned, now filled with the heady feeling of mastery over the entire population, 'Ladies, have no fear. For you, my viewing room will be available between the opening hours – of television, I mean – from five-thirty to nine o'clock at night. You will be at liberty to view the programmes in peace and privacy without fear of being molested or insulted in any way. In fact, I'll make it a "Ladies Only" time in the bar, if you like. I might even manage to serve tea and biscuits – for a small charge,' he added hastily.

'Hmm,' sniffed a fat woman at the front – 'Considerin' no one hits your pub before half eight anyway, you're not doin' us much of a favour. An' the first hour only runs the children's programmes.'

However, the Canon was weighing up the situation at a fast rate. He disapproved of television to begin with; it gave the female population too many independent ideas about sex, female equality and labour-saving devices. In the Canon's view women kept out of trouble only in two instances, when they had a houseful of children and a bar of soap as their major piece of household equipment, or when they joined a purely contemplative religious order – he had his own little differences with the Reverend Mother of the parish school, apart from his pastoral difficulties with his female flock. In his opinion the women of Knockpeddar had been spending entirely too much time sitting before their television sets when they could be better occupied in housewifely duties and, if he had his way, he would have made juvenile television illegal by act of government. Regarding the possibilities of an increase in village drunkenness, the Canon had long since resigned himself to the fact that, for his male parishioners at any rate, getting drunk was a career and not a hobby. Besides which, it suddenly struck him that it would be a dandy time to run a Retreat. So he stepped forward and pronounced judgement in favour with pious and heartfelt exhortations to control the agility and rapidity of the elbow lifting within the confines of Clancy's pub.

Ned Clancy was dreamily calculating what his newest move would mean in financial terms. It was only fair, he told himself righteously, that a little extra should be added to the drink prices to balance the wear and tear on the snug, and the television. Even adding on an extra twopence, since the snug could now qualify as a lounge area and the liquor be charged for accordingly, there was no doubt that he would only break a little above even, with all that traffic in and out of the snug. He was considering the idea of an additional five pence when he felt Miss Dunphy's steely glance on the back of his neck. He turned unwillingly.

'I wouldn't Ned,' she said with infinite and repelling silkiness. 'Twopence extra is plenty. If you add any more I'll buy a television set myself and get the women to come to my house, which means the men will have to stay home and look after the children at night.'

Ned shivered. He very nearly crossed himself. That old bitch should carry a broomstick, he told himself nervously. Still, he reminded himself as the cold sweat dried on his forehead, there were lots of ways a clever publican could reap a little extra money from his customers, once he put his mind to it.

Over at the Grange, the Earl was not unaware of the events of the moment. On the surface an apparently easy-going, vague and handsome man in his forties, his well-bred and genteel exterior hid a razor sharp acumen, handed on by his North of Ireland forebears, which had mated very well with the Corkonian ancestry on his mother's side. This provided him with a hard-headed practicality and a firm ability to set his sights strictly with an eye to the main chance. Such a well-feathered friend indeed had been his late wife, a whey-faced insipid distant descendant of the Irish nobility, who came well endowed with gilt-edged securities if not with physical beauty. Fortunately for his aesthetic sensitivity she shook off her mortal coil within five years of matrimony, but it was the Earl's abiding regret that he had been unable to assist her departure, when he learned that, whey-faced or not, she had been maintaining her chauffeur in considerable comfort and had so depleted the gilt of her securities as to make them little more than plain plated. So the Earl was faced with the arduous battle of living his life as a working nobleman, until such time as the marriage market turned up a suitable candidate for his honoured name, and he could again live up to the family motto which, translated from the pig Latin on the family crest, stated firmly that 'All Service Has Its Price.'

Reviewing the current possibilities it appeared to him that some revenue might come his way at executive level. Here he was with a stately home filled with all abortions of noble taste in furniture and heirlooms, even down to the suit of armour worn by a battle-happy ancestor. One would not stoop so low as to suggest that he should take in boarders into the Grange, but it might be suggested that as a personal favour he could be persuaded to allow the top brass of the forthcoming film unit to pay through the nose for the hospitality of Grange Peddar. The leading actress, the Producer and the Director, the Earl thought sagely, would certainly need a little more than the village accommodation could provide. Grange Peddar might be a little shabby, but if they wanted atmosphere it could provide it in plenty.

The Earl also reminded himself that a deal on the side might be arranged for the use of the Grange and grounds for some of the scenes. He might even dig out that play he wrote all those years ago when he was at Oxford – something might be done to bring it up to date. He began to feel that things were looking up. He glanced out of the study window – the weeds would certainly have to be rooted out of the driveway, and perhaps his credit would be good enough to have Fonsie O'Malley send over a man to clean up the lily pond and get the filter working again, and while he was at it, he'd get an estimate for that repointing job at the far end of the coach house. He even contemplated a little trip to Dublin, which would take the tedium out of life in an all-male household, and when Miss Dunphy and James Brodie arrived at the Grange with similar ideas of accommodation for the film unit in mind, he received them with unusual warmth, allowed himself to be convinced that he was doing Mr Lipperstein and Miss O'Day an enormous favour, and closed the deal with only the most genteel haggling for a sum far above what he originally hoped to receive.

James was also successful in organising the vacant garage flat, once inhabited by the gilt-stripping chauffeur, as accommodation for Susan. He was already arranging to stay in the lodge himself, since he felt the village was a little too far removed from his lady love. However, the Earl decided that James might be useful to have on his side in the event of putting through negotiations for the leasing of the grounds, and insisted that a guest room in the Grange would be allotted to him as part of the original deal.

Having got so many of his arrangements well under way, James cheerfully wired Susan to give the green light to Mr Lipperstein and sat back to await the arrival of the airlift that was going to start Knockpeddar on its road to prosperity.

Chapter Eight

Two weeks later a stream of long black automobiles whipped through the main street of Knockpeddar, observed with considerable interest by Brenno O'Mahoney who was resting in the ditch just beyond the village, contemplating the journey home to his farm.

It was, he told Beauty later over the nightly can of stout, an inspiring procession and every bit as good as the funeral of the Earl's late wife, even without the special hearse which was laid on to take the funeral wreaths the day they buried Her Ladyship in the family vault of the de Luceys. 'Cars the length of the street they had,' said Brenno, wiping the foam off his upper lip.

He had an inspiring glimpse of Oscar Lipperstein, whose bulk was not enhanced by the sheepskin coat he had purchased at Shannon Airport's duty free shop, and which on Oscar appeared more sheep than skin. The tantilising whiff of Oscar's discarded cigar filled his nostrils – Brenno had been fortunate enough to have been struck on the right boot by Oscar's Corona as the Most Adventurous Producer hurled it from the automobile window while making a point of conversation, and Brenno had instantly salvaged it, removed the mangled end and was happily smoking the remains as he discussed the evening's happenings with his pet.

Oscar had indeed arrived. His limousine swept through the rather battered gates of the Grange and pulled up outside the main door. Oscar looked around. 'Jeeze, dis dump ain't exactly the Waldorf,' he said, eyeing with disdain the elegant frontage, surrounded by slightly unkempt, but still beautiful lawns.

'No sprinkler system, no patio and I bet dere's no swimmin' pool or sauna either. Dis jerk could do wit a good decorator.' He eased his coat out of the car and lumbered up to the door. He was halted in his tracks by the dulcet voice of Miss O'Day, who was still arranged in the front seat, encumbered by her mink wrap, her crocodile handbag and her poodle, an evil-tempered, spoiled canine whose temperament was only equalled by that of his mistress.

'Oscar! I know your mother wasn't married to your father, but do you have to prove that he never took his hat off either? Come back here and help me get out of this horsebox!'

Oscar gritted his teeth but reminded himself that some day, when Miss O'Day's poundage moved from her chest to her hips, he would be in a position to shake down her family tree in complete detail and, pinning a conciliatory smile on his lipline, he hurried back to the car.

Miss O'Day flung her wrap at his head, managed to almost pulverise him with the impact of her handbag and swung the famous frame onto the driveway. Damaged as he was, Oscar still got a hot feeling as her skirt rode up thighwards. Miss O'Day eyed him.

'Put your eyes back Oscar . . . even you haven't enough dough to get there,' she snapped, as she straightened her stocking seams. The Grange front door swung open and Miss O'Day switched on her press relations smile. Riordan, the Earl's butler-valet-cook-gardener-marketing manager-betting advisor-and-general fact-otum, stood to attention. Riordan's job was unique in the annals of butlering – sadly, his Lordship had had to reduce the domestic staff at the Grange to a drastic level from the days when his late wife was still in possession of real folding money. Riordan now had to make do with the help of a local girl who turned up most days, and they both fought a losing battle with weeds, cobwebs, dust and a somewhat temperamental black range. But the butler soldiered on in the hope of more affluent times to come.

Impassively he watched the party approach. Well, we've got a right lot here, he told himself – a fat lech, a high class call-girl, a poof if I ever saw one, down there in the silk socks and suede shoes and a poor bastard that looks as if he can't call his soul his own. I wonder what his Lordship will make of them.

Riordan (only his mother remembered that he had also been baptised Columba to his lifelong revulsion) had discarded his usual working gear of battered corduroys and an old army issue shirt, for an ancient but well-preserved lounge suit of the Earl's. He felt it was up to him to present an initial dignity within the manor, to offset the unfortunate peeling of the varnish on the entrance doors – an occurrence he had expected to happen because of the Earl's complete lack of do-it-yourself know-how. With all the aplomb and well-bred suspicion which even the gentry leave to their butlers to perfect, he waited silently for the visitors to enter the great hall.

Oscar waddled forward importantly, jamming the cigar back into his mouth and extending a fat hairy hand. 'Oirl – glad to meetcha. I'm Oscar Lipperstein. Nice little place ya got here, even if it needs a little dis an' dat. Remind me to give ya de name of a good decorator I use. He'd be glad to fly in an' give your place a face-lift that'll send ya.'

Riordan gazed down his nose at Mr Lipperstein who for the moment failed to recognise the advent of the frozen mitt, as he beamed happily at the Grange's retainer. The silence lengthened, until even Oscar began to feel puzzled.

'I,' said Riordan with majestic detachment, 'am his Lordship's butler. His Lordship does not open his own hall door. May I take your coat . . . sir?'

Miss O'Day shrieked in delighted laughter. 'Oscar, you've fallen on your fat fanny again. That's what comes of never watching anyone else's movies except your own.' She sauntered over towards Riordan, laying on the famed Frivvle. Dawn believed in making new fans every day whenever possible. Added to which she worked hard at building up the profitable but quiet sideline she ran with the publicity men in the marketing of particularly specialised photo stills personally autographed in real ink, which they sold independently of the studio publicity department. With a rake-off of seventy/thirty between them, Miss O'Day was taking care of her old age in more ways than investing in stocks and real estate. Personal contacts with her public ensured that the enraptured requests for something particularly 'special' had the sting removed to some extent when the bill for the prints was presented.

'Mr Riordan, I'm Dawn O'Day. I'm going to have to rely so much on you and so is Ching, my little pet. Will you see that he gets something to eat right away? Travelling never agrees with him, so just grind up a little lean T-bone steak very fine please, and positively no fat. Later I can give you his diet sheet.'

She handed over her poodle and her most charming smile to the butler. The pooch promptly sank its teeth into Riordan's thumb and then leered at him, before jumping down to leave a large dark puddle on the delicate Chinese rug outside the door of the Earl's study.

'Oh dear,' Miss O'Day put on her little girl pout, which normally caused her male fans to drool and her women fans to rush home and practise before their mirrors for hours. 'I'm afraid Ching has made a boo boo. Still,' she said consolingly, eyeing the priceless rug with the ingenuousness of complete ignorance, 'I guess it's one of your old things anyhow from the look of it, so there's no harm done. I'd just hate it if the rug was only bought lately. Dawg pee is pretty tough to remove. We had quite a job training Ching when I first got him.'

Again she smiled winningly, and moved around the hall, examining the pictures and the ancestral suit of armour that guarded the approach to the staircase.

'Gee, Oscar, look – a coat rack! Ain't it cute? Very progressive. I must get me one of those before I go back to the States. I got just the spot for it.' She draped her mink stole around the shoulders of the suit.

Riordan gazed at the scene impassively, his expert eye rejecting the mink as definitely studio grade fur. 'I shall inform his Lordship that you have arrived,' he said coldly, and stiff-backed he tapped gently on the morning-room door before disappearing from the fascinated stare of the visitors.

Susan, who up to now had been a silently convulsed observer of the little introductory scene, decided it was time to put Oscar on the straight and narrow path to friendship with his host.

'Oscar,' she said kindly, 'button up about the condition of the house. The Irish upper classes prefer their gentility to be donated by their forebears, and their homes and furniture to be weathered by generations of ownership. Anything under a hundred years old is merely junk unless it's a horse, but it includes whiskey, wine and carpets which were antique when you were pinned into a diaper.' She threw Miss O'Day a dirty look. Miss O'Day was now idly plucking the petals off an arrangement of roses in a cut glass bowl.

'Jeeze,' said Oscar plaintively. 'I was only tryin' to be friendly. How in hell was I to know dat guy wuz de butler . . . Mind you,' he continued with more enthusiasm, 'I wouldn't mind havin' him in a movie. He's got a kinda class. Couldn't we change the script around a bit an' work him in? Then we could film it back in the studio and save money.'

'No!' said Susan positively. 'After all,' she continued with infinite cunning, 'Dawn wants a deeply sincere story about a simple Irish girl, awakened to perfect love by a simple Irish boy. Where could you work in a butler and not spoil her part?' Miss O'Day looked at her a little suspiciously, but Susan nodded at her earnestly and Miss O'Day relaxed.

'I ain't flying back to the States when I just got here. I wanna to make the movie here, just like we planned, so I won't pass any changes like working in butlers and saving money. You always were a piker, Oscar . . . I'll bet when the doctor delivered you, you snitched his watch,' Miss O'Day snapped, ripping yet another bloom to shreds.

Oscar's blood pressure went up another five notches. However his attention was diverted by the arrival of Mr James Brodie, and he gladly vented his temper on him, instead of damaging his contract position with his leading actress.

'Where in hell have you been? You shoulda been here to meet us. I don't pay ya to lead-swing around.'

Three weeks of Knockpeddar's way of life had done quite a bit for James. He had taken to the Irish diversities of doing even the most simple operation as a native takes to Guinness. His already well matured self-survival instincts had developed to a surprising degree and he was now emerging as that undefeatable mutant, an Irish-American con man. Already he had a number of side schemes perking nicely, not the least of which was a quiet deal with the Earl to lease the Grange stables for property storage, and the Friars' Walk for use as a set. Down in the village his credit was as good as Fonsie O'Malley's, since he had prudently agreed that a rental be paid for the use of the thatched cottages in the movie, and he had a neat scheme under discussion with Ned Clancy to market American cigarettes to the company on a fifty-fifty split, provided that Ned was given the sole concession. Other minor ways he had made friends and influenced the population included promises of passes to watch filming, an arrangement to use his influence with Miss O'Day to show her Frivvle off, clad in an Irish tweed suit, the guarantee of a lecture on stage craft to the local dramatic society by one of the assistant producers who did the real work in Oscar's movies, and he had an unexpressed but clearly understood agreement with the mothers of Knockpeddar, that any female deflowering results would be nicely submerged in American dollars, negotiable at slightly more than the current bank rate in the unit's pay department.

Consequently Oscar's irascibility affected him to a much lesser degree than it would have done prior to his arrival in the land his father had loved and left.

'Well, Mr Lipperstein, may your road be short and your day be long! Everything is under control – you don't have to worry about a thing. The Earl has running water, a loo, a telephone, a bell service, provided you don't mind waiting a little for an answer, and even an icebox in the kitchens. Your creature comforts will be well taken care of.'

Oscar refused to be placated. 'Dis place is like a morgue. It ain't got no steam heat an' I don't see no elevator. Am I supposed to climb up dem stairs all de time?'

'Maybe it'll reduce the size of your belly and you'll be able to see your shoes for a change,' said Miss O'Day inelegantly, smoothing her hipline. By now decapitating the flowers had begun to bore her.

Mercifully, Riordan returned. His face broke into a smile when he spotted James. 'Ah, Mr Brodie, how pleasant to see you, sir. His Lordship was wondering if we were to have the pleasure of your company for dinner tonight. He is anxious to continue the chess match.'

Even Oscar was impressed. He began to feel he had done the right thing in hiring James after all. Riordan frightened him to death – for the first time since the day he kicked his mother and got kicked back, Oscar had come up against a personality stronger than anything in his immediate circle and of a nature that he hadn't a clue how to handle.

Oscar may have been fat, but he wasn't slow. Beneath all his complaining noises was a certain satisfaction at being a guest in a stately home, crumbling or not. It would make good dinner conversation when he got back home to be able to throw out airily, 'when I was stayin' in Ireland with the Oirl.' However, being the Most Adventurous Producer carried with it certain responsibilities, of which never being pleased about anything was only one.

'I'll be delighted,' said James politely. 'Unless of course Mr Lipperstein has other plans for me.'

'No, no,' said Oscar hastily. 'We have a conference sharp at noon tomorrow. No business talk tonight.' He nodded obligingly at James and then followed Riordan's beckoning wave as the butler shepherded them into the morning-room to meet their host.

Not for nothing had Riordan lingered in the morning-room when he went to announce Mr Lipperstein's arrival. The Earl had had a complete rundown on his new paying guests and had already penned in the little black note book he had purchased on his butler's advice, in which to keep an account of the extras with which he expected to swell the board and keep figures, a neatly written item covering the damage to his Chinese rug. After he got his first glance of Oscar's girth, he made a quick mental note to put down wear and tear on his bed and chairs as well for a start.

'Delighted, delighted,' he murmured graciously when James made the introductions. Miss O'Day fluttered her lashes at him and wriggled happily as he bent over her suede gloved hand with old-fashioned courtesy. She began to feel there was potential at the Grange after all. His quick and approving glance at her legs (his Lordship was far too much of a gentleman to mentally measure her northern advantages so initially) did not go unnoticed by Oscar's leading lady either.

'What a darling place you've got Earl,' she trilled, moving closer to him. 'You simply must show me around your estate just as soon as possible. You know, I just adore the country – all that air and trees and flowers and – and – those darling cattle just standing like statoos!'

'In an elephant's eye,' muttered Miss King, recognising Dawn's blatant line lifting, not to mention her objectives. Miss O'Day, to Susan's certain knowledge, firmly believed that flowers grew in long ribbon-tied boxes, and until cows were permitted to walk down Fifth Avenue and shop for model dresses the only time Miss O'Day was likely to be seen fraternising with any maverick was when it faced her T-bone fashion on a restaurant plate, garnished with a fried egg.

'You will dine with me in the evenings,' said the Earl politely, even if his heart was sinking already at the thought of having to watch Oscar masticate his food. At first glance his Lordship could already tell that Mr Lipperstein would be a messy masticator.

'We have arranged a private sitting-room on the second floor for your use while you are here. This way your personal privacy will be respected.'

His Lordship had no intention of having his personal routine disturbed by his paying guests unless it was by his own choice. 'The ladies also have a small drawing-room which was used by my late wife for entertaining her friends.' A slight shadow passed over the Earl's face as he mentioned her Ladyship. The awful perfidy of that chauffeur still rankled even after all those years of happy widowerhood. It wasn't that he felt cuckolded. It was just the realisation that his wife actually paid for the privilege as well, that got him. It was, he reasoned with a certain nostalgia, a *man's* prerogative to conduct such a transaction.

'Mm, a widower huh?' said Miss O'Day with interest. As she studied the Earl's silvered good looks a misty expression came into her eyes. A lonely looking man she decided – one to whom the understanding company of a lovely woman would be a godsend. A man of the Earl's calibre would have little in common with the common herd in the village, she decided. He could do with a more experienced and sophisticated form of company and indeed, it was almost her bounden duty to see that his Lordship had feminine companionship that would please – such as her own, for instance. His Lordship was fated to become a project of Miss O'Day's whether he liked it or not.

'You will find our village a most unworldly spot,' remarked the Earl, who had been well tutored by James in Oscar's production needs. 'Our requirements are few and our people of a simple nature. We do not subject ourselves to the horrors of television or the puerility of the cinema westerns. Our people make their own entertainment with our national song and dance in the evenings. They are simple folk to whom your arrival will be a major excitement in their lives.'

'Just what I told Mr Lipperstein,' said James heartily, giving the Earl an approving look. 'He wouldn't find a more unsophisticated spot if he searched the whole country from one end to the other.'

'Yeah' said Oscar dubiously.

'Think of the untapped acting talent you'll find for your extras, Oscar,' Susan cut in hurriedly, for it wouldn't do if Mr Lipperstein got cold feet at this stage. 'No problems with unions or actors who want to direct themselves, no bother with trying to film in between television aerials, electricity cables and automobile parks. I'd say you'll cut your filming timc in half working down here. As Producer/Director the financial saving and the natural assets must stand for something in your book.' Oscar began to look more cheerful – of course his right-hand woman was making good sense and anything that saved him money and time was all right by him.

He puffed upstairs in Riordan's wake to his suite, preceded by Miss O'Day whose Frivvle was so much in evidence that Oscar at once began to regret his parsimony in refusing to bring his newest and most willing young starlet with him to keep his blood pressure down. But, optimistic as ever, he was sure that among all these innocents in Knockpeddar there would be one nubile female who would be sufficiently ambitious to singe her wings against the movie arc lamps, to keep his libido on an even keel.

Chapter Nine

Later that evening after a somewhat disastrous dinner, during which Oscar disgraced himself by drinking out of the finger bowls Riordan had provided to put on a show for the Earl's new guests, Oscar being under the mistaken impression that this was the Irish way of serving straight gin, James and Susan took a stroll down towards the village.

'You've got yourself well dug in with his Lordship, in a very short time,' Susan remarked.

'I tell you, I've been a real godsend to that man,' said James with pride. 'He's been lost for intelligent company. If he had business concerns I guarantee I'd be his managing director by now. I've put him wise to a number of good schemes which will help to make a dint in his overdraft by the time Oscar hauls his fat rump back to the States.'

'Don't you think showing someone how to cheat your employer is a bit unprincipled?' Susan asked disapprovingly.

'Not at all, you know as well as I do that Oscar will cheat him from Monday to Friday. Anything he can put over on our beloved Producer will be more than earned. And anyway, the Earl will have to put up with Dawn breathing at him out of her plunging neckline for the next few weeks, and that, my dear Susan, one wouldn't wish on a dog. I saw the look in her eye when he said he was a widower. That woman has designs on his Lordship, you mark my words.'

'Do you think so?' Susan said. Then she thought about it. 'You could be right, James. After all, Dawn must be getting worried about her poundage apart from her age. She packed her weighing scales, her electro-massager and four books on diets before she came. And but for the fact that Oscar would have gone doolally, she'd have brought along her masseuse as well. So if she could snaffle the Earl for a husband, she could retire gracefully and get fat in peace in a stately home with the advantage and snob value of a title to go with it.'

'Well now,' said James. 'We must help love along then, mustn't we?'

By now they had approached the environs of Knockpeddar. It looked a charming spot, bathed in the evening sunlight. Between them, James and the villagers had done a worthwhile job on the exterior. There wasn't a television aerial in sight. Every house sported a brand new thatched roof, and a number had done a quick conversion to a half door. One cottage had a spinning wheel strategically placed beside the step, its owner even now devoutly praying that Oscar would not ask to see it in operation, for there was little more left of the mechanism than the wheel. A freshly scrubbed pig resided in some surprise in a child's latticed playpen at the side of another cottage, making vain efforts to remove a pink satin ribbon from around its neck. A brand new and unused shiny milk churn rested in a prominent position on a table at the bottom of the street. Even the duck pond had been cleaned and restocked with four white ducks. At regular intervals when they surfaced after dredging the bottom of the pond for worms, someone rushed out and removed the mud off their bills and backs.

Down in the pub the ballad group was busily downing pints to whet their tonsils before the evening performance, due to begin when Oscar would arrive. There were four of them and they presented an awe-inspiring sight. Miss Madigan in the local drapery shop had had a record sales week. She hadn't an inch of red flannel, grey tweed or white calico left in stock and she said a nightly prayer for James with deep gratitude. The two girls perspired unhappily in ankle-length flannel skirts and cambric aprons, and the bright green taffeta which Miss Madigan had bought from a travelling salesman five years back and never managed to sell to the selective customers of Knockpeddar, now crackled sweatily on the singers, made up into tight blouses that left long-lasting weals on the unfortunate wearers, since Miss Madigan's pattern service happened to be low in sizes when the rush came. The two male members of the group stood uneasily at the counter – Miss Madigan, who also doubled as the village dressmaker, had unfortunately forgotten to line the grey tweed trousers when she ran them up. The wardrobe of the dramatic society had provided two rather battered caubeens, neither of which fitted the boys, but which looked impressive sitting side by side on the top of the bar. The football club came across in white knee socks, and even if the tops carried a red stripe, it was felt that the Americans would not be sufficiently conversant with the local club colours to notice.

The musical instruments had presented some difficulty. There were few talented musicians in Knockpeddar of the traditional type, but Jem of the aforementioned 'Jumpers' was pressed into foresaking his beloved clarinet for a flute, and Breeda Cosgrave gallantly learned three chords on the small harp lent by the Earl, which, they all hoped, she would play at the proper moments to provide a little harmony to the group. They were, however, most fortunate in that Humphrey Quigley, the second of the balladeers, had, over the years of perfecting his swallow in Ned Clancy's pub, also perfected his performance on the spoons, and could flick and tap with the best of them. The bodghran, that undefinable Irish escape from the drum, was in the enthusiastic hands of Miss Marita Doherty, who had to be given regular kicks on the ankle bone to remind her not to drown the singers during the performance. Ned too had really put his back into giving his premises the ancient look of Celtic twilight. Indeed, what he was saving on the fluorescent lighting alone, more than offset the cost of the three oil lamps he had bought secondhand from a couple of tinkers who passed through Knockpeddar the week before.

Ned was already chalking up a neat profit in short measures which, so far, his customers had not noticed in the dim light of the lamps which he had placed well away from the servery. He had a standing order for a daily delivery of sawdust from the local sawmill and, even if the spittoons were not authentic, in that light it was hard to spot that they were really toffee tins given a quick coat of paint. The striped wallpaper that had nauseated James on his arrival was no more, being now whitewashed over and the wall hung with a few out-of-date calendars Ned had salvaged from the storeroom.

In the centre of the village square where there was once a small traffic roundabout, Fonsie, who also just happened to own the local building supply company as well as the construction firm, had provided ready cast cement paving stones which now covered the grass centre and converted it into a temporary dance area. Fonsie was somewhat anxious about his paving stones – he hoped the dancers would not get so enthusiastic in their stamping that they would fracture the cement squares, because Fonsie had actually already sold them to a householder thirty miles away for use on his new patio. Even now that unfortunate man was making frantic telephone calls to find out if he could expect delivery this side of the summer and, all being well, Fonsie hoped that when the film crew returned to their transatlantic base, the paving stones could then be lifted and dispatched whole and entire to their original destination. The rent he prised out of the council fund for the use of the blocks would, he hoped, more than offset the abuse he would surely have to take from his irate customer.

It was amazing the effect that a couple of gallons of free paint had had on the shopkeepers of Knockpeddar. They had a rush of paint to the head so to speak, and the result was arresting. There was light green, Kelly green, mid green and in fact forty shades of the stuff, freshly applied to every shop in the street and Festy Finegan, the local painter, had taken to his bed with an acute case of nausea when he completed his mammoth repaint job. Only one exterior broke away from the green cult – Ned had sagely decided that the exterior of his premises should be easily discernible by the strangers, so he had it done over in a fluorescent orange – the result looked somewhat like a fried egg yolk on a plate of cabbage, but one thing was certain – you couldn't miss it.

Old Mrs Murphy had been persuaded to resurrect her Kinsale cloak, and she was now sitting on a milking stool outside the pub, sustained by regular pints of Guinness while she fought a losing battle to keep the hood of the cloak from smothering her.

James thought it all looked marvellous. 'Well, what do you think?' he asked Susan happily.

'It's unbelievable,' replied his lady in a hushed voice as she neatly side-stepped a hen, which a small boy was hunting back and forth across the road on instructions from his mother, stationed at one of the windows in the street. 'Oscar will love it. James you really have done well.'

They nipped into the pub for a final check around which was just as well, since Ned had not been able to resist putting a stock of rye whiskey in prominent view on his shelves.

'You're not supposed to have such a thing in the house,' James remonstrated. 'This is a Guinness and Irish booze house only, so get all those foreign brands out of sight.' Ned sulked. How was a poor publican to make a crust if he couldn't serve up what the visitors were accustomed to drinking?

'Now remember, if you're asked for bourbon, you look puzzled and you don't know what they're talking about. You give them Irish whiskey instead,' Susan told him. 'You can charge for it at the rate for bourbon if you like – they won't know the difference,' and Ned began to feel a little less hard done by.

Chapter Ten

It was well after nine o'clock before Oscar heaved himself out of his limousine into the village square. James in the intervening time had sympathetically helped to oil the throats of the balladeers, the feet of the dancers and the endurance of old Mrs Murphy with regular applications of the national brew, and taking things all round the entire village was, at this moment, viewing Oscar, the film and its own future prosperity in a happy haze of enthusiasm. The late evening light bathed the street in a gently deceptive glow and the dancers were even now doing their best jigs on Fonsie's paving stones, somewhat inexpertly it is true, but with an earnestness of intent that only a well-oiled Gael can bring to any task set to him. Someone poked the pig in the playpen into annoyed wakefulness with a discreet jab of a broom handle where it counted most, and old Mrs Murphy, by now fast asleep under the folds of her Kinsale cloak, was jerked into instant awareness by the rapid installation of yet another pint of porter into her gnarled hand. James shifted the balladeers as far as the doorway of Ned's hostelry where they struck up a chorus of 'Danny Boy', the one song everyone had a fair working knowledge of.

Oscar too, was not exactly sober. The Earl had fed him pretty well, but Riordan had flatly refused to produce anything remotely approaching the best brandy. Instead he served the visitors a vintage which was best described as 'Instant', but which, emptied into a decanter of finest old Waterford cut glass, and ceremoniously served in warmed balloon glasses to match, sufficiently impressed Oscar as to make him believe that his palate was unable to live up to the quality. A couple of snorters of Riordan's Revenge (he still owed Miss O'Day for the pooch bite) and Oscar was suffering from slight double vision, while Miss O'Day discovered in herself a delightful sense of instant supremacy over every male in sight and a hot tightness round her heart, which she mistook for sexual desire but which tomorrow she would discover to be acute heartburn.

'Jeeze!' said Oscar hazily as the car stopped. 'Would ya looka dat? De real dippidoo. If we'd abuilt the set we couldna done it better!'

'Mmm...' replied Miss O'Day with unusual warmth as she eyed a tall young man with black curly hair whose fingers were busily working a braille system on the rounded rump of his female partner. 'We couldn't have asked for more, Oscar... not a thing!'

She swung her legs out of the car, just as the young man whirled by her and he promptly fell over her feet, landing most fortuitously into her lap. Dawn's ample bosom pillowed his cheek and, almost like a homing pigeon, he sighed and snuggled into its warmth. Then Oscar had to go and spoil it all by yanking him back on to his feet. Dawn smiled brilliantly at him and held out her hand for assistance from the car seat. Slightly bemused, the young man shook it and Dawn, holding on firmly, eased herself from the seat, teetering slightly as much from the after-dinner brandy as from the pleasurable contact with the hefty young Allo O'Brien of the braille fingers.

As they made their way to the pub the Canon was also out and about and taking his evening constitutional, and planning his sermon for the following Sunday's Mass. To his surprise, he found an almost embarrassing air of respect coming at him from everyone he passed. The men were tugging at their forelocks and the women were actually curtsying as he went by. The Canon couldn't understand it – usually everyone turned tail down the nearest lane or into the most adjacent shop when they saw him approaching. He wished he had brought his spectacles with him. Perhaps they were trying to tell him something – in a panic he felt for his flies and heaved a sigh of relief when his hand told him all his buttons were fastened up. He raised a hand in blessing and almost bumped into Oscar who was watching the villagers' reverential displays with some surprise.

'Good evening, sir,' said the Canon politely, hastily averting his eyes from Miss O'Day's décolletage which, lacking spectacles or not, the Canon could see more visibly than he would have wished, what with his vows of chastity so long untempted.

Oscar calculated that with all that saluting and bowing the cleric must be at least a bishop, so he was, for Oscar, quite respectful.

'Dis is a real nice place ya got here, your Holiness,' he said chattily, teetering forward toward the Canon who stepped back as the alcohol fumes hit him in the same familiar wave as they did on Saturday nights in the confession box over in the church. He sighed slightly, as it began to dawn on him that from now on, what with all the extra cash which the local population would acquire by one means or another from the film unit, it was an odour he would have to learn to live with if he was not to sit in the fustiness of the confessional without any penitents at all for two hours every Saturday night. The Canon had long ceased preaching about the evils of drink to his flock – every time he ran a sermon about it he noticed that the line outside the confessional depleted itself of all the menfolk for at least three months afterwards. When all was said and done, the only practical way of keeping tabs on the more obvious social disorders in the village was by analysing the current crop of sins retailed through the grille by the males of Knockpeddar. The women usually pared their misdemeanours down to whether they said yes or no – either way, in the Canon's book, they were getting it wrong.

James swiftly straightened Oscar up before he collapsed on top of the Canon.

'This is Mr Lipperstein, who is the Producer and Director of the film, Canon Hackett,' he said. 'He is taking a little stroll to see the whole village – we trust the church is still open? Mr Lipperstein is very interested in epitaphs on ancient tomb stones – he collects them. I've been telling him that some of the stones in the parish graveyard are most unusual.' Oscar blinked. He wasn't quite sure what an epitaph actually was, but he calculated that if it was on a stone then it had to be graffiti, and he was always in the market for a good piece of lavatory humour.

The Canon nodded, smiling vaguely; trying to keep on ignoring Miss O'Day was beginning to give him a slight headache which wasn't at all helped by the strains of 'Danny Boy' from the ballad singers, by now on the fourth repeat and growing more hysterical and untuneful by the second. The tweed-trousered boys had a distinct tendency to counter tenor notes in the upper reaches, and the Canon was surprised to note that old Mrs Murphy had suddenly joined the group of dancers on the roundabout. He was doubly amazed when she lifted her skirts and began an inexpert jig, because to his certain knowledge Mrs Murphy had been bedridden for over six months – at least that's what her daughter had told him when he asked why he hadn't see the old lady in church of late. He hoped her apparent improvement was due to the bottle of Knock holy water which he had sent her after his last visit to the County Mayo site of pilgrimage.

'Perhaps his Reverence would like Mr Lipperstein to send him back to the Parish House in the car?' suggested Susan as she moved in to take the Canon's arm in a deceptively gentle grip.

'Yeah, why not? Guess we'll stick around here for a spell – you see de guy – I mean the Reverend – home, Sue, an' then come back here.' Oscar nodded obligingly and the Canon, with the look of a child to whom Providence had suddenly donated an entire sweetshop, clambered into the fur lined recesses of the seating, resting his aching head against a cushion whose softness and depth moulded itself around his earlobes in a truly decadent fashion. As he ran his fingers over the seat rests, almost miraculously a compartment slid out from the side and displayed a glass, and ice cube container and a couple of bottles of amber fluid.

'Well, good gracious me, what will they think of next?' said the Canon in surprise, and Susan had a double poured and into his unresisting hand before the limousine had begun to pull away from the kerb.

With the Canon safely out of the way James steered Oscar along the main street, to show him the rest of the wonders of Knockpeddar while the Most Adventurous Producer was still bemused by Riordan's brandy.

In the evening light the village looked a pretty place – the plastic roses which were carefully stuck in the old three-legged cast iron pots which James had bought from the last tribe of tinkers to go through Knockpeddar, looked just like the real thing in the early dusk. The pig had fallen asleep in the playpen and someone had thoughtfully placed a little red cushion under its head as it lay in the pen, its back legs twitching spasmodically, as much from delayed shock at its new sty as from its dreams. The ducks had come ashore and had been carefully tethered to a stake on the bank of the pond, since they were known to have a wanderlust that might take them out of the village for days, and no one wanted them to go missing at the crucial moment. Even the hen, worn out by the exercise of crossing and recrossing the roadway had settled down to sleep in the exact centre of the street where everyone understandingly stepped around it. In the windows of the cottages the women were lighting oil lamps, praying fervently that the whole lot would not go up in flames before Oscar went away again and they could switch on the electricity. James was proud of his efforts and he could see that Oscar, slightly hazed or not, was more than a little impressed.

When they reached Clancy's pub the ballad singers struck up with a renewed enthusiasm and Oscar did a quick button count on the girls as he went through the doorway, but decided not to do anything rash, as there seemed to be a fair lot of female talent about that he thought he could look over later. Too early a commitment could make problems if something better should hap-happen to come along, he reasoned. After all, it was early days yet.

Meanwhile Miss O'Day was doing a little viewing of her own. Allo of the braille fingers was still hovering on the edge of the company and Dawn felt that a little encouragement might be used now to pay dividends later. She scrabbled in her handbag for one of the publicity stills she rarely travelled without, and with a brilliant smile, only slightly spoiled by a small belch of ill-digested brandy fumes, she pressed the photograph into Allo's hand, breathing throatily at him, 'this is one of my more special photographs, just for you, dear boy.' Allo had a pretty good track record, even for Knockpeddar, and he knew a come-on when he saw one – after all, the girls had tried it with apple tarts, hand knitted sweaters, tickets to the football matches, free passes to the school variety concerts and so on.

'Are ye idle?' he asked, jerking his head towards the dancers, and before she knew it Dawn was grasped around the waist, her bosom was pressed into Allo's chest in a close encounter of a most intimate nature, and he whirled her into the middle of the jig. Dawn didn't know whether to feel pleased or insulted – she was used to most of the people she knew grovelling before her, flattering her with a continuous stream of studio clichés, and nobody ever hot-handed her well-insured buttocks unless she allowed him to earn the privilege by way of a pretty bauble such as a diamond bracelet, the odd condominium or even a daintily wrapped block of stocks and shares. Now here was this yokel, showing absolutely no respect for her fame at all, acquiring a most detailed knowledge of her anatomy without putting up one damn thing to deserve it.

Still, Dawn told herself dizzily, he had the cutest curly black hair that caressed the nape of his neck in a very sexy manner indeed. He had eyelashes as thick as a feather duster, and she was sure that his Gaelic machismo could offer an exhilarating change from the over-experienced textbook prowess she was familiar with. However, eyelashes or not, Allo was due for a disappointment if he thought he was going to prove his manhood to this Yankee glamourpuss when, and if, she let him walk her back to the Grange. Dizzy Dawn may have felt, but stupid she was not.

The only memory Miss O'Day retained of her mother was the latter's one piece of advice which she gave her daughter, 'Always make 'em sweat a little before you give it out, and the stake is sure to double.'

It was this that had taken Miss O'Day so far up the star-making ladder and which she vowed would take her further along the dollar studded road to ultimate security, when her version of her famous Frivvle grew too familiar to stir the sexual excitement of her public. She could certainly not afford any gossip which might filter its way back to the Earl and spoil her chances of a little brow-soothing on his Lordship. Allo wasn't going anywhere, and his potential could be explored in the near future – right now Dawn needed to retain her reputation for exclusivity, so with a reluctant sigh she slowly removed his hand from her hipline, and her bosom from his Aran gansey, patted his cheek and teetered her way back to where Mr Klatch and Leonard, the suede-shoed Artistic Director, whom Riordan had so correctly classified, were standing in attitudes which could have guaranteed them a fifty yard headstart in any relay race. To their amazement Dawn linked arms with each one of them, (the brandy and the Irish jigging by now getting to her vision just a trifle) and said 'Fellas, don't you just adore the rural life?'

Leonard was not so enthusiastic – he had a feeling that Knockpeddar's male population operated on one kind of current, and it certainly was not his. If Oscar had not been so rotten about bringing over extra personnel he could have brought young Clifford along to this godforsaken bogheap. As it was, the naughty swine would probably race the hell out of the new sports car while Leonard was marooned in Ireland, and heaven only knew who he would have in the apartment in the meantime . . . the more he thought of his problems with Clifford, the more depressed Leonard grew. He decided he would get back to the

Grange and put a telephone call through to Hollywood and see how things were going. (It was hours later before he discovered that all telephone calls out of Knockpeddar took a minimum of two days to achieve, even providing that Miss Dunphy condescended to operate the exchange at the post office, once it came to six o'clock in the evenings. Since she was usually somewhere else most nights, the population of Knockpeddar had long learned to live very happily without the continuous availability of the telephone system).

Meantime Susan, having deposited the Canon safely back in the Parish House, had rejoined Oscar in Clancy's pub. Oscar was clutching a generous measure of bourbon and was surrounded by what can only be termed as a swallow of the local male drinkers, all of them regulars at Ned Clancy's. Oscar, in fact, was the centre of attention, no less for his hospitality (James had rapidly called for the first three rounds of drinks on Oscar's behalf), but also for what was turning out to be a unique talent. Oscar was setting a new record up for the longest spit in Knockpeddar, and Knockpeddar was mildly famous for the length and talent of its local spitters. But Oscar was already four feet ahead of the village champion, and he was having a marvellous time. Farther and farther down the floor of the snug went the base line between himself and the spittoon. Clancy's had been a haybarn in its original state before Ned had inherited his father's farm, sold off the grazing and converted the barn into a decent sized pub, fit for the hefty male population of Knockpeddar to drink in. So Oscar was more likely to run out of spit than space before he missed the spittoon. Paudie Quinn, who was now the last remaining contender, finally gave ground to Oscar's superior prowess, slapped down a pound note in front of Mr Lipperstein and with his last remaining spit anointed his own hand and saluted Oscar as the better man.

'Sign on dis guy – he spits real good and we'll use him in one of the bar scenes in the movie,' said Oscar, pocketing the pound with the air of a performer who has just received a favourable contract. He proffered cigars all around, and as the smoke quality in the snug moved up the social scale from black shag tobacco to middle price Corona, Oscar removed himself back to the Grange, having, in his mad moment of success, promised to represent Knockpeddar in the local spitting contest at the end of the month.

'How clever of you Oscar,' Susan trilled at him, as they drove back to Grange Peddar. 'Nothing like getting on the good side of the locals before filming starts! You're certainly making sure of their co-operation.'

'Yeah,' replied Oscar dreamily. 'Jeeze, did ya see that last spit I did? It was all of twenny feet I reckon.'

'I never knew you were into spitting,' said James. 'That's quite a talent you've got.'

'Neither did I, but I guess I got the muscle power deeze guys don't have,' said Oscar, puffing at his cigar with satisfaction.

'All gained from yelling at everybody else,' muttered his secretary, as she deftly removed the mutton-like paw that Oscar was placing quite absently on her thigh. It was all very good-humoured with no offence given or taken, as Susan was wont to advise James whenever he grew incensed at Oscar's constant hand manipulations when Susan sat without the width of the Most Adventurous Producer's mahogany desk between them.

Miss O'Day dozed quietly in the front of the car dreaming that she was winding the curly black hair of young Allo O'Brien around her toes, while he lay on a fluffy green and yellow striped towel by her swimming pool in Hollywood, clad only in the very briefest of swimming jockstraps, all of which went to show that the new paintwork and the digital expertise of her new acquaintance were combining to have a mind-bending effect on Miss O'Day. Had he known, Oscar would have had cause to be thankful to Allo, because from then on Dawn's Frivvle grew even sexier than it had been before, particularly once Allo took to spending most of his time watching Miss O'Day while she was on the set, and the rest of it trying to get her to examine the confines of his father's barn with him when filming was over for the day. And as he escorted his original female partner home that evening, Allo too, was looking ahead to future times which, with all the optimism of the Irish male, he was quite sure were going to prove highly satisfying for him one way or another. Meanwhile, didn't he now have within his grasp a young bird whose willingness to nest was only equalled by his own solidly ingrained refusal to either build the wherewithal or emulate the cuckoo. However, young Bernie Kelly was prepared to do a little rehearsing in advance of the main event, and who was Allo to disappoint her!

Chapter Eleven

Next morning, after downing a tumbler of liver salts, a Bloody Mary and two cups of black coffee, Oscar called a meeting of his executives, deciding that they might as well get on with the business side of the film before the camera crew and technicians turned up in Knockpeddar. Susan was delegated to accompany the Artistic Director and the Production Manager to recheck the locations James had organised, since Oscar was doing most of the interior shots back in Hollywood, give or take a scene or two. Mr Klatch was doing yet another re-write of the script, now that he had actually seen Knockpeddar at close quarters, in addition to which both Dawn and Oscar were already suggesting additional ideas which they had each come up with during their morning ablutions in the Earl's surprisingly well-equipped bathroom. Oscar was still keen to include some sort of spitting scene, preferably one in which he could, like Alfred Hitchcock, arrange to appear as a performer in his own film, even if it was only to be as a competitor in a 'Hit the Spittoon' contest, while Miss O'Day had spotted a painting of the Earl's great-great-grandma sitting side-saddle on a jet black colt, and she had a deep desire to include a scene which would feature herself in a similar attitude. She felt the publicity stills would sell very well in a land where horses beat sex by a short head, and the Earl too was a keen equine fancier, so it couldn't harm her chances to be seen on, beside, at the head of, or with, a four-legged friend.

Not that Dawn was in any way expert on horseback, but she was a trier, and if the scene called for it then Miss O'Day would always come up trumps for the final take, even if her stand-in had to do the real work. Mr Klatch had found that the atmosphere in Ned's pub was to his liking and it seemed only natural that he betake himself to the village hostelry with his notebooks, where, he felt, if he soaked up the local colour along with the local brew he could well end up with a script worthy of an Academy Award.

James was spending the morning making arrangements with a convent of nuns established twenty miles away, to board out the camera crew and the technicians. The order had been forced to close down its boarding school following a somewhat embarrassing affair in which the local gardener overreached himself in planting seeds of a non floral kind with disastrous results among the Upper Sixth, and the Sisters were finding it a bit difficult to meet the bills. They were happy to accommodate the film crew for the duration of the film. Later, three of their prettiest young postulants went missing when the crew pulled out, but then as the Reverend Mother reminded Sister Burser, when you win some, you usually lose some too.

All of which left Miss O'Day on her own, and at somewhat of a loose end. She decided to take a walk around the gardens in the hope that she might perhaps run into the Earl, or even a neighbouring representative of the local gentry with whom one could dally a little – after all, everyone knew that Irish landed folk had nothing to do all day but roam around each other's estates with fishing rods, guns and a couple of Irish hounds at heel. She collected the poodle from Riordan, who handed out the quivering bundle of white fur without comment, from one of the kitchen pantries. Dawn grabbed the pooch, with her usual extravagant shrieks of affection. 'Diddums then miss its Mommy, poochie pet?' And did nice Riordan give poochie pet a bitsy steak?'

To her utter surprise, Ching cowered back from her, huddling behind Riordan's left leg, nose to the ground and rump tucked in as far as he could get it. Both eyes closed tight and one ear twitched toward the butler.

Dawn stared at her pet. 'Has he eaten somethin' he shouldn'?' she enquired. 'He looks real sick to me.'

Riordan glanced down at the poodle. 'There is nothing wrong in the slightest with your pet, madam. He is settling down nicely. Give him another day or so and he will be a different dog.'

Dawn again bent down to pick up the poodle and again the pooch bellied away from her behind the butler. Miss O'Day could not understand it. She opened her handbag and produced a chocolate peppermint which she knew Ching just adored, and broke off a corner of the candy to feed to the poodle. Ching moved in to accept the morsel. Riordan coughed, and immediately the poodle stopped, shook his ears and retired again behind Riordan's left leg.

'If I may say so madam, animals do not need sweetmeats in their diet – it disturbs their temperament,' said Riordan, carefully fastening what Dawn observed to be a new-style collar and lead on her pet.

'Where's Ching's lovely red velvet and rhinestone collar?' she demanded. 'That collar cost me one hundred an' fifty bucks.'

'The collar is in your sitting room madam, I recommend that you use the one the animal is wearing – you will find he now prefers the choke chain and lead he has on him.' Riordan gave the lead a chuck and almost bowled over the poodle in the procedure. But Ching merely grovelled a bit and it was only when Dawn picked him up and tucked him under her arm that he opened his eyes and eased up on the shivering. As Dawn took him away toward the morning-room from which French doors led onto the rose garden, he suddenly pushed his head out from under her arm and gave forth a series of ringing barks at Riordan's back. Then, his self-respect slightly regained, he bit a piece out of Miss O'Day's crocodile handbag.

By the time the shooting was completed, Ching was suffering from a clear case of split personality and a permanent twitch in his right eye from the strain of trying to be two dogs to two people, neither of whom he could stand at any price. Miss O'Day continued to feed him chocolate drops and bits from her plate when she felt like it (and with Miss O'Day's fondness for food, Ching was not exactly stuffed to the back teeth with titbits). Riordan, having torn up the detailed daily menu given him by Miss O'Day, continued to put out a sensible canine food plate once a day, which, Ching soon learned, was his lot and which, if he failed to swallow it immediately, disappeared down the eager gullet of the black and white tomcat who was Riordan's nearest and dearest object of affection. Ching took revenge through the house – he piddled in odd corners, he gnawed furniture legs and curtain hems, he buried kitchen utensils in the reception room chairs and settees, just to embarrass Riordan. He even managed to get into the butler's bedroom and drag away a rather saucy looking pair of red silk pyjamas he found there, which the Earl had vaguely missed some months back but never thought much about afterwards, believing they were still at a certain flat in one of the better quality squares of the Irish metropolis.

Miss O'Day, however, discarded the lead and choke chain, which allowed Ching to run freely ahead of her. Like a white streak, he disappeared into a small potting shed in which Dawn could see a figure in the inner gloom, clad in soil-covered grey flannel trousers whose ends were tucked into a pair of turned down wellington boots. A battered felt hat was pulled down to cover the face and the owner was busily mixing a nauseous-smelling liquid mix with a stick in a rain barrel. He scooped up a watering can filled to the brim with the noisome mixture, and as he placed the can down again on the ground, Ching got caught in the slop-over which thoroughly soaked his immaculate white coat. Dawn was furious and she rounded on the yokel with all the skilled vituperation of a native Brooklynite.

She had already gone rapidly through his father's ancestry, when she realised she was actually tearing a strip off her host, the Earl of Grange Peddar, who was staring at her with total fascination.

'Oh – er – Earl, gee, I dinn't know it was you. Guess I kinda lost my temper some, nuttin' personal, you unnerstand? I'm a little sensitive this morning... Anyway, Ching shouldna been in here... please don't pay any attention to my little spat!' Miss O'Day could have kicked herself. To think she had cut loose like a cat house madam on his Lordship. But on the other hand, when did the books ever tell you that a titled member of the higher echelons would be mixing cow crap and water in a shed, wearing gear that a pan handler would have turned up his nose at?

The Earl hastened to assure Dawn that her little mistake had caused no ill will. On the contrary, he was quite enchanted by the lady's vocabulary. Not since his father's reaction when his younger sister had run off to Kenya with a penniless but persuasive coffee planter, thereby ruining the family chances of acquiring cash through a suitable matrimonial alliance, had he heard such turns of phrase, even though some of them were quite new to him.

He escorted Miss O'Day from the confines of the potting shed into the more salubrious area of the rather charming Victorian Folly, whose octagonal shape enabled one to see all sides of the rose garden from the windows at once. This could turn out to be most useful, since it was not as easy to be crept up on by anyone spying on one's activities, a fact the Earl now rather regretted, once he realised where in the garden his wife had spent a fair share of her time without the flower beds appearing to show the results of her labours.

He fussed around, unfolding garden chairs, fixing cushions, and lining up a table between them so that he could serve Dawn a cool gin and tonic from the little store he had in a corner cupboard. 'I sometimes come down here by myself, away from everyone,' his Lordship said, pouring them both a hefty slug.

Dawn nodded, her eyes big with sympathy. 'Guess you have a lotta responsibility what with the estate, ownin' the village an' all,' she commented, searching madly through forgotten scripts for the rights and duties of the Lord of the Manor, as seen by various Hollywood writers she had known and discarded.

The Earl closed his eyes as he again remembered that chauffeur. But for him he would not have the continual worry of keeping the estate even half ticking over.

Dawn leaned over and touched his hand. 'I know you must feel lonely at times,' she said throatily. 'You must always remember I want to be your friend – even though we don't know each other that long. I do kinda feel we have a lot in common. I'm a lonely sorta person myself. The responsibility of bein' a star is just awful – every damn thing you do gets chewed over in the noospapers.'

She touched her eyes with a tiny wisp of lace handkerchief and batted her eyelashes at his Lordship with considerable expertise.

'You see, Earl, I don't have a husband to lean on, and my Momma . . . isn't around . . . so I can say I'm on my own.' Miss O'Day's mouth tightened for a moment. Her mother's perfidy in taking off complete with Dawn's spare cash, her blonde mink jacket and her live-in boyfriend of the time was still a sore point, especially since her mother was now married to the same boyfriend, and had been one of the top hostesses in Kentucky ever since. It wasn't that Dawn had wanted the guy, who tended towards overweight and halitosis, but he was the first well-heeled swain who had actually walked out on Miss O'Day before she collected a more lasting souvenir than a fond memory, and her mother's departure had also left a gap in the domestic arrangements that Dawn now had to pay dearly to fill. So all in all, Miss O'Day considered that mothers were for other people.

His Lordship was quite touched. 'Please my dear, couldn't you call me Charles and perhaps I will be permitted to call you Dawn?'

Dawn wriggled happily – she was definitely making progress this morning. 'Sure – that'd be just dandy,' she cooed, and automatically she bent down to pick up Ching, clutching him to her white sharkskin suit, before she realised that the dog was in no state to be touched, not to mention pressed to the bosom. Ching had occupied himself in the interval between the potting shed drenching and his arrival in the Folly with an ecstatic roll in the newly dugover rosebeds, and the soil had embedded itself well and truly into his fur. He managed to deposit a fair share of it on Dawn's jacket before she dropped him rapidly back down onto the ground. Her jacket was not only filthy, but it smelled to high heaven.

Now Miss O'Day's dressmaker was under permanent orders to cut the star's garments so tight that it was just possible for Dawn to get into them. So there was room for nothing more under the sharkskin jacket. Miss O'Day was in somewhat of a quandary – she wasn't quite sure how his Lordship would react if she whipped off the jacket to reveal two of her major assets at eleven o'clock in the morning. At the same time there was no way she was going to sit around in a smelly coat until she got a garment down from the house to replace what she was wearing.

Gambling that Earls are also men, Dawn opened the buttons and with considerable gallantry his Lordship turned his back, receiving for his virtue a grandstand view in the antique mirror which his wife had hung in between two of the windows. Dawn tied her scarf bandeau fashion around the famous pulchritude, and the Earl thereupon made himself a vow that Miss O'Day was going to be the next Countess of Grange Peddar – assets like hers only accrued to the favoured few, and he was going to make sure he was among that happy band.

As for Miss O'Day, his Lordship's apparent gallantry so affected her that she decided that she was quite tired of fighting for her technical virginity among the smart-asses of Hollywood, and to be able to go through life without worrying that, at any moment, some huckster would make a grab at her, was well worth giving serious thought to. Besides which, she was getting mighty tired of living half the year on a diet of a lettuce leaf and four prawns in order to maintain her measurements

Life in the Irish countryside was becoming more appealing by the minute, especially if it also happened to include a real live Irish Earl plus a curly haired admirer on the side. So Miss O'Day too decided she would make a highly satisfactory Countess of Grange Peddar, where her assets would not only be respected but appreciated one way or another.

Chapter Twelve

Miss Dunphy the postmistress wasn't altogether idle behind her post office counter. She had put together a list of available accommodation in the village and had persuaded James that she was the best person to offer hospitality to the Casting Director, since, she pointed out, if he was housed anywhere else the locals would persecute the poor man for walk-on parts. That she was herself determined to obtain a speaking part in the movie she didn't bother to mention.

In the shop window was a printed list of room and board availability and charges (Miss Dunphy was making sure that no one was going to go over the prevailing rate behind her back), and as well as the accommodation list there was also an announcement reminding the locals that the film unit would be in the market for a number of props, such as horses' collars, farm carts, hand ploughs, flails, if anybody still had them, a couple of donkeys and an unnamed quantity of cow manure plus a sizeable quantity of soot.

Leonard was redesigning the river bank to include a hump-backed bridge, upon which most of the romantic scenes were due to be played. He was installing a white cement wall which needed to get an instant look of mellowing, and a liberal application of soot and cow dung was what Leonard decided would do the trick. If there was one thing Knockpeddar always had plenty of it was manure, not only of the bovine variety, but also of a porcine type, since at least half the local farmers went in for pig breeding. They were already having their problems with the disposal of the pig slurry, and Leonard's poster looked to them what one might safely term heaven-sent. They rightly calculated that a townee like Leonard would be unaware of the basic difference between the varieties anyway. Consequently, bright and early next morning, the village presented a somewhat unsalubrious sight, as a double line of dung-laden farm carts formed down the street. By the time a slightly distraught James had sent for Leonard, scuffles had already broken out among the early arrivals and the latecomers, who were accusing each other of breaking the queue, undercutting the quality and fouling up the roadway. Once Leonard arrived he was surrounded by the purveyors who demanded that he close the dung deal on the spot so that they could unload and get back to their lawful pursuits down on the farm. Leonard, eyes watering visibly as he stepped back onto the path out of the wind of the laden carts, could see he had a situation on his hands, and Leonard was really no good in situations. He called James.

'If I settle on one guy with his load of cow crap, the rest of them will kick my ass off,' he whispered, keeping a panic-stricken eye on the burliest of the farmers who was carrying a hefty looking blackthorn stick which he was waving about in a somewhat threatening manner.

James patted his shoulder reassuringly. 'Relax Leonard, you'll think of something – in fact, you'd better, and pretty damn soon too!'

Leonard got a sudden stroke of inspiration. 'We'll take the trailer loads. Those of you with horse-driven carts forget the cow crap, but we'll use your tackle, or if you have old farm machinery which I have already listed, bring it along tomorrow morning. OK?'

There were ominous murmurs and Leonard hastily spelled it out carefully for the farmers. 'We'll pay the same rates for the gear and tackle as we'll be paying out for the cow crap.'

The murmurs immediately changed to more satisfied sounds and Leonard escaped into Clancy's for a reviver. The farmers were half-way home before they realised that the labour costs were going to be a lot lighter for those of them who were renting out the farm equipment. Which explained why the next morning just after dawn there were five trailer loads of cow manure carefully dumped so that they blocked the only exit road through Knockpeddar, and they later had to be removed at treble rates (naturally) by the five lorry owners who had placed them there. After that, Leonard left negotiations to James to handle.

The next few days were busy ones for James and Susan, and their respective notebooks were full of lists and reminders. James was finding that the mechanics of film making were knee deep in details, most of which everyone wanted attended to instantly. He didn't get much opportunity to relax with Susan and let romance take over, for Oscar kept her working till all hours, running back and forth between Mr Klatch, Leonard and Mr Finkel, the Casting Director, who was by now well settled into Miss Dunphy's best room and being so well taken care of that he was seriously considering divorcing his fourth wife for retrospective neglect. Miss Dunphy was an excellent cook when she put her mind to it, and the little things which Irish husbands take for granted, such as warm slippers, pressed and cleaned clothes, freshly ironed shirts always at the ready, unopened newspapers by the breakfast plate, undivided attention in conversation and total acceptance of masculine opinions on everything, were suddenly part of Mr Finkel's daily life – he couldn't believe his good fortune, and best of all, he had no demanding offspring nagging at him for cash injections.

Ned wasn't doing too badly out of it all so far – he was already contracted to rent his haybarn plus a few odd sheds for storage purposes, and it went without saying that he got the contract to supply beverages to the catering section. Unfortunately, he had not been quick enough to realise that he could sub-contract the provision of the actual food for the film crew, a little arrangement that Miss Dunphy had taken over in company with a committee of local females, who were prepared to do the meals on wheels bit for the unit at a consideration which they divided between them, less a small percentage extra for Miss Dunphy. It was all very co-operative and turning out hamburgers, doughnuts and bowls of spaghetti bolognaise made a nice change from plates of bacon and cabbage, or mutton stew, which was almost compulsory diet in Knockpeddar, whose male population totally refused to accept even the faintest touch of cordon bleu cookery on its tables.

With Knockpeddar undergoing a theatrical face-lift, Fonsie was also a busy man. His problem was to get the lucrative work of remodelling the village well advanced, while managing to keep his ordinary clients, who were foolish enough to have contracted him to build their houses, in a state of reasonable contentment. As it was, he had to do a fast run around the various building sites where the houses were in a state of construction and remove most of the building materials in a hurry, since deliveries to Knockpeddar from the far reaches of Cork were, to say the least, very spasmodic. But Fonsie reasoned that since he wouldn't be doing any house building until the film unit job was completed, it seemed the sensible thing to use the materials already to hand, rather than waste valuable financial time sending for fresh orders which might, or might not, turn up inside of two months anyway. Consequently, at least three young married couples saw their first-born starting school before they moved into their first home, contracted to Fonsie when they were still single and ignorant of the ways of the Knockpeddar building industry.

But by far the most interesting event of the week in the village was what became known in local lore as 'Took On Day'. The current greeting in Clancy's was 'Were ye took on?' It even gave rise to a sort of new social system, those who were Took on and those who were not. While any dog or devil could get a working job on the set, being Took On referred exclusively to working in the film proper as an extra, and whether it involved being in a crowd scene or having a special walk-on part, or better still a line to say, made a definite distinction among the natives.

Oscar had hired the Parish Hall for audition holding and long before he turned up in his black limmo a long line had formed outside the doors, mainly composed of the younger population of Knockpeddar and district, who had nothing else to do in the mornings anyhow. The ballad group which had tried so valiantly to entertain Mr Lipperstein on his arrival had come along in their sartorial splendour, only the lads' mothers had managed to add a lining to the grey tweed trousers, so that they could at least stand and sit more comfortably. As he went by the crowd Oscar ran a quick eye over the feminine talent. There was something a little odd about the sight, and it was only when he had looked over a couple of them and heard them 'recite a little something' as the Casting Director asked them to do that Oscar spotted what it was.

All their hairstyles were similar – tightly crimped waves ending in sausage roll curls and only the lengths were different. Ever after Oscar believed that all Irish girls had this peculiar type of hair, and in future quests for realism he was to spend a lot of good dollars trying to get the Hollywood stylists to reproduce the phenomenon. If he had asked, anyone would have told him that the style was readily achieved by dextrous use of old fashioned curling tongs, providing what was locally known as a 'Marcel wave' since the village didn't run to a professional hairstylist.

Half-way through the morning Oscar's total boredom level had been reached. Most of the male aspirants, when requested to show their acting prowess, had obliged with Robert Emmet's speech from the dock, and by now Oscar felt that had he been on the jury, he would have long ago moved for a verdict of guilty. After twenty declaimers of the famous Irish dissertation on justice, no one could really blame him if he felt less than sympathetic toward Bold Robert. It was quite a relief therefore when a late arrival in the person of Miss Carmel Corcoran turned up for audition.

By any opinion Miss Corcoran was several cuts above the rest of the female talent. A year before Carmel had taken herself off to a charm school in Dublin, where she quickly found out that hair looked infinitely better when curled with heated rollers and curling brushes, that a pair of large green eyes were useful when you hadn't the price of a meal, and a well-shaped pair of legs crossed and recrossed at regular intervals could control the course of any job interview.

Unfortunately, like the Mona Lisa, Miss Corcoran had her flaw – her two front teeth had a definite tendency to protrude, which limited her modelling career in the Irish metropolis to a considerable degree. Within eight months Carmel had exhausted her financial resources, her sources of free dinners, and the patience of the modelling school director. She found herself a job as a receptionist in a filling station, which she relinquished on hearing from her mother in Knockpeddar that the film company was about to make the village into an Irish Shangri-La. She beat it back home to see how she too could get on to the bandwagon and make the price of an orthodontic job on her teeth.

With her newly acquired experience Carmel weighed Oscar up in a trice. Carefully she swept her long lashes up and then shyly down again and then back to look deep into Oscar's small black eyes. It never failed to get the subject's attention, she had found. As she netted Oscar's, Carmel gave a sort of absent-minded flick to her short flounced skirt, effectively lifting the fabric from her knees to reveal a stretch of smooth tanned skin disappearing in an upward direction back into the fold of her skirt. Oscar pulled his jacket over in a vain effort to control his stomach width. He even removed the stogie from the side of his mouth as Carmel approached him.

'Well . . . what have we here?' he asked with a leer, keeping his eye firmly pinned on Miss Corcoran's undoubtedly captivating limbs, and failing utterly to notice those unfortunate teeth. Miss Corcoran was used by now to keeping her naturally friendly smile well under control, since she had lost several good modelling assignments by laughing heartily before the contract was signed. Carmel came from a Knockpeddar family whose expertise in lying was the admiration of the entire district – a talent which now stood her in good stead as she gave Oscar and Mr Finkel a totally spurious account of her theatrical experience, which was in reality all gained, apart from the annual school play over at the convent up to the age of twelve, from the film magazines and library books with which she had been obliged to pass those lonely nights in Dublin while she was awaiting a suitable meal ticket to turn up. She was so impressive that Mr Finkel didn't even ask her to do a little something, and Miss Corcoran exited with a small speaking part in which she was going to play the loving best friend of the film's heroine Miss O'Day, and which Miss Corcoran was determined she was going to handle so well that she would act Miss O'Day off the screen, Frivvle or not. Meantime, she prudently tracked down Susan and signed on the dotted line before Oscar got a good look at those front teeth of hers. And as she left the hall Oscar felt his spirits and his libido take a lift. He just knew this movie was going to go well . . . he could tell that the natives would be full of co-operation!

Chapter Thirteen

Brenno O'Mahoney was the last to hear that the film company was holding auditions. Brenno had missed his nightly stint in Clancy's due to the fact that Beauty had been somewhat off form. The goat had been foolish enough to have chewed his way through half a packet of discarded mothballs which gave him a severe bout of camphorated hiccups, and Brenno hadn't the heart to leave him tied up in the haybarn while he sat cosily in Ned Clancy's snug with a pint of stout.

Consequently it was two days after Oscar had held the auditions that Brenno called into Ned's and caught up on the latest gossip which centred around the abilities of those who had been 'Took On.'

Brenno listened to the drinkers with what amounted to complete despair. 'Diya mean that all the parts in the fillum is gone be now?' he asked, and it was a clear indication of his seriousness that he didn't even take a swallow of his first pint before checking on the disastrous news he was hearing.

'Aye,' said Ned with some relish (between Brenno's normally unsavoury pong and Beauty's residue of camphor, Ned would willingly have ejected Brenno there and then, were it not for the fact that Brenno owed so much on the slate that Ned was determined to give him no excuse for non-payment when the summer harvest came around and Brenno again had a temporary cash flow.)

'Had ye a part for yourself in mind now? Like did you want to play the leadin' man, climbin' all over that blonde lassie, or maybe throwin' a leg over 'er in the lovey dovey bits!' The drinkers guffawed – everybody knew that by the time Brenno's Mam had gone to her just rewards, whatever shape they may have actually taken, she had traumatised her son sufficiently to ensure that he would never get any matrimonial ideas about any female, young or old, ugly or good looking, which probably accounted for the deep and abiding affection between Brenno and his goat. He felt safer with Beauty than with any other living entity.

'I wanted them to hire my Beauty – isn't he the cleverest

Christian in Knockpeddar,' said Brenno. 'There must be a bit of a part in it for him. Shure I could train him to do anythin'.'

'Could you ever train him to drop dead?' asked Ned sourly, casting an eye on the old cuckoo clock behind the bar. It was coming up to six o'clock and the Set Designer and Production Manager had got into the habit of stopping by for a couple of quick ones before dinner. Ned had no intention of having them accosted by the odoriferous Brenno within the confines of the snug, because the refusal which Brenno would obviously get from them was bound to provoke, and Brenno had been known to cause a deal of damage if he got mad enough to start a row. Not only that, but he had in the past returned later when things had quietened down, complete with his goat, and caused even greater destruction by giving the animal the highly secret correct cue to charge into the plate glass windows of the pub. What the phrase was that turned Beauty into a speeding demolition machine no one in the village could find out, since even at his most inebriated Brenno refused to divulge the information.

'Ah, you should have been here a couple of days ago – shure they hired horses an' harness and all the oul' wrecks of ploughs and I hear they wuz in the market for an oul' donkey as well. Ye missed it Brenno so ye did! Begod, they might have paid top money for that oul' goat of yours if they hadda seen it!'

Brenno moaned as if he were in dire pain. To think that the first night in ten years he had not come into Clancy's everyone else should have known about the auditions and beaten him to it. 'Who had the givin' of the jobs?' he said anxiously. 'Maybe I could get a word with him before I go on home?'

'Shure, won't he be in...' commenced one of the imbibers helpfully, until Ned clattered a couple of empty pint glasses together to drown out the voice, and glared at the helpful one who subsided rapidly into his pint again.

'You'd have to talk to the Big Man himself and he's up at the Grange,' said Ned, swiftly removing Brenno's empty glass from in front of him, and wiping down the counter in a most dismissive fashion. It was Ned's time-honoured gesture, that advised there was no refill about to be put in front of the customer, and it was a brave drinker indeed who would even question the proprietor's decision.

Brenno silently proffered his customary tin can for Beauty's evening tipple, and Ned filled it rapidly and ushered Brenno off the premises by the side door, just as Leonard and Mr Finkel turned in at the front entrance. Leonard sat down and sniffed. 'Jeeze,' he remarked, 'I can still smell that cow crap in here.' And he shuddered as he extracted a pink silk handkerchief from his jacket pocket and waved it vigorously about, filling the atmosphere in the immediate vicinity with 'Bal des Fleurs' which immediately fought and lost the fragrance battle with Brenno and the camphor.

Brenno slung the can over the handlebars of his bicycle and set off for home. As he wobbled along the road he brooded over this additional injustice in a life which was, up to now, kind of top heavy with inequalities. He had been the one to remain at home with the Mammy, hoping that over the years she would shuffle off her mortal coil before he got too old to appreciate the joys of being able to come and go as he pleased and to run the farm as he saw fit. Then, when she held on limpet-like to her uneventful life until extreme old age and boredom took her, it was too late for Brenno to enjoy the fruits of freedom, and when he checked on his mother's financial resources he found she had none to speak of, and what she did have she had hidden somewhere in the house so successfully, that after eight years Brenno still hadn't managed to locate the hidey hole.

So any plans Brenno might have had for farm improvement fell by the wayside and as it was he had barely enough to keep his thirst at bay from one unemployment payment to the next. Now here he was with financial stability and fame for his pet in sight, and he was to be foiled simply because he was in the wrong place at the wrong time. It was almost too much when his front wheel sprang a puncture just outside the Grange gates, which, unusually for them, were standing wide open. The avenue curved away around either side of the house, and on the distant terrace Brenno could see the unlovely outline of Mr Lipperstein, splayed out in a deck chair, obviously snoozing off the effects of his lunch, since he had a yellow handkerchief spread over his face and head, from what Brenno could see.

Suddenly the puncture became what Brenno saw as his Chance. He shoved his bicycle into the hedge inside the entrance gates and hared off down the road, covering the last half mile to his dilapidated abode in Olympic standard time. Puffing into the shed, where Beauty was lying on a discarded pile of his mother's old clothes, he grabbed the goat's chain and hauled him back up the road to the Grange. Beauty didn't want to go up the avenue – somewhere in his mind he knew such a journey would probably end badly, otherwise he would have been up that avenue before now, since open gates were open season for goats going walkabout. However Brenno removed the can of stout from the handlebars of his bike in the hedge and shook it enticingly before Beauty's nose, and the goat followed the scent of his favourite liquid at a brisk trot. Brenno worked his way around to the terrace, moving quietly so as not to bring Riordan out to see who was the unannounced caller who didn't use back or front doors. Oscar was a noisy spectacle – the yellow square of best silk was floating up and down in rhythmic semaphore with the thunderous snores that the Most Adventurous Producer was emitting from his adenoidal nostrils. The sound was quite melodic once you tuned in to the beat – a sort of cross between Tannenbaum and the Wiffenpoof Song.

Brenno stopped in front of Oscar's chair. There was a half-smoked cigar lying in the ashtray and, since it was not alight, Brenno considered it would ultimately be consigned to the trash can, so he slipped it into his jacket pocket believing that man's first commandment was 'waste not what others chuck away'. He absent-mindedly put down the can of stout on the ground, and like a shot Beauty had his nose into it, slurping the contents with a volume that competed well with Oscar's snoring.

Brenno moved cautiously over and prodded Oscar in the rolls of flesh that hid his trouser belt. Oscar only shrugged and changed his rhythm a little as he settled back into his noisy slumber again. Beauty was puzzled at this large human with the ability to make such funny sounds, so he pushed an enquiring nose into Oscar's left eye.

Oscar came to with considerable rapidity, to be faced with an apparition worse than he would ever expect to see in any horror movie back home.

'Jesus H. what's that?' he yelped, mopping his streaming eye and endeavouring at the same time to hoist himself up from the deck chair, a feat he would not have managed unaided, even if he had the use of both eyes. Beauty leapt back in surprise, managing to insert his hind leg into the stout can in his retreat from Oscar's wildly waving feet and arms. The goat hastily shook himself free of the can, which unfortunately flew upward and struck Oscar smack on the nose before continuing its way through the window with a resounding crash. This brought Riordan out onto the terrace at a gallop and he surveyed the unfortunate Mr Lipperstein, his nose pouring with blood and rapidly doubling itself in size which, considering the original proboscis Oscar's father had donated to his only son, was going to be quite something when the swelling ceased.

'Heavens above, what is going on – sir?' Riordan asked, hiding his satisfaction when he saw Mr Lipperstein's condition. Riordan had, after a week, had a plateful of the Most Adventurous Producer and his domestic habits, and the sight of his injuries produced in the butler a sense of exquisite pleasure. But appearances had to be kept up, and also there was the little matter of the broken window to be accounted for. True, Oscar would ultimately pay for the damage, but meantime Riordan would have to spend the time mending it, on top of all the other extra duties he was now handling in his various capacities.

'Mr Riordan, it was all a bit of an accident – shure I only wanted the gentleman to see Beauty, so's he could give him a part in the fillum. Tell sir that he's the cleverest goat in the country – he could learn anythin' an' I can teach him whatever sir wants 'im to learn.' Brenno, with his request out in the open at last, looked with infinite pleading at Riordan.

It was unfortunate that Oscar chose that moment to explode. Mopping up the stream of blood cascading down his cream and yellow check wool waistcoat and holding his rapidly increasing nose in agony, Oscar was hysterical with temper. 'Get that sodding goat the fuck outta here,' he bellowed. 'There's no way you'll come within a mile of my movie ya mad bloody jerk, or your goddam goat either!'

Riordan closed his eyes disapprovingly at Oscar's language, even if he understood the cause of it, and Oscar turned away, stamping off towards the French windows en route to the bathroom to do something about the mess his face and clothes were in. Which was a pity. Beauty took considerable umbrage at the tone of voice this purple-faced bloody-nosed human was adopting to his beloved Brenno, and he decided that Oscar needed to be remonstrated with in a way he would be unlikely to forget in the future. So the goat lowered his head and took off, ramming Oscar accurately into the butt, and landing him head first among the rose bushes, whose mulch had earlier been enjoyed by Miss O'Day's pooch and which had since been rewatered by his Lordship from the odoriferous contents of the water barrel.

Brenno grabbed Beauty's chain and hauled his pet to heel. 'Ye had no call to say them things to my Beauty,' he said chidingly.

'You'd better hop it,' said Riordan, slipping Brenno a pound as he made his way to the rosebed to extricate Oscar from the bushes. 'This is no time for favours – leave it for a day or so.'

Brenno retrieved the milk can from inside the drawing-room and made his way down the drive with a now untroubled Beauty trailing quietly behind him. He collected his bicycle at the entrance and both of them ambled home to the farm. Brenno sat by the fire until very late, trying to think up some way by which Beauty could join the other Took On people, but he realised that short of a miracle there was no way Oscar would allow either of them within a mile of the film set. He even thought of putting one of his mother's old dresses on his pet and passing him off as a human, but came to the conclusion that it would take too long to teach Beauty to walk about on two legs instead of four.

'If ye hadn't them horns on ye me lovely, ye might cod them ye were a little donkey pullin' a cart,' he said fondly as he rubbed the goat's bony nose in the dying firelight. Beauty snuffled sympathetically.

'Maybe if I asked that Brodie lad what he could do, he might fix you up,' said Brenno suddenly. 'Didn't I often give a hand to his uncle with the potato pickin' and maybe I should remind him about it!'

Brenno felt better as he settled down for the night – James Brodie, he told himself, was almost a local, a Knockpeddarite, and Knockpeddar people were clannish unless they were courting the same girl, bidding for the same beast, or playing a hand of poker. James would surely not see his Beauty left out of the money pot at the end of Knockpeddar's rainbow. With all that American knowhow James would surely think of a way to get the goat Took On, and Ned Clancy would no longer dare to refuse both Brenno O'Mahoney and his goat the bar service they would, as film stars, be entitled to expect.

Chapter Fourteen

Canon Hackett had still not come to grips with the changes which were daily overtaking the simple life in Knockpeddar. He had taken quite a fancy to Susan, in whom he discovered a kindred spirit when it came to an interest in archaeology and local history, and he was particularly touched when Susan told him that she had obtained several books about Knockpeddar and its environs before she even set foot in the country. He promised to take her to the ancient eleventh-century abbey, to show her the various holy wells in the district and the remains of the old Irish Sweat House which lay deep in the woods to the east of the village.

Susan appeared to be the sort of young woman who would wear a head covering to Mass, join the Altar Society after marriage, and in between sewing for the Foreign Missions produce what the Canon was fond of calling 'A fine Quiver of Young Arrows to the Bowstring.'

About Miss O'Day his feelings were just short of uncharitable. In her he saw the temptations he preached about, in particular during the Lenten season when self-denial and renunciation of the pleasures of the too willing Irish flesh of Knockpeddar's female population were occasions of sin before which he fought a Canute-like battle.

Only Mammon, he felt, could have endowed Miss O'Day with the sort of figure he had to avert his eyes from every time he met her in the village, and her method of walking along the public street should, in Canon Hackett's view, be declared illegal. Already, he knew for a fact, there were four accident cases in the County Hospital, all of the victims being locals over the age of seventy, who had fallen off their bicycles on seeing Dawn frivvelling her way down to Clancy's bar, clad in a skirt, the split pleat of which told them more in sixty seconds about the female form than they had learned in three score and ten years.

Nevertheless, the Canon had a sneaking fascination to extend his initial acquaintanceship with the star, and he awaited an invitation to dinner at the Grange with an impatience and anticipation that had put an onus upon him to say a second Divine Office daily in reparation.

As the full crew descended upon the village the Canon began to feel that a grave mistake had been made in allowing the whole business to get under way at all. He was already receiving complaints from the convent that only six of the final year girls were turning up for classes and those were the ones who had decided to become nuns, teachers, or Civil Servants, and were therefore not among the girls who had been Took On for the crowd scenes in the film. He also noticed that there seemed to be a considerable increase in the number of couples wandering in and out of the woods and the bar in Clancy's, and he was quite sure it was neither the wildlife nor the quality of the lemonade that lured them. And he was tired to death of checking the various laneways and byways around, since if he aimed to catch the culprits in flagrante amoroso, so to speak, he had to walk very quietly and his corns were currently giving him hell. It was strange, however, that no one seemed to be watching television at night any more – normally the Canon was able to see what was being viewed on the box as he walked around the village after supper, since no one ever bothered to draw their curtains. But there wasn't a telly in sight. Not that the Canon complained – he loathed television and its only merit in his eyes was that the weekly chat show from Dublin usually provided him with the subject matter for his sermons for Sundays. The sudden dearth of flickering screens vaguely bothered him and at the back of his mind lurked the thought that, whatever alternative entertainment was being pursued by the females of Knockpeddar to replace the nightly serials, kitchen dramas and romantic films, the end result was not going to be one the Canon would ultimately welcome. It was in all probability a case of the disease being a lot more permanent than the cure, Canon Hackett reflected, which brought the additional thought that in five years time he would have to build on another infant's classroom to the local school.

On one of his evening strolls he came across Miss Dunphy weeding the tubs of flowers which were her sole claim to a front garden, and he asked about the sudden lack of interest in the world of television particularly among the mothers of Knockpeddar.

Miss Dunphy was about to tell the truth until caution got the upper hand – she couldn't be sure how the Canon would react to what amounted to a massive deception on Mr Lipperstein.

'Well, Canon,' she said ingratiatingly, 'we've been having little chats with Miss King about life in America and she told us about the "ladies only" clubs they have over there, where all the local wives get together and – well – do good works for the good of the community, so to speak.'

'Really? How interesting,' said Canon Hackett, wondering if there was any way he could utilise the idea to his own advantage.

'Oh yes indeed,' continued Miss Dunphy. 'They visit the sick, for instance, and they have sewing groups for deprived children. They have improving discussions about the quality of life and they even run to poetry sessions and musical evenings . . . All very good for the soul, don't you think? So, now that we're organising this kind of thing for our women here, they don't seem to be as interested in the television as they used to be.'

Devoutly Miss Dunphy prayed that the Canon would not ask why this improving venture was centred around a discreet annex at the back of Clancy's bar, or why he had not been asked for the loan of the Parish Hall or his canonical presence as Committee Chairman. But she need not have worried. The Canon was not overanxious to add another group to the sizeable list that seemed to need his attendance and which left him very little time for his beloved chess games. He was only glad that the females had something to occupy themselves with in the evenings, and he felt that if Susan had a hand in the affair then it would not go too far astray.

Miss Dunphy felt a bit guilty about bringing Susan's name into the deception, and she made a mental note to warn Miss King that if his Reverence the Canon asked about the social club, Susan would back up her compatriots who, after all, were sacrificing several hours of nightly escapism for the good of the film and Jim Brodie. They deserved support, she felt, since their worst fears about the quality of early evening television had been realised, and if it hadn't been for the free tea and the sweet sherry Ned stocked it would not have been bearable at all. Their menfolk of course fared better – they could see the detective programmes, the westerns and the odd horror movies in what were idyllic surroundings – anywhere that wasn't home. It was taking regular pep talks from both Miss Dunphy and Susan to prevent the murmurs of discontent from Knockpeddar's women developing into a roar of rebellion, and Miss Dunphy was at her wits' end to know what to introduce to keep the ladies from packing the whole thing up and salvaging their televisions from the wardrobes and attics to be reinstated in the front rooms once more.

It was while she was subjecting her stringy grey hair to its nightly torture of being rolled up tightly onto the old-fashioned steel curlers which had once belonged to her mother, that Miss Dunphy came up with what she felt was going to be the perfect solution. It took a couple of hours solid planning out, but when she finally turned out her bedlight she settled down to satisfied sleep, in the sure knowledge that she was going to change the entire life of Knockpeddar's women for ever more, whether they liked it or not. That it would have far-reaching effects on the males of the village bothered her not at all. Miss Dunphy had long felt that Knockpeddar's men had had things far too much their own way and it was well time that things took a turn which would favour the women.

Looking ahead Miss Dunphy could see an equal sharing of domestic labour, regular husband and wife excursions to places of entertainment, rather than the segregated system which currently operated. She could envisage new divisions of family spending money, financial independence from a regular cash injection rather than dependence on the egg money or the carry-over from the housekeeping pittance, which constituted the wealth of most of Knockpeddar's females at present. Best of all, she could see a community of women who would have the choice of going out to work on their terms, rather than the current adherence to the system of being a working wife whose activities were strictly confined to the marital factory.

In short, Miss Dunphy was about to launch a scheme which would make over the women of Knockpeddar. Social Education was to be the name of the game and from the film crew she would extract a panel of lecturers on things like electrical repairs, fashion, make-up, finance and accounting, creative writing, organisation and methods, poise and personality development, work study and anything else she could think up as the time went on. And best of all she was going to ensure that Knockpeddar's First Citizen of government, Fonsie O'Malley, would arrange yet another respectable financial grant to make it all happen. Knockpeddar, she reckoned, could safely be described as a 'deprived area' and as such should be made to qualify for the financial assistance that a benevolent tax-paying public was press-ganged into providing for their luckless fellow natives.

Next morning therefore immediately after breakfast, having dealt with the early arrivals at the post office, she shut shop and tripped off to Fonsie's where she found Mr O'Malley nursing a somewhat tender head and an even more delicate stomach along with a hot whiskey.

As she put her head around the door, Miss Dunphy smiled knowingly at the dark grey bags beneath Fonsie's eyes. 'Another late night up there in the Government buildings?' she asked sweetly. 'What a powerful lot of work you do for all of us, to be sure, Fonsie . . . spending a hot summer evening working away in your government office . . . especially when the rest of the Dail members are on the summer holiday recess, from what I read in the papers. But then everyone doesn't leave Dublin for the month of July, I'll be bound.'

She stared at him unwinkingly and Fonsie took a convulsive swig of his drink. 'Come now, Fonsie,' said Miss Dunphy gently, 'there's no need at all to feel nervous – I'm not going to tell a soul what I might know of your . . . activities; that's our little secret, isn't it? Anyway, at the moment I've far more important things on my mind.'

There seemed to be a veiled suggestion in her tone that at some future date Miss Dunphy just might revive her interest in Mr O'Malley's extra-curricular pastimes and it made Fonsie even more nervous. Miss Dunphy's information files were reminiscent of time bombs for which she alone carried the detonator. And it often took very little flak to cause an explosion which could have very long-term domestic repercussions for the victim, particularly if there was a little something he would rather keep in a very dormant state.

'What can I do for you Maggie?' Fonsie asked cautiously. He knew Miss Dunphy well enough to be sure that it wasn't to ask after his health that she turned up at his home.

'Well now, it's a small matter of a little grant I want to talk to you about – a very small one really, so I'm sure you will have no trouble at all organising it for me,' said Miss Dunphy, seating herself in Fonsie's chair behind his desk. Without the slightest compunction she quickly flicked over his papers as she set down her handbag in front of her, noting with a single rapid glance that Fonsie had been awarded a sizeable contract for a sewage-laying scheme just twenty miles south of Knockpeddar, which was going to prove most profitable to Mr O'Malley both on and off paper, if she knew anything about the way Fonsie worked. And she had also spotted a couple of bills from a Dublin boutique which was most up-market and certainly one at which Mrs Fonsie would never ever shop. So all in all Miss Dunphy felt she was on strong ground with Mr O'Malley.

Too late Fonsie followed her gimlet eye and swept the papers into a drawer. Miss Dunphy merely smiled, and Fonsie silently took the document she held out, gave her pen and paper so that she could list all her requirements and waited while she enumerated them with infinite care and in considerable detail. He had no desire to have Miss Dunphy back on his doorstep to provide additional facts which were immediately available. Indeed, Fonsie devoutly hoped that never again would he have to suffer the sight of Miss Dunphy across his desk at eleven thirty on a summer morning, or any other time of day. Furthermore Fonsie prayed that the next occasion when he would have any contact at all with the post mistress would be as he followed her coffin to its final resting-place in the parish cemetery, and if he had the choice he would, he vowed, bring along a wooden stake to make sure the old witch didn't rise again and return to persecute him. In fact Fonsie was so anxious to be rid of Miss Dunphy that he paid little attention to her reasons for wanting the grant at all. He vaguely took in the information that it was for the cultural improvement in the area of female interests, and that was where he stopped. Which was somewhat of a pity as it turned out later, when Mrs Fonsie suddenly developed considerable expertise in accounting and business methods and moved into Fonsie's office where she finally discovered exactly how much money Fonsie really made, and life was forever changed for the unfortunate Mr O'Malley.

'One more thing,' said Miss Dunphy as Fonsie ushered her out of the dining-room. 'I think it would go down very well with everyone if you matched the amount of the grant with a donation, as a gesture of confidence in the whole scheme.'

Fonsie spluttered.

'Of course Knockpeddar has been waiting twenty years for a decent sewage system for the village... but I suppose that the proposed housing scheme over in Killsheelin needs modern plumbing too. Weren't you fortunate to sell that building land to the County Council all the same, Fonsie, when they decided to erect those houses. And to think you originally bought the land for a song... or so I heard.' Miss Dunphy widened her eyes innocently. 'Of course, if the people here heard they were being left without the new plumbing in favour of a housing scheme twenty miles away that isn't even built yet, and in which you have more than a passing interest... well, I don't know what the local reaction might be.'

She moved away down the garden path with a totally pulverised Fonsie behind her. 'What a pretty garden you've made... it's really a credit to yourself and Alice... a love of nature is very commendable.' Miss Dunphy closed the garden gate behind her and nodded brightly at Fonsie.

'I'll expect to hear from you within the week then,' she said. 'I knew it would turn out all right once we had our little chat.' Fonsie nodded silently and staggered back to the house where even a second hot whiskey failed to improve his disposition one little bit.

Chapter Fifteen

Meantime the great first day of shooting was approaching. All the local working talent was gainfully employed much to the satisfaction of the Canon. He observed with unclerical glee that they were being kept well and truly on the hop by the Americans who, when their first polite requests to speed up the job had little effect, were now weighing in with blistering language which, though the Canon didn't understand the half of it, appeared to be having results of a favourable nature on the speed with which they were getting on with the work.

There was, unfortunately, a strong aroma of pig slurry drifting downriver from the bridge, where half a dozen stalwarts were busily slapping wet dung along the concrete wall. The Canon stopped to admire a little blue painted rowing boat tied up with stays from the bank to the centre of the river, at the stern of which a young man was busily erecting a little wooden stand, obviously destined for the morrow's shooting schedule. The Canon was too polite to interfere, but he felt that the young man was making a slight error of judgement – the daily morning downpour in Knockpeddar would certainly leave the boat with a minor flooding problem, that is, if the craft was left there at all, since the village boasted several kleptomaniacs who stole everything that was not nailed down. But then these were little experiences that the visitors learned quickly, once the shooting schedule got under way.

He met Mr Klatch who was wending his way towards Ned's. 'How is the script coming along?' the Canon asked, delighted that he could converse with some authority with these strange people, thanks to a few sessions with Susan up at the presbytery.

Mr Klatch was pleased that someone was prepared to ask about his work without the intention of knocking his efforts, and he gave the Canon a rundown of the story as they sauntered down the village street.

The Canon was somewhat dubious about the plot but he didn't like to criticise since films were not his field, though he felt that he could have told Mr Klatch a thing or two about nature running true to form. After all, he reflected, there was no way that one could really believe that Miss O'Day was the sort of heroine who would, in any guise, fall in love with a simple, poor Irish fisherman, settle down in a simple Irish cottage, shun the advances of a dark and handsome stranger, dash in between her young husband and the dark stranger who also happened to be an expert swordsman (for some reason known only to Mr Klatch), when honour had to be defended, and inevitably receive the blade aimed at her husband into her lovely heart, all of which was to be followed by a dramatic deathbed scene and the slow Irish procession to the graveyard.

But Mr Klatch was so pleased with his plot that Canon Hackett hadn't the heart to discourage him. Actually the Canon rather liked the storyline – it appealed to his illusions, and who was he to query the expertise of a Yankee film maker on what might and might not sell? And didn't the whole idea promote the view that Irish females were saintly enough to die for the high standards of purity and marital fidelity they had always been famed for – Ireland was the isle of saints and scholars with an equal division to the sexes well-defined under each category, and justly so in the Canon's view, since he firmly believed that female education was the road to anarchy. Women, he was fond of remarking, should do the praying while the men did the saying, and every time he crossed swords with the nuns in the convent school his opinion gained a firmer hold on him.

The daily call sheet advised attendance on the set for six thirty the following morning, but at that hour only the visitors were to be seen making their way down the village street in the morning rain. The wiser members of Knockpeddar emerged at nine o'clock, when the shower ceased and the sun had dried up the ground again, just as it always did. It was after ten before Miss O'Day appeared, causing a considerable hush among the population as she emerged from her dressing caravan. She was clad in what America firmly believed was typical Irish garb of the 1800's – a bright red petticoat with lace underskirts, a Kelly green satin bodice heavily embroidered with yellow harps and shamrocks overlaid by a black wool shawl. She had her blonde hair in two plaits tied at the ends with green bows, her feet were bare and she was being led by a sizeable Irish wolfhound at the end of a length of baling twine.

Dawn was wearing what she believed was the simple innocent colleen look demanded by the script, and which she had practised for a good half hour in front of her mirror last night in Grange Peddar manor. So busy was she trying to maintain her expression that she utterly failed to observe that the wolfhound was veering left of an arc-lamp while Miss O'Day was veering right, and there was a crash as the baling twine wrapped itself around the shank bringing the lamp to the ground.

Allo, who had been an interested bystander, was quick to seize his chance to be a hero. He dived at Dawn, sweeping her up in his strong arms out of the very path of the arc-lamp, managing to include a quick feel of her bare leg as he caught her up in his arms. Dawn shrieked, as much from the shock as from the surprise at Allo's dexterity at that hour of crisis. The personnel on the set applauded with relief when they saw Dawn suffered no more than a bruised dignity. Someone located the wolfhound, now cowering behind a hedge at the other end of the village, and forcibly dragged him back onto the set. This time Miss O'Day held on to his collar and managed to make it as far as the rowboat without accident.

Her leading man was already installed in the boat and Miss O'Day was about to lean over the bridge, which had now acquired a landing stage to simulate a quayside, and utter her first lines of the day.

She sniffed suddenly. 'Oscar!' she shrilled. 'Have ya got a bag of dead skunk stashed here or what? The smell is terrible and I ain't goin' to stick around to make any scene with this stink everywhere. Get rid of it!' She stamped off the set and back into her caravan while everyone else stood around trying to decide how to get rid of the smell of the cow manure.

It was Susan who came up with a solution, thanks to her several visits to the Canon's house. She had a quick check with the property man and they drove up to Canon Hackett's, where his Reverence was in the vestry of the church sorting out the hymn books. Although the Canon was a little unsure whether or not he was about to commit a minor blasphemy, he could see the predicament the unit found itself in, and he willingly donated as much of the church incense as he could spare, plus the burner and a young altar boy to work it; when the take resumed after tea-break Knockpeddar's locals began to feel they were going through the third Sunday in the middle of the week, as they took in the aroma of incense mixed with Chanel No Five, which Dawn had liberally sprayed over herself before rejoining the set. As the cameras tracked her again to the rowboat, where she was to lean forward so that her décolletage would make a good camera shot for her fans, and at which she was to utter the immortal words, 'Ah, shure and begorra, Bran and I will miss ye,' while she threw an arm around the wolfhound's neck, Miss O'Day slightly mistimed her dramatic gesture and released her hold on the dog's collar.

Like a racehorse out of its gate, Bran took a flying leap off the bridge and landed fair and square in the rowboat which promptly upended, landing its occupant, the tripod and camera, plus the sound boom in the unsalubrious waters of the Knockpeddar river, and sending a minor tidal wave upwards which drenched Miss O'Day from head to foot. It was a pity too that it washed up against the concrete wall, dislodging a good portion of the pig slurry from its tenuous hold on the surface.

'Cut, goddam, cut!' Oscar yelled rather unnecessarily, while the locals, thinking it was all part of the plot, cheered with considerable enjoyment. Meantime Bran used the moment to swim away upriver and disappeared into the woods where he was not recaptured until long after the film was in the can and the unit departed back home to the States.

The leading man was having hysterics while two electricians endeavoured to rescue him from the foulness of the river, and Miss O'Day was busily reducing the newly built landing stage to bits, as she threw whatever was handy off set. Several years of starring roles had perfected her aim to a commendable degree, and Oscar from past experience kept out of her line of fire until she had exhausted herself.

Allo was faithfully standing by in the background among the camera accessories which interested him greatly, mainly because he felt he could use a couple of the batteries lying around. As he watched Miss O'Day's overarm prowess he was filled with admiration. 'Jasus,' he remarked to no one in particular. 'But couldn't she do real well with a couple of hay bales at harvest time?'

'Whatsalldat?' asked Oscar, pausing in the throes of a full scale argument with the leading man, who had just resigned from the entire movie, as he overheard Allo's remark and tried to remember where it was he last saw the handsome young man.

'Hay bales – we pitch 'em up on the buggy at harvest – you'll see how it's done next week when we cut me father's upper field,' explained Allo obligingly.

Immediately Oscar's mind moved into visuals – he could see shots of little Irish donkeys grazing in the lush summer meadows; he could see vignettes of tiny fieldmice sitting up nibbling barley stalks, not to mention the Irish summer wind, wafting across golden fields of corn or whatever it was that the Irish grew in their patches. But most of all he could visualise torrid love scenes for Miss O'Day among the cocks of ripened hay, with flashes of her long slim thighs, crane shots of her cleavage, and close-ups of her leading man's hand actions for as long as they were decently filmable. The thought of hands immediately brought back to Oscar just exactly where he had seen Allo previously.

'You're de guy that just saved Miss Dawn from the arc-lamp, ain't you?' he asked. Allo nodded. 'An' didn't you bump her the foist night we came here?'

Again Allo nodded. Oscar considered him more closely. He was presentable, Dawn seemed to like him, and Oscar now had no leading man. The delay while he re-negotiated for another actor with whom Miss O'Day was prepared to work, or who was prepared to tolerate Miss O'Day, would cost him plenty. Oscar prided himself that he could turn a tailor's dummy into a passable actor if necessary, and he was prepared to convert Allo O'Brien from farm boy to romantic lead, with much the same success as he achieved when he turned Miss O'Day from second grade stripper to leading sex symbol. His only error, which Oscar was determined not to repeat with Allo, however, was to allow Miss O'Day delusions of acting talent. With Allo, Oscar could see that all he had to do was reinforce Mr O'Brien's belief in his bird pulling ability and a happy relationship would be enjoyed by all.

Once he explained carefully to Allo, just what a leading man in a Dawn O'Day film would have to do, Allo couldn't wait to get on with it. But it was too late to do any more that day, what with the ruined landing stage, the upturned boat and Miss O'Day's costume ponging to high heaven by now, so Oscar decided to call a halt, and after James had explained to him about the regular morning rainfall Oscar and his director moved the daily starting time forward.

The unexpected break in schedule gave James and Susan an opportunity to go calling on James' Uncle Pat of the farm and no immediate heirs, whom James had had no time to visit since his arrival in Knockpeddar. James felt a little foolish driving up the rutted track in the long black limousine, but it was the only vehicle available and Knockpeddar did not run to a car hire firm in the village. However, the sight of the big car did not affect his uncle in the slightest. Patrick Brodie had little time for motor cars large or small, since his girth was far too massive to allow him to climb behind the steering wheel of anything smaller than a tractor. Anyway Pat Brodie was far too busy to waste time driving around the countryside – he was one of the busiest business men in the district, whose dedication to his activity was almost a legend over four counties. Indeed, his attachment to his commercial concern was one of the prime reasons for his overweight. Patrick Brodie ran the finest and most profitable poteen still in the south. Since his proud boast was that not a drop was sold until it was two years old, one could see why he had to work an eighteen hour day in order to satisfy the hundreds of customers he serviced.

After a five year battle with the local fuzz Pat now had a firm agreement with the sergeant of police. They would notify him in advance when they proposed to raid him, and he would install a couple of gallons of his brew in the unused outdoor water closet at the bottom of his garden. The police dutifully raided the outhouse, while Patrick's maturing stock remained undisturbed beneath the four enormous turf stacks at the edge of his turf bog. No officer of the local law was daft enough to enquire why Pat Brodie continually bought logs and coal, when he had stacks of such excellently matured peat which never seemed to be utilised.

In return for their lack of attention the minions of the law had a visit from the good fairy every Christmas, Easter and St Patrick's Day, when a two gallon container of best poteen was deposited inside the porch of the police station for their personal use and benefit. Only once in all the years, when a ridiculously ambitious young officer, so newly appointed to the constabulary that the shop creases were still in his jacket, came to do temporary duty in Knockpeddar did Pat get raided without being prepared for it. The raw rookie unearthed a sizeable cache in one of the turf stacks and was all set to pull down the other three, when by the good offices of a number of Pat's more influential customers he was suddenly recalled to Dublin, where he found a more congenial occupation handling the local brothel keepers at which he subsequently did very well.

In no time at all Pat had both of them sitting down in the big farm kitchen, where Susan's lap was immediately taken over by a large black and white cat which promptly and ecstatically kneaded her nylons into shreds as Susan gently tickled behind its ear. Pat eyed her approvingly. 'I see that cat of mine has taken to you,' he said, as he deposited three tumblers and a bottle of colourless liquid on the scrubbed wooden table and poured out measures big enough to choke on, which Miss King did immediately she took an uninformed swallow of what looked like an innocuous draught of clear spring water.

'I don't trust people who don't take to cats, and cats who don't take to people are usually smart enough to know they can't trust 'em,' said Mr Brodie as he solicitously pounded Susan on the back until she stopped choking.

'Now,' he explained, 'take a small sip to get your taste in, and then you can take a decent sized gollop of it.'

By the time they were half-way down the measure in the glasses Susan felt as comfortable and relaxed as the cat on her lap. She found she had flashes of conversational wit she never would have believed she was capable of; James seemed to be the most handsome, clever and charming man she had ever known, while Mr Brodie himself was, she told herself, cuter than a bug and a priceless treasure that some woman had failed to find and keep in the matrimonial stakes.

She loved everybody, even Oscar Lipperstein, as the glow of Pat Brodie's best brew massaged her senses. In the couple of hours that followed James and his uncle caught up on the family news while Susan dozed quietly in the big armchair, lulled by the purring of the black and white cat, the easy conversation of the men, and the unexpected effects of Ireland's answer to Indian firewater. Before they returned to the village she helped to make supper for all of them, and thought that the smoky bacon which Pat Brodie took down from a hook in his dairy and cut in solid slices was the most delicious meat she had ever tasted. There was home-made bread in the dairy, wrapped in a clean linen cloth as it cooled, though she saw no signs of a resident female around the environs of the farm kitchen. She concluded that Pat Brodie was equally efficient at domestic chores and fending for himself as he was at illegal brewing of poteen.

When she later remarked on his abilities to Miss Dunphy, the postmistress sniffed. ''Tisn't right that a man should be out there lookin' after himself without kith or kin around him. Of course by the time the mam passed on the father was long dead, the brother gone to America and like many another Irishman whose mother makes a tin god of him, he was too fly to get caught by anyone lookin' for a husband,' she told Susan with some asperity. For in her secret heart Miss Dunphy had once seen herself happily installed in the Brodie homestead with Patrick, and had spent many hopeful Sundays entertaining old Mrs Brodie to afternoon tea. But alas, once Pat gained the freedom of solitude, Miss Dunphy's chances with him disappeared for good.

Another soul who used the cancellation of the day's shooting to what he hoped would be useful effect was Brenno O'Mahoney. He decided that the only way to take advantage of any opportunity that might arise was to be around wherever it might occur, so he decided that his best chance was to stay close to the place they were shooting the film, with Beauty alongside him. He was taking the whole business very seriously. Not only did he give himself a reasonable wash, but he even changed into his Sunday blue stripe suit, wore a shirt, ragged of collar and cuff it is true, but nevertheless a shirt with which he could actually sport a tie – had he such an item in his meagre wardrobe. However he did turn up a knitted belt belonging to his mother which he felt did just as well. And most important of all Brenno actually gave Beauty a good sluice in the old tin bath which had been abandoned in the cow shed after his mother had died. He found a remnant of toilet soap in a drawer, and when he was finished he felt that Beauty was splendid enough to sit in the parlour of Grange Peddar manor. It had all been achieved with considerable effort – Beauty now stood, red-eyed and glowering at him, as he tied the knitted belt under his shirt collar and put on his Sunday cap. It had been quite a battle to get the goat into the bath, and indeed poor Brenno had had to fill it twice with water, after the goat had kicked it over him, locked in what was just short of a death struggle to break loose.

'It's all for your own good, me oul' segocia. You'll be meetin' a grand lady and ye'll have to look nice or maybe they'll run us again,' Brenno pointed out, but Beauty didn't seem to get the message and butted Brenno in the stomach in protest, and when he folded up from the blow followed it up with a vicious kick from his front hoof into Brenno's knee. Brenno could understand his pet's confusion, and was patient with him. He placated Beauty with an extra ration of porter until he calmed down, and then Brenno led his pet back down to the village, Beauty staggering slightly, since he wasn't used to a double measure of the black stuff so early in the day.

The village gossip level was at full pitch over the rowboat fracas, and only the original owner of the wolfhound was unhappy, although he was even now calculating how high he could send the price of his dog in the event of Bran not being located, so that he could resume work on the film. Brenno listened to the talk and, had he been a religious man, he would have breathed a prayer of thankfulness to a Providence who somehow seemed to have decided that, just for once, Brenno O'Mahoney and his pet should get a second bite at the cherry of good fortune.

Without a wolfhound, Brenno reckoned, there was now a vacancy for Beauty to step into, so while they were both still relatively sweet-smelling he decided to go in search of Miss O'Day herself, so that she could observe Beauty at close quarters and realise how ideal he was to replace that no account canine who reneged on his commitment at the first moment of theatrical pressure.

Finding Miss O'Day was no easy task. Brenno tried her dressing caravan but found it tightly locked and bolted. There was only an empty chair outside the door on which someone had left a pair of black lace panties, decorated with gold Lurex rosebuds, and Beauty promptly seized hold of them in his mouth, and chewed away happily as he and an anxious Brenno trotted back to the village where they tried Ned's lounge, from which they were immediately ejected by the proprietor. Brenno decided to make his way to the Grange, only this time he would not attempt to enter the grounds as he did previously, but he would hang about hoping to see someone from the Big House, who might tell him the whereabouts of Miss O'Day. Beauty was still ruminating over the remains of the lace panties when Brenno caught sight of his quarry, sauntering in the rose garden with his Lordship.

At the same time Ching, Miss O'Day's poodle, came gambolling down the drive and suddenly caught sight of the pair standing outside the gates. Without further ado he launched himself at Beauty with more nerve than wisdom. Beauty did no more than scoop the pooch up with his horns and toss him back up the drive, where he fortunately landed on the grass verge. Dawn, hearing the shrieks of her pet, came running while Brenno, having quickly looped Beauty's chain over the ironwork of the Grange gates, picked up the dog, smoothing him carefully before handing him back to Miss O'Day.

Suddenly Dawn caught sight of the shreds of black lace and a stray rosebud which was sticking rakishly out of the goat's mouth. 'Goddam . . . those are my drawers that blasted thing has in its mush,' she yelled, dropping the poodle and darting toward the goat, only to halt in her tracks as the goat lifted his head and his eyes suddenly glowed coal red at her.

Brenno moved swiftly over to his pet. 'Give the lady her . . . whatevers,' he commanded, and Beauty obediently opened his mouth and deposited a small tattered bundle of soggy rags into Brenno's horny hand. Brenno timidly proffered them to the star. 'Maybe you could put a little stitch in them ma'am, and then they'd be as good as new?' he suggested, stepping smartly backwards when Miss O'Day lifted her high-heeled pump and scattered the lace rags to the winds of Knockpeddar. For one brief moment Dawn said nothing, simply because she was having difficulty in getting her tongue around the phrases which were racing with the speed of light toward her lips.

Then she cut loose on the unfortunate Brenno who waited patiently until she paused for breath, and then somewhat unwisely asked her to consider using his pet to replace the vanished wolfhound. By the time Dawn had finished recommending what Brenno could do with his goat, what she would do if she even smelled either of them within a mile of the set, and the legal possibilities in front of Brenno, should hair or hide of her poodle be injured through its contact with the mad brute that had attacked without any provocation, Brenno had to face the fact that he would not gain the necessary support from the movie's leading lady to obtain a part for his pet.

'He's a real quiet animal, ma'am. I know well the two of ye would get along fine if you'd only give him a chanst,' he called conciliatingly through the gates as the star stamped back up the drive, followed by the poodle who proceeded to drag a back leg whenever Miss O'Day looked round at him. Brenno could not be sure what comment passed between the two animals, but suddenly Beauty belched loudly and tossed his head, while Ching deliberately stopped, turned, and peed. Then he yapped twice and continued up the drive in Miss O'Day's wake at a fast trot.

Brenno shook his pet's chain in despair. 'When will ye learn to take it easy?' he scolded as they made their way home. 'If ye keep on pickin' fights I'll never get ye Took On.'

Chapter Sixteen

Next day most of the village turned up to watch the resumption of shooting, especially when they had been told that Allo O'Brien was in the process of being turned into a real live film star. Already one of his friends had opened a book with the odds at five to four on Allo getting Miss O'Day into the back of the O'Brien haybarn by the close of play, so to speak. Dawn was quite looking forward to her first artistic confrontation with Allo. As a rule she couldn't stand the sight of her leading man, which made it difficult for her to display any kind of convincing involvement in the love scenes. This time she had a distinct tingle in all the important little places when she stepped out of her caravan and onto the set and beheld Allo, resplendent in dark green knickerbockers, a blue hunting coat, yellow silk stock around his neck, and a black bowler with a curly brim, plus a riding crop long enough to pass for a fishing rod under his arm. She thought he looked gorgeous and when the Assistant Director had managed to still the ribald laughter from the natives, by threatening to remove them immediately from the set, the scene got going.

Dawn frivvled towards him, holding out her arms at a level which would enable the tracking camera to get a proper outline of her bosom, her jawline and the carefully half-opened pucker of her mouth which Oscar had decided, with considerable accuracy, would always devastate her male fans. This was the moment when Miss Corcoran, as Dawn's faithful friend, was to dart forward and beg her not to be led astray by the handsome landowner, who was, of course, the personable Mr O'Brien. Carmel, careful to keep herself full face on to camera so that those unfortunate teeth would not precede her in profile, moved swiftly across, successfully blocking Miss O'Day from the shot but giving Oscar a grandstand view of the upper reaches of her elegant thighs as she did so.

For once Dawn did not halt shooting as she would undoubtedly have done had her mind been totally on camera angles and colleagues who could upstage her. She was too anxious to get to the close quarters part with Allo. She shook off the restraining hand of Miss Corcoran as directed, and only Dawn knew that Carmel managed to give her the most delicate of pushes which projected Miss O'Day onto the manly chest of Allo, who promptly clamped his hands over Dawn's buttocks, pulled her tightly against his well-filled knickerbockers and gave Dawn her first extra-terrestrial contact of the day.

Dawn didn't see it until the rushes were shown, so she was more than delighted with her facial expressions during her brief scene with Allo. Never, she believed, had she 'emoted' so well and as she remarked to the lighting director Mr Schlimminger, with his talent and the Irish light she was going to look better in this movie than in any other she had ever made. And of course Allo, Dawn already felt, was like a soul spirit who might yet become to her what Pidgeon was to Garson, Bogart to Bacall or even Travolta to Newton John. Mr Bennie Crisp, the Director, was also more than happy, especially when he saw the close-ups of Allo whose dancing fingers were almost poetry in motion. (James felt it incumbent on himself to advise that these particular frames be reserved for the American version when the film was finally completed.) Allo, too, had quite enjoyed his day – it was a lot better than counting cattle, shearing sheep or baling hay, and since his dialogue for the takes consisted only of a couple of 'Ahs' and a few well-timed gasps, his intellectual capacity was not exactly taxed. By the end of the first week's shooting he had built up quite a fan club. He was followed by a number of nubile young teenagers who seemed to have turned up out of the apparently deserted countryside and the outer reaches of north Cork, and they hung around the set all day waiting to escort Mr O'Brien homewards in the evenings, preferably by way of Knockpeddar woods, which Allo was more than happy to explore with them.

Meanwhile Miss Dunphy was busily laying the groundwork with Mr Finkel for a small part. Her ambitions did not stretch as far as a leading role, but she had hopes that some little cameo role would emerge that Mr Finkel would immediately decide was perfect for her undoubted talents and use his influence with Oscar to secure for her. She waited on him with an assiduity that turned her into a living legend for Mr Finkel when he returned to America. She even managed to produce an ancient cure which got rid of his perpetual indigestion, and she fed him more information about Irish life than he would ever have discovered in any library.

She was totally unscrupulous about reading through his manuscripts, which was how she found out that the young hero of the film was to have a mother in the movie, a part Miss Dunphy thought would suit her down to the ground, since it involved the sort of Gaelic maternal scheming which came so naturally to the postmistress anyway. And she quite fancied being in a position to attack and revile Miss O'Day even if it was only to be theatrical make believe, because from the moment she had laid eyes on the movie sex symbol Miss Dunphy had taken an unaccountable dislike to her. True, Miss O'Day had come into the post office and verbally laid about Miss Dunphy the first time she tried to make a telephone call and got cut off in midstream, because Miss Dunphy announced that it was six-o-five and the switchboard was closing for the evening; which left Dawn without the special range of body lotions that she had been in the process of ordering from New York, after a two day wait to get her transatlantic connection at all. Miss O'Day had not been informed of the importance, not to say the essential desirability, of staying on the good side of the postmistress. To her Miss Dunphy was only another inefficient Irish state employee, which shows how disastrous an ignorance of the local pecking order can be when one is a stranger, especially if the district happens to be Knockpeddar.

But Miss Dunphy did not intend to harass Mr Finkel as she saw other aspirants to fame try to do. She, instead, hovered around him in the evenings as he studied Mr Klatch's script notes, and almost before he knew it Mr Finkel was trying out phrases of dialogue with her in order, as she delicately put it, to get the true Irish phraseology and flavour to it, so that the Irish audiences both in America and on the home ground would not have their artistic senses insulted by words alien to the country and its culture.

Mr Klatch was enchanted to have her help and guidance, and after a few consultations it was only a step to Miss Dunphy regularly reading the various parts and giving what one could only describe as a sterling performance of the hero's mother, so much so that Mr Klatch and Mr Finkel actually besought her to test for the part! She was looking forward with much anticipation to her first appearance on the set when, she believed, Mr Crisp and Oscar were going to be exposed to a whole new dimension of Irish acting talent.

Down in the village the new prosperity was already beginning to make itself apparent. Now that the full line-up of technical and executive staff was established, the visitors outnumbered the natives by four to one. All of which meant a number of advantages – the local girls were splitting their social arrangements into two-hour stints, since there was a dire shortage of feminine company about. This did not exactly please the local male population, who now had to watch what they had constantly criticised in the most ribald terms, being wooed, wined and whoopeed by the Yankee visitors, while they were reduced to downing pints and playing pitch and toss to while away their evenings.

Ned, of course, was packed out every night mainly because there wasn't another hostelry within a ten mile radius of Knockpeddar. He was putting in an eighteen-hour day and was almost reduced to being teetotal since he never had time to enjoy a decent session in his own pub any more, what with bottling, cleaning up, stocking shelves and swabbing down. Not that he minded – that pile of lovely money was more than enough to console him, but he promised himself a really massive booze-up when the film makers had departed; only this time, he vowed, he would have it on the best brandy – after all by then he would be able to afford that luxury.

But the great business success of the entire occasion was Miss Madigan, whose drapery shop had undergone what could only be regarded as a metamorphosis. Under her genteel exterior and lace-collared navy serge shop dress beat a heart full of well concealed ambition. The arrival of the film unit presented to Miss Madigan a unique opportunity which she grasped instantly. Within two days she had commandeered the assistance of a local handyman who hadn't been quick enough to get 'Took On' when the Art Director was looking for carpenters for the building of the sets. She willingly sacrificed her front parlour which backed on to the shop, so that she had a display room with white shelves and a central wrapping counter. A quick trip into Cork and she was back with a consignment of Aran gansies, linen hankies, Irish tweed ties and waistcoats, and a range of pottery and souvenir goods which were the best the agent for the diligent workers in Hong Kong could provide. Her very best seller to date was a piece of granite, set into a plastic cube attached to a keyring and labelled on its accompanying card as being 'a chip off the Old Blarney Stone', which she had been most fortunate to discover in a small production outfit in a side street off the dock area in the southern city. Miss Madigan couldn't keep enough of them in the china bowl on the display counter, and she was already negotiating with the producers to go jumbo size and turn the keyring cubes into bookends, which she felt would go down a real treat with the Yanks.

Then there was the other big seller, a sod of turf screwed on to a wooden plinth and labelled with the name of each county of Ireland. These were doing big business also for Miss Madigan, since everyone seemed to have relatives from a different part of the country and they all wanted to bring back 'A Piece of the Ould Sod', as the pieces of turf were labelled, to their families. The fact that all the sods actually came from a local bog outside Knockpeddar, and were mounted on their wooden plinths by the same local handyman to whom Miss Madigan paid an honourable fifteen per cent of the retail price of a fiver apiece, was a business secret that neither of them was prepared to noise abroad. As it turned out the handyman was a fellow with considerable ingenuity in thinking up new lines for Miss Madigan's souvenir trade, and in the long run he did financially a lot better than his compatriots who got Took On by Stupendo Films Inc. property department.

Indeed Miss Madigan discovered she had entrepreneurial abilities she had been totally unaware of, and as she saw her commercial future grow continually rosier, her gratitude to the visitors and to James Brodie and all who belonged to him was rapidly becoming a religious fervour. So when James called in to buy a gift for his lady love Miss Madigan naturally brought out her finest wares for him to choose.

James passed up the knitted wollen caps, the thick scarves, the bainin cardigans and the pampootie slippers. He almost settled for a finely knitted evening stole until Miss Madigan brought out a box from under the counter. 'I think your lady friend might look nice in this,' she said almost in a whisper. 'I got in only the wan of it because it'd be fierce dear, bein' hand crocheted by an old woman who lives outside of Cork. I thought somewan off the film might buy it, but if you want it you can have it for what I paid for it meself.'

James looked at the contents – it was a delicately crocheted blouse with long sleeves, which closed with tiny pearl buttons down the front, and it was quite the most delightful thing he had ever seen. He knew Susan would look ravishing in it. Miss Madigan wrapped it as carefully as if it were the Golden Fleece and James paid her the fifteen pounds she insisted was all she wanted to charge for it.

James' gift could not have been more welcome – the Earl was giving a dinner party so that his friends could meet the American visitors for the first time, and Susan felt that an Irish lace blouse would pay a subtle compliment to her host and his neighbours, apart from which she knew Miss O'Day had nothing to compare with it in the wardrobe provided by the studio for her trip to Ireland. She was even happier about it when she heard from James that it was the only one of its kind in Knockpeddar.

So at seven thirty she descended the wide staircase into the hall, where already a small group of dinner guests was occupied with knocking back copious draughts of best Irish malt whisky. Susan, in her new blouse and deep wine-coloured velvet skirt which set off the rather charming old garnet earrings given to her by her grandmother on her twenty-first birthday, made quite an impression on the company. At least three of the men put down their glasses and veered towards her on the spot, but the Earl beat them to it and introduced her round the group, whereupon Susan immediately proceeded to charm all the females with her infinite wisdom and considerable knowledge of subjects like Irish tweed in American fashion, growing herbs in window boxes, Marilyn Monroe's skin problems, Robert Redford's love life and how to care for old paintings, Miss King being a remarkably widely read young woman in between fending off Oscar's amorous attempts.

Miss O'Day, of course, was late in joining the party as had ever been her wont back home, since she believed the star of any show should be the last to make the grand entrance. Unfortunately she stretched it out a bit more than was acceptable to Riordan. He had already allowed the usual half hour delay common among Irish guests, plus the established forty-five minutes' drinking time before the meal, and had prepared a rather delicate mushroom soufflé for an hour, which would coincide with what he was accustomed to, where timing was concerned.

As the assembled company waited – and waited – and Riordan's soufflé rapidly disintegrated in the oven, the butler actually did what he felt was unheard of in any civilised well-run household – he rang the dinner gong a second time. It was an action he had only once previously had recourse to – which was the day the Earl's sister and the coffee planter had disappeared to Kenya and no one had remembered to inform him there would be one less for dinner. Easygoing he might be, but the butler had one inflexible rule about being on time for the evening meal – indeed, it was said that the Earl's late mother had actually climbed out of her sickbed to sit in her accustomed place at the head of the table, and had considerately waited until the port was being passed before keeling over in her death throes.

Oscar, who had had to await Miss O'Day's pleasure to escort her downstairs, finally waddled onto the landing ahead of the star. Oscar was a riveting sight in a white lurex dinner jacket, and as he puffed down the staircase he looked like the Mont Blanc in an avalanche.

Miss O'Day had given long and careful consideration to her attire and had at last settled on a gown which was more remarkable for the bits which weren't there, than for the sections which were. The entire top of it was made of flesh coloured net with two embroidered butterflies settled at a level which would conceal the pink tips of Miss O'Day's well-publicised bosom. The bodice swept down to a deep V-shape well below belly-button level, where another butterfly spread outsize wings of brightly-coloured silken stitching, highlighted with sequins that caught the light in a somewhat lecherous manner. The collarline was modestly high under Miss O'Day's lovely throat and the skirt was voluminous in layers of chiffon which picked out the colouring of the embroidered butterflies. Dawn thought it was the best of all the knock-out dresses she owned and she did so want to impress his Lordship and the local gentry. After all, she would yet be holding court at the manor over the lot of them, so inspiring a little awe would not do any harm. The shocked expressions of the womenfolk who were, to a woman, clad in either plain silk jersey dinner dresses with long sleeves and bodices modest enough to display the family diamonds or the inherited real pearls, or in black taffeta cocktail suits and cameo jewellery, Dawn took for straight envy, so she turned her most dazzling smile on the Earl and the Colonel-type with the military medals.

His Lordship swallowed convulsively as Dawn moved close to him and waggled her eyelashes at him over her glass. 'Aren't you going to feel a little – chilled – my dear? Should I ask Riordan to fetch you a wrap?' he asked solicitously, carefully averting his eyes from the sequinned butterflies which now appeared to be winking at him from crotch level.

'Gee no,' replied Dawn ingenuously. 'I'm real warm-blooded. I feel just fine – I guess your steam heatin' is pretty efficient over here; at any rate, the Colonel here looks like he needs to take his jacket off. You poor man . . .' She turned to the Colonel who was panting somewhat. 'Let me give you a little rub of my cologne stick. I always carry it with me an' it's iced. I use it often on the set.' She charmingly dug into her evening bag and produced a large phallic-looking tube of perfumed iced cologne which she carefully wiped over the Colonel's forehead. Since she had to move closer still to him to reach up to his perspiring brow, the Colonel was so overcome that he had to take a tablet to restore his equilibrium.

Mercifully a tight-mouthed Riordan announced that dinner was served, and before she could do any more harm his Lordship took Dawn by the arm and ushered her into the dining room.

Riordan now proceeded to have his supreme revenge on Miss O'Day. While everyone else scoffed with great enjoyment the prawn-stuffed avocados, with loud congratulatory remarks to the butler about the high quality of the mayonnaise, Miss O'Day could only manage a single spoonful because the overdose of vinegar in her serving made it impossible for her to eat it. Her soup was so well-laced with pepper that tears sprang to her eyes and caused her eyeblack to run at the corners, rather destroying the smouldering look she had gone to such pains to create. Her helping of duck à l'orange was so larded with salt that she had to leave it to one side, and then she discovered that her helping of vegetables and roast potatoes had been similarly treated. She couldn't understand how everyone else cleared their plates and had second helpings as well. Dawn had been saving herself for this dinner and, in order to enjoy it while not having to worry for once about her weight, she hadn't had lunch at all and had only downed orange juice and black coffee at breakfast.

She was starving by the time dinner was finally on the table and now here she was, unable to get down the slop that everyone else was saying was total Cordon Bleu. One of the ladies actually confessed to his Lordship that she would be prepared to double the butler's salary if he would only come and work for her and cook meals like the one they had just eaten. Dawn couldn't understand any of it. She smiled weakly when the Colonel remarked what a tiny appetite she had, because whatever she lacked, it wasn't what the Irish are pleased to call a 'good stroke' at the table. When the coffee came around she ravenously gulped down half of it and then nearly spewed it all up again, because it had so much sugar in it that it tasted like treacle.

Since she wasn't eating over much Miss O'Day had more time to study the other guests, and it began to occur to her that there was something not quite right about them. There was, she told herself, not a decent dress among any of them and not a boob in sight. And when she looked at Miss King's crocheted blouse she noted that Oscar's secretary seemed to fit a whole lot more easily into the general picture than she did herself, knock-out dress or not. The women, who studiously avoided speaking or even looking at her directly, were flatteringly charming to Susan. The Hon. Mrs O'Kane, for instance, commented on the beautiful workmanship of that damn blouse she had on, and asked where she could come by a similar exquisite handwork. Miss O'Day was well aware that her own dress would cost nearly a year of Miss King's salary, yet no one had a single compliment to pay it. And already Susan had been invited to three homes for various entertainments and occasions, while she, Dawn O'Day, leading star of Stupendo Films Inc. was being treated like an antisocial disease. Even Oscar was neglecting her – he was engaged in a technical conversation on film processing with one of the men who displayed a keen interest in capital investment in the movie business. Dawn downed a couple of fast brandies and rapidly followed them up with a brace of double gins while they were going round, none of which did her a lot of good on her empty stomach. She began to feel quite light-headed and while the company was in the middle of a detailed discussion of the last fox hunt, a subject of which Miss O'Day knew nothing and was even less desirous of learning about, she moved out onto the terrace leading down to the rose garden.

She teetered slightly on her high heels as she fumbled around for a seat in the summer darkness and suddenly turned her foot on the tiles, which the Earl's great-grandfather had originally imported from Italy to lay on the sun terrace. Over Miss O'Day went, landing unceremoniously on her rump in the fish pond. Her screams brought the others running onto the terrace. Dawn was eased out of the pond and her rapidly swelling ankle gently but eagerly massaged by the Colonel, who laid an instant claim to first aid experience from his army days, even though his lady wife happened to run the local Red Cross classes in their area. His Lordship dispatched Riordan for the local doctor who turned up in record time when he heard he was to treat a movie star. He was a practitioner who had spent a lifetime in Knockpeddar without a great deal of financial gain to show now that he was close to retirement, so the chance of a decent fee was one which would have dragged him out of his grave to say the least of it.

Solicitously he manipulated Miss O'Day's foot, decided to strap it just in case, bandaged and wrapped her up to her knee, dosed her with anti-shock tablets, produced a box of sedatives and recommended that Miss O'Day return to bed and not lean out of windows again.

'But I ain't been to bed – I was just out from the lounge for some air,' Dawn explained drowsily as Dr Kelly packed his medical bag again and delicately dropped a sizeable account for his services in her lap, whose chiffon folds were now dripping all over the Earl's brocaded couch (a reckoning for which later turned up in his little black account book), and Dr Kelly stared over his spectacles.

'Oh, I thought you were already in your night attire,' he said airily as he went away. 'I should get to bed my dear, you could catch a chill from shock you know, particularly in those garments.'

As Riordan and the Colonel carried her up the stairs to her suite

Dawn began to understand a couple of things, and she immediately collared Susan who had come up to see if she needed any little thing.

'Do you see anything wrong with this dress?' she demanded, as she removed the gown and kicked it into a corner.

'It's quite a garment – for a movie,' said Miss King carefully, 'but in a backwater like this it's not likely to be appreciated as well as it might be.' Dawn was mollified.

'I wanna buy a blouse like the one you had on tonight – I guess it's more suitable for these old biddies anyhow. Where did you get it?'

With a deep but well-concealed pleasure Miss King informed her that the blouse was one of a kind, almost unique in fact, and Dawn got steamed up again.

'Well – I want one . . . I don't give a darn where it came from or who made it. She can make one of a kind for me, an' you can send someone down to that crappy shop and order it for me.'

Too late Miss O'Day had realised why she was getting the cold mitt from the rest of the female dinner guests and right now it was important that everyone should like her, if she was to make any headway with the Earl. No one knew better than Dawn just how subtly a female could bury the stiletto in another female's unwary back. If crochet and Irish tweed would win the popularity stakes then Miss O'Day was quite prepared to swamp her charms in either, or both – for the moment at any rate. When she hog-tied the Earl in well knotted matrimonial cords then, she told herself, she would set those schmucks on their equinal asses.

'Why don't you stop by the shop yourself?' Susan asked casually. 'After all Miss Madigan has lots of things you might find suitable while you are staying in Knockpeddar, and now that your foot is injured you won't be able to go shopping very far afield.'

Dawn, who was now cramming the contents of a box of chocolates into her ravenous stomach, calories or not, decided to take Susan's advice. It was obvious that she would not be working on the set for a couple of days at least, until Dr Kelly removed the bandages from her ankle, so she could while away a morning rooting through the stock down in Miss Madigan's.

His Lordship put an anxious head in around her bedroom door to see how she was recovering from the unfortunate accident. For one dreadful moment when he had seen Miss O'Day's foot he was afraid that, not only would the unit decide to pull out of the Grange altogether, thereby losing him a highly lucrative temporary income, but he also visualised a massive lawsuit for damages to Miss O'Day. So when Riordan suggested he should pay a courtesy call on the star, he immediately collected a cut glass bowl full of his best roses from its place in the drawing-room, and trotted upstairs to visit Miss O'Day.

When he announced himself at the door Dawn hurriedly stashed the box of chocolates under the bed, where it was immediately swallowed by Ching, and as promptly regurgitated again, thereby costing the studios the price of another Chinese carpet. Then Dawn draped the folds of her bed-jacket modestly over her bosom and bade him enter. As he sat uncomfortably on the edge of her bed the whole scene reminded Dawn of one of her earlier movies. She leaned forward, took his hand between both of her own and softly told him not to worry one little bit, that she would be fine.

'I cannot bear you to be sad on my account,' she said, falling into the very lines of the script she had played so well, even if she could hardly stand the smell of garlic from her leading man's breath at the time. She pressed his hand to her chest, and the Earl almost dropped the vase of flowers he was still holding rather awkwardly in his other hand.

'How brave you are my dear,' he said. 'I do hope you are not in too much discomfort.' Miss O'Day wanted with all her heart to inform him that her chief discomfort at the moment was the gaping void in her stomach which only a good steak would fill, but she could see she had a slight advantage and she didn't want to lose it. Instead she brushed back her hair from her forehead and looked into the middle distance.

'I simply can't wait to get back on my feet – after all, the show must go on,' she murmured bravely, and his Lordship regarded her with new admiration. Miss O'Day, he was convinced, quite erroneously, was the sort of young woman who would instantly climb back on a horse which had thrown her in a ploughed field or over a six foot wall. He was equally sure that Miss O'Day could also wrestle with the most stubborn of salmon on the dirtiest of days upriver, or could walk miles in the pouring rain on a beagle hunt. She was so obviously the dedicated type. And he was certain she would have no trouble in subduing the Income Tax inspector who called regularly and intimidated the Earl within minutes of his arrival. And of course, he reminded himself, she would make an infinitely more attractive sight across a breakfast table than any other female of his acquaintance. He shuddered slightly, recalling the long-nosed slightly collie-like appearance of his late wife, whose receding chinline never failed to irritate him. It quite spoiled the effect of the rather lovely de Lucey diamond medallion which each heir's wife automatically received for her lifetime, whenever the late Countess decided to wear it. Surreptitiously eyeing Miss O'Days décolletage, which by now was showing remarkably well through the transparent folds of her nightgown, his Lordship felt that the family jewellery would have a most charming and worthy resting-place on that creamy pulchritude.

'Can I get you anything my dear?' he asked solicitously, 'a cushion perhaps, a book from the library?'

Dawn smiled at him. 'I would love a little pot of your lovely Irish tea and perhaps a little brown bread?' she said delicately, 'and maybe you'd like to keep me company for a while. We could have a little chat. Guess there must be lotsa things to tell about this castle? Maybe you would have a little snack with me . . . I do hate to eat alone.' Dawn was being crafty. She had observed that the Earl's favourite night-time snack was a plate of fresh salmon, and she had high hopes that he would put a portion of it on the tea tray, which she could dig into without seeming to be healthily hungry so soon after dinner.

His Lordship went off to locate Riordan and a tray of tea for her, but Dawn's ploy was successfully foiled by the butler who suggested to his Lordship that he would leave a supper tray in the Earl's bedroom, so that he could enjoy the salmon with a cool glass of chilled white wine before retiring. Miss O'Day had to make do with plain brown bread which Riordan made sure was three days old and just about to be put into the chicken bin. True it was sliced wafer thin and delicately served on a silver plate (Riordan was good at that sort of thing), but it made poor enough fare for an appetite as sharpened by hunger and too much salt as Miss O'Day's.

The Earl was only too pleased to have an audience to whom he could recount the history of the castle, all three hundred years of it. It took quite a time and Dawn dropped off into a light doze at intervals, coming to at regular moments to widen her eyes and utter little murmurs of encouragement to his Lorship to continue. But his mention of the castle's resident ghost brought her to with a jolt.

'Ya mean ya have an actual hauntin' here?' she cried in considerable trepidation, huddling back among her pillows.

'Why of course,' replied his Lordship calmly. 'Grey Lady has walked the tower turret for over two hundred years and she turns up on occasions in the red drawing-room and in the grove of trees half-way down the back avenue. Some of the servants of years ago often told my mother that they had met her in the corridors, opening and closing room doors as though she were checking up on their work or looking for someone. They got quite used to it.'

Dawn shivered. If there was one thing she could do without, it was a Grey Lady peering around her door jamb to see what she might be up to. 'Gee, I'd just drop in my tracks if I ever saw anythin' like that,' she told the Earl.

'But Grey Lady would never frighten anyone – she is a happy spirit, according to family history,' explained the Earl patiently. 'She was an ancestor who loved Grange Peddar so much that she never wanted to leave it, so her spirit still remains in the building, and anyone who ever saw her said she laughed and smiled at them before she disappeared.'

'I don't care – I'm sure I'd just go crazy with fright,' replied Miss O'Day, as she looked cautiously around the bedroom.

'Well, she hasn't turned up in this wing of the house so far,' said the Earl consolingly. 'So you will probably never catch a glimpse of her. It is only on very rare occasions these days that Grey Lady materialises.'

Just before she dropped off to sleep, Dawn recalled that Oscar had his room in the tower turret which consoled her somewhat. After all, she told herself, maybe Grey Lady herself would take off for somewhere else, once she caught a good glimpse of Oscar in his purple and green striped pyjamas.

Chapter Seventeen

Next morning Dawn departed for the village, followed by the film's Publicity Director, a young man named Marvin Heimer, whose first major assignment this actually was. Marvin had handled a dozen or so very minor movies for Stupendo Films Inc., a few television one-offs, but nothing outstanding for as important a star as Dawn O'Day, so he was eager as a bird dog to flush out all the publicity quarries he could raise. Miss O'Day, with her lovely leg well bandaged, hobbling around on crutches and shopping in the little local village store like an ordinary unsophisticated local girl, was great for media openers, so Marvin betook himself and his photographer along at a civil distance until Miss O'Day declared herself ready and willing to be photographed.

Miss Madigan took the party's arrival at her emporium with a professional calm that did her credit. After all, she had had the advantage of an early morning visit from Susan to clue her up about the blouse and what she might do to turn the financial tide to her advantage. Dawn ordered a couple of kilted skirts, a linen blouse or two, and a couple of Aran gansies, threw in one of the gossamer knitted wool shawls and then came to the main event.

'About that blouse you sold the other American girl,' she said. 'It's not bad looking. I might buy one if you have my fit.'

'Well now, miss,' said Miss Madigan rather offhandedly. 'It's not so much have I your fit, but have I a blouse at all for you, and the fact is – I haven't. That wan was special, and I haven't another in the shop.'

'Can't you order me one?' persisted Miss O'Day.

'Ah, well now, there's the trouble, you see,' said Miss Madigan. 'The woman that crochets them can only do one at the time, an' she's an oul woman of eighty-three or so. It takes her a fair length of time to work – her eyes not bein' what they used to be. In fact I hear she's thinkin' of giving up the whole business altogether.'

Dawn was not pleased. 'You must talk her into doing one for me,' she insisted. 'An' what's more, I need it fast. I don't care what it costs, I gotta have one.' She had decided that it was time his Lordship took her away from the castle for a quiet dinner à deux, and this time she was going to be dressed as he was used to seeing his dinner companions clothed, all nice and modest.

Miss Madigan seemed to consider the position most carefully. Then she smiled, and had Miss O'Day been familiar with Irish feline behaviour she would have instantly recognised the expression as being exactly similar to the one seen on Riordan's cat, when he trapped the mice behind the kitchen stove and gave them the option of being roasted or captured.

'Well now, Miss, I could go specially into the town and see her meself tomorrow. Shure maybe she would have one half done for someone else that she could let me have for you, seein' as how it's yourself that's wantin' to buy it.'

Dawn was delighted and full of smiles again, and Marvin took the opportunity to get a few quick pictures of Miss Madigan and Miss O'Day at the shop counter.

'Now about charges,' said Miss Madigan delicately. 'Them blouses aren't cheap at the best of times and what with havin' to make a special trip to persuade old Mrs O'Neill with a few extra pounds to hurry things up, I'm afraid it'll cost you around the seventy pound or so.' Dawn waved a careless hand dismissing the subject. (Later when she found that the Irish pound in Knockpeddar was on an exchange rate of five dollars which set her blouse at a sum of 350 dollars, she rather regretted being so casual, since there was no way the studio wardrobe department would agree to pay for it and Dawn hated spending her own money at any time.)

Miss Madigan totalled up her purchases, wrapped them up in the bright green paper she had now taken to using and Marvin began the lengthy photo session in and outside the shop with Miss O'Day to get the best possible pictures, for which Miss Madigan, in true Knockpeddar tradition, later sent an account to the studio's Publicity Director to cover the use of her time and premises.

On the set too things were moving along well. After two weeks Oscar had progressed to the odd exploratory reconnaissance half-way up Carmel Corcoran's thigh, before she found it advisable to halt his trip which she had so far managed to achieve with the most innocent of attitudes. In fact Mr Lipperstein sometimes felt quite guilty over his own persistence and was now doing his best to make up to her for his temerity. Now that Miss O'Day was unable to turn up on the set, Oscar decided that Miss Corcoran could do stand-in for her on the long shots and he was quite astounded how like the star Miss Corcoran became, once she donned a blonde wig and showed Oscar how successfully she had mastered Miss O'Day's famous Frivvle. Oscar congratulated himself not only on having saved the cost of bringing Miss O'Day's regular stand-in all the way from America, but also on his perspicacity in engaging as talented a young woman as Carmel Corcoran for the picture. By which it can be gathered that Oscar was making long-term plans for Knockpeddar's ex-model. They may not have been exactly honourable, but then Miss Corcoran's aims were not above reproach either. Already she was squirrelling away as much loot as she could into her local friendly Building Society deposit account so that the final exodus of the movie unit from Knockpeddar would not see her alone in a hard cruel Gaelic world, when her personal sights were set on a kindly American cosmos well-illuminated by backlights, fillers, kickers and keylights. Carmel was headed for the land of great white opportunity and if she could get there on a complimentary ticket then, she reasoned, her little fund would last all that much longer until a well-heeled dinner date, or better, turned up to ease the cash flow problems which might occur temporarily until she found her artistic feet.

However it was taking most of her experience as an unmarried female Knockpeddarite, used to fighting the good fight over the years, to sustain the virginal state in which she still technically could classify herself. Carmel held to the local adage that no one bought a cow while the milk was going for free, and the most she was prepared to offer was a small sample of the product, until someone made her an offer she couldn't refuse. And it was beginning to seem as if Mr Lipperstein might come up with the golden number, but Carmel felt her timing would be all important. Which is why Oscar was still only at the negotiating stage.

Meantime they both met each morning in Ned's for a pre-lunchtime drink, and if it occasionally crossed Oscar's mind that he was changing ten dollar bills with considerable rapidity over the course of an hour or so, due to the high rate of exchange at the Knockpeddar hostelry, Miss Corcoran kept his mind off things financial by occasionally pressing her splendid thigh against him in a manner that promised endless delights once Oscar became bold enough to look for them. The difficulty was that Carmel's actions belied her ingenuous prattle as she chattered about all sorts of simple and unworldly subjects, so Oscar could be forgiven for remaining in a state of continual uncertainty as to the extent of Miss Corcoran's knowledge of the world of carnality. And the luminosity of her dark eyes shining with a childlike innocence from the morning dusk of the lounge corner seat, was a definite inhibitor that made Oscar feel like a dirty lecher for even thinking the things he was considering. He had never met anyone quite like Carmel, which wasn't surprising, since she was a breed of female particular to Knockpeddar, where the nubile woman had to be fleet of foot and wily of wit to avoid being deflowered before she was tall enough to decipher the sexual graffiti on the lavatory doors at the convent school.

One of the more interesting developments was the emergence into the world of administration of his Lordship's butler. Like Miss Madigan, Riordan had discovered an entirely new career for himself and quite by accident, which made it even more satisfactory.

Miss Dunphy, having put the women's educational and social programme in operation so to speak, since Fonsie, as expected, came up with the required grant to fund it, was in need of an administrator and Programme Controller to take over the scheme, now that she was about to join the galaxy of movie stars in the making. She attempted to make out a list of persons to whom she could entrust the allotment of the fund, the organisation of the lectures and training sessions, and the general co-ordination of money and resources. Apart from his Lordship, the Canon and herself, she couldn't come up with another soul she felt would be entirely trustworthy – floating cash around Knockpeddar was usually quickly submerged by someone or other without trace, which was why there was no possibility of ever raising charitable funds through lotteries, bingo, weekly collections or other games of chance which involved someone collecting and delivering cash from or to the citizenry. Now this all left Miss Dunphy in somewhat of an awkward situation. She mentioned the problem to James and Susan, hoping that James might take on the co-ordination arrangements. But James had to point out that local opinion could prove very sensitive to a stranger handling the finances of the new scheme, and it was almost an inspiration when he advanced Riordan's name as a possibility for the job.

Riordan was not given to mixing too much with the villagers, but on the rare times he turned up at the pub for a draught of Ned's best whiskey he was always pleasant, bought his round with the best of them and never talked politics, religion or sex in the bar. The more she thought of it the better Miss Dunphy liked the suggestion. Anyone who could organise Grange Peddar so that it even paid half its way, as she knew from her interest in the mail for the Grange that Riordan managed to do, obviously had an ability beyond the average. Riordan had enough 'presence' she felt to subdue the more vociferous among the females, enough sophistication to charm the shy ones and enough drive to make sure that whatever was begun was also completed. Miss Dunphy was looking far beyond the current period of prosperity in Knockpeddar and was determined to train her female associates accordingly, and Riordan was quite obviously the man most likely to ensure the plan would be successful. Best of all, she knew he was as honest as the daylight over any monetary transactions, since he paid all his Lordship's bills, put on his racing bets, balanced his estate accounts and attended to small financial transfers to a certain discreet Dublin address, which Miss Dunphy knew all about but would never in a million years dream of divulging, since she felt his Lordship deserved all the good times he could afford after the perfidy of his wife with her mechanically minded paramour.

Riordan was quite touched to be asked. Miss Dunphy had made a point of going to the Grange herself to see him in private, and as they sat companionably over tea and some of Riordan's home-baked apricot gateau, she explained her plans for the women of Knockpeddar after the movie team had departed.

'You know, there's an awful lot of untapped talent here in this village,' she commented, delicately wiping the crumbs from the corners of her mouth. 'If we could turn it into a business co-operative we'd have a little industrial mecca down here in no time, that would make mincemeat out of Killarney as a tourist centre. We'd have no competition in this part of the country at all and no need of it with the sort of ideas I have in my head.'

Riordan looked interested. In the quiet of his sitting-room at the Grange, on many a night he had given thought to ways in which he could get rich with reasonable speed before he grew too old to enjoy the benefits. Miss Dunphy gave him the feeling that they were on the same wavelength, except that she had moved further along with her ideas and might even have a practical programme to put in motion.

'The men in this village are never going to be smart enough to do anything to improve what the politicians are pleased to call our "quality of life",' Miss Dunphy went on. 'So I feel we must motivate the women to get the business started and then make sure they are properly trained to run things instead of letting the men get in and ruin every operation we might start. We have a golden chance now to make use of all these film people to teach us what they know, and when we have the knowledge then we'll have the strength to do things our way.'

Riordan nodded – the idea of a matriarchal society suddenly operating in Knockpeddar had enormous appeal. 'And when your ladies have the expertise in commerce, finance, arts and crafts, law and whatever else you are planning to have them taught, what will you do with them?' he asked curiously.

'We'll build a tourist complex . . . you know about Disneyland in America, don't you?' Miss Dunphy asked.

Riordan nodded again.

'Well,' continued Miss Dunphy, settling back in her chair, 'we'll build a Tir na nOg, the Land of Heart's Desire or whatever you want to call it, but it will have leprechauns, fairy princesses, castles, enchanted lakes and magic caves filled with lovely expensive souvenirs. You'll be able to join the Fir Bolg and fight with the Fianna, or ride in Queen Maeve's chariot, or swim with the Children of Lir down on Lough Bawn – in short we'll re-create ancient Ireland in Knockpeddar and make a real bomb of money out of the Yanks and the Germans. After all, if the Americans can do it with Donald Duck and Mickey Mouse, I think we stand a fair chance of making a few bob out of Brian Boru or Deirdre of the Sorrows, don't you?' She sipped her tea, studying Riordan's expression over her teacup.

'Of course we'll have fairy gold to use instead of your real money, until settling-up time comes at the end of the holiday. We'll board visitors in Irish cottages and reconstructed beehive-style huts. It's surprising how much comfort people will sacrifice for atmosphere. We'll also get in on the medieval banquet racket. If we do it all right, I'm telling you everyone will make a stack of money.'

Riordan was enchanted. 'You know, I think you might be on to a good thing,' he said, pouring Miss Dunphy out a sizeable glass of the best port. 'I went to a couple of medieval banquets and they were booked solid every night and all the customers got was a glass or two of mead, a couple of spare ribs to gnaw on, and some very indifferent madrigals performed by a troupe of overweight young women. But the tourists loved it.'

'And take Spain,' continued Miss Dunphy, who had never been abroad in her life, but who kept well up to date through the travel brochures she ordered from several Cork tourist agencies every year, on the off-chance that she might someday decide to treat herself to a two week package holiday in Benidorm or Torremolinos instead of settling for a week in Kinsale as she usually did.

'Now the Spanish have those bullfights and these Flamenco affairs that they bring the tourists to, and by the time they've downed a couple of glasses of Spanish Red Biddy, they don't give a damn who's dancing or what they're eating. Now couldn't we come up with something just as good as your bullfight or your Spanish dancing?'

'I have no doubt at all that the whole project will prove a model for the rest of the country's tourist centres, Miss Dunphy, and with your excellent mind behind it I can only anticipate considerable success,' Riordan said, generously refilling the postmistress's glass. Wild horses would not have kept him out of the plans – Riordan recognised organising genius when he saw it, and he wanted to be part of the good life which he was certain was about to come. Meantime his job was to make sure that the ladies did their homework, developed their minds and commercial talents, nutured their artistic leanings and kept from getting pregnant, since women in Knockpeddar were old-fashioned enough to believe that a mother stayed at home with her hand in the cradle once she had some human bundle to put into it, and it just wouldn't do if the group were to lose even temporarily the new talent which he hoped would emerge from Miss Dunphy's Social Education scheme.

In a matter of two days Riordan had a file of lists, schedules, bookings and a full complement of guest lectures organised. He had the advantage over Miss Dunphy with his lecturing staff, since they all turned up at the Grange throughout the day one way or another, and he was therefore in a prime position to approach them, mention terms and clinch the deal all at the same time. He worked long into the night to sort out his budgets, having deducted a reasonable percentage for his own salary as Administrator/Controller, and finally he made his way down to Ned to arrange about the availability of the back lounge for classes and lecture sessions.

Initially, Ned was delighted to hear that the lounge would be required all day up to and including the hours he had already allotted to the ladies for television viewing, but not quite so pleased when Riordan informed him that he would no longer be serving the sweet sherry nor would he be offered any extra reimbursement for the use of the snug during the non-television hours. Riordan was quite adament when Ned protested there was no way he could sacrifice the snug without payment of some kind. And after all, he had already ordered four cases more of the sickly tasting barrel rinsings that passed for sweet sherry in his hostelry, and if he couldn't offer them for sale, how would he sell the stuff otherwise, since the only people who would drink it were the matrons who knew no better or could afford nothing else.

'Not a penny, Ned,' said Riordan firmly. 'This is a socially orientated scheme for the ladies and like all potential plans for improvements in living standards it doesn't have any cash flow behind it. After all, you can always make a little on the side if you offer morning teas and biscuits, or even a sandwich or two if you know how to make them. So you won't be at a complete loss.'

'It can't be done, Mr Riordan, with the best will in the world – shure where will I put the regulars who like to use that snug?'

'Ned, I happen to know that the snug in question was a store room for empty cartons before the film unit arrived. But if you really feel you cannot continue to allow the ladies to use it, and make it available throughout the day as I request, then perhaps I could persuade his Lordship to allow us the use of one of the drawing-rooms up at the Grange. I could, of course, also organise a buffet service from our own kitchens so that the ladies would be able to avail themselves of a pleasant break in their studies for morning coffee,' said Riordan silkily. 'Did I mention that we expect to have up to thirty ladies each day at our classes?'

'Now that won't be necessary at all, at all,' said Ned hastily, doing a fast calculation as to the profits on a minimum of thirty cups of tea, sixty sandwiches and treble that in biscuits. As the sum clicked into place he grew visibly more cheerful, especially when he added another ten per cent on to the cost as a distribution fee. And who knows, but maybe some of the women might have a hidden fondness for alcoholic beverages in mid morning, and if they were available, who could tell what impulse buying might go on through the day?

So good were Riordan's powers of persuasion that the turn-out each morning of potential entrepreneurs was highly encouraging. It was quite amazing how many secret desires suddenly surfaced among the down-trodden women of Knockpeddar, once the means of dredging them up became available.

Mrs Fonsie O'Malley, for instance, discovered an unusual flair for bookkeeping, auditing, company law, diversification of assets and transference of stock, and her ability within a couple of days' tuition from the film's Financial Director to draft foolproof schemes for tax avoidance was nothing short of brilliant. A mouse-like spinster, Queenie Regan by name, who lived in unbroken boredom with her elder sister, found a whole new dimension to her life after attending lectures on communication, script writing and media utilisation given by Mr Klatch, and she plunged into an excitingly torrid new world, writing soft porn novels under the name of Lucian Saint Clair.

A comely young matron who had recently married a carpenter, now working full time with the movie unit, gave her sagging marriage and her own talents a new lease of life when she took up the trade for herself after instruction sessions from the Head of

Props. Not only did she modernise the primitive cottage her husband had presented her with and which he never seemed to have time to improve, but she was later in demand for improvements, design and modernisation, quite apart from the course on interior decoration she managed to fit in between her first and second offspring. When she opened her own business she refused to employ her husband because she said his standards weren't high enough. But as she told Miss Dunphy, he made a great stores manager because he never stole so much as a screw, due to the fact that she gave him shares in the supplies subsidiary and if stock was missing his bonus was accordingly reduced.

Knockpeddar later got itself the finest health and beauty salon in the south, after a younger sister of Carmel Corcoran got clued up on the potentials from the head of the movie make-up team. Later it all did Miss Dunphy's heart no end of good to see the expensive transport parked outside Delma Corcoran's 'World of Venus' where the visitors subsidised the costs of glamorising the local girls, and new standards were set for any Knockpeddar male interested in dating the local feminine talent.

'You know, Mr Riordan,' she confided one evening as she strolled over to the Grange with a cake of her whiskey bread for the butler to try, 'I must say I never thought you had such organising talent, even though I knew you were his Lordship's right-hand man. The way you've got this whole course worked out, not a hitch, and the women tell me they are all doing extremely well in their chosen subjects.'

Riordan nodded a trifle smugly. Even the Canon had complimented him on the way the women were occupied these days – indeed it was hardly worth Canon Hackett's while to sit in the confessional now, because the ladies had so little to confess, which meant they were well occupied and out of temptation as far as the devil was concerned at any rate. And wherever the unmarried girls were hiding, he was not finding them in the grab-and-grope situations down the laneways to thc the same extent as before. (It was only later he found out there was a motorised shuttle service between the village and the boarding school housing the film crew, which took up much of the romantic slack during the long warm evenings.)

'It is to be hoped that you won't let it all go to waste once the film unit has returned to America,' said Miss Dunphy gently. 'I feel that there must be a more inspiring future for you than being butler – important as the job is, of course,' she added with haste. 'I know that you are much attached to his Lordship's family; didn't your father work for his father, as I recall?'

Riordan nodded. 'Indeed he did, and I never expected to do anything else, but go into service. It is strange how a single instance can change a lifetime decision, Miss Dunphy.'

'Do you know,' said the postmistress suddenly. 'I think you would make a first class politician. I could just see you in the government, administering and organising on a grand scale, just as you do here. You'd be a sight better than Fonsie O'Malley, who's only in it for the perks he can get out of it for himself.'

'I doubt it, Miss Dunphy,' Riordan replied. 'Fonsie does manage to "pull strokes", as he puts it, in a manner I could never stoop to. A great many of the people in Knockpeddar use his abilities for their own ends too.'

'But it always costs them when Fonsie does them a favour,' cried Miss Dunphy. 'I'll bet in a month you'd be just as clever at pulling a stroke as ever he was, but you would never screw people down the way Fonsie has always done.'

Riordan smiled, not ill-pleased at the thought. She was really saying what he had been considering himself of late, and if Miss Dunphy put her mind to a little promoting, then who knew where he might end up? 'Let me pour you a little brandy, my dear Miss Dunphy, it is so good for one's energy,' he said gently, and Miss Dunphy settled herself in the armchair with a sudden feeling of being treasured – a sensation she had not experienced for a considerable number of years.

Chapter Eighteen

It was the week after Dawn's little accident that Susan was entertaining James to a quiet dinner in the flat over the garage, where she was installed thankfully well away from Oscar's demands. Mr Lipperstein truly believed that a secretary's job should be a twenty-four hour occupation, and previous location work had convinced Susan that if she wanted any free time at all, then the only way she would get it would be to have accommodation as far away from Oscar as she could manage to find, and hopefully with no telephonic communication whatsoever between her accommodation and that of Mr Lipperstein.

The garage flat was a charming place. Her ladyship had spared no effort in making it attractive for her friendly chauffeur and if the pink silk curtains, white carpet and rose-coloured eiderdown were perhaps more to feminine taste in the main bedroom Susan didn't complain, and James felt more than comfortable in the living room among the real hide leather armchairs with their deep buttoning, the well-placed mahogany tables and the built-in hi-fi system, which was positioned at a level that did not necessitate having to get out of the armchair to push the buttons. It was peaceful and relaxed and a soft evening breeze drifted in through the open window as they sat replete after their meal, lazily sipping their coffees in companionable silence.

'My Uncle Pat likes you,' said James reflectively. 'He said he hoped I'd use my common sense and not let you get away from me. He also said he thought you would make a great farmer's wife.'

'Did he now?' said Susan softly. 'And what do you think then?'

'I,' said James mischievously, 'think you probably have the best child-bearing hips in Knockpeddar!' and Miss King promptly threw a cushion at him which missed him and sailed out of the open window.

'Now see what you made me do,' she chided, going over to the window to see where the cushion had landed. Down below Brenno and Beauty were standing mesmerised – at least Beauty was standing, the unfortunate Brenno had taken the force of the cushion straight in his face, which had by its very suddenness from above caused him to fall backwards onto the ground. Beauty was still looking up at the window from which the assault had come and then he lowered his head and gave a protective lick of his tongue to Brenno's face and hair.

'Arragh, I'm kilt down dead,' Brenno moaned, and James hurried down the stairs from the flat, closely followed by Susan who had thoughtfully picked up the brandy bottle as she passed the drinks tray. She poured a generous draught down Brenno's willing throat, who, when he spotted the bottle in her hand, opened his mouth automatically as a fledgeling in a nest. A second mouthful and Brenno allowed himself to be helped to his feet. Beauty, having observed that his owner was once more upright, had moved companionably over to Susan's side and she was engaged in rubbing in between his horns in a most friendly fashion, of which the goat showed his entire approval by gently nuzzling her knee.

'Goodness, I am sorry,' apologised Miss King with concern. 'I didn't mean to hit you with a cushion ... we were just having a bit of fun.'

'Aah ...' replied Brenno with a world of meaning, looking from one to the other. Susan blushed and Brenno felt ashamed that he had credited what he could see was a well-stood young lady, of whom his pet hugely approved, with any sort of base behaviour. 'No matter Miss, twas nothin. I'm as right as a trivet,' he assured her. 'I really came to have a little word with yourself and Mr Brodie, if you weren't too busy to talk to me for a minnit?'

'Perhaps you'd like to come upstairs,' Susan suggested hospitably, but then she remembered Beauty. 'Well, perhaps another time when you're on your own,' she amended, and James quickly steered Brenno and his pet over to the garden seat that decorated the small lawn in front of the garage entrance.

'It's me goat, Beauty, here,' Brenno began. 'They won't give him a part in this fillum, you see, and they have chickens, an' donkeys, an' cows and God knows what else booked to be Took On, but no one will give Beauty a chancst, an' I've set me heart on it ... shure Beauty would be a real addition to that fillum, I know he would.'

'I'm sure he would,' said Susan still rubbing Beauty's head, 'but you see Brenno, the script doesn't really call for a goat – of

Beauty's particular talents. He's really too good for this particular movie.'

Brenno was only slightly mollified. 'But ye see, I promised Beauty I'd get him in the picture, and every wan in Knockpeddar thinks I'm an oul' eejit to be attached to this animal, an' I want to show 'em all that Beauty is a real prize. That's why I want him in the fillum, Miss, not for the money, but just to show that Beauty is the cleverest goat in Ireland.'

James looked at Susan in despair. Even he was sorry for Brenno and Beauty, but he had already heard the instructions from Oscar and Miss O'Day loud and clear, to keep Beauty and Brenno as far away from the set as human endeavour could manage.

'Beauty can do all sorts of things,' Brenno was explaining to Susan, whose tender heart was quite touched by his devotion to his ripe smelling pet. 'He can break up a fight between a gang of tinkers once you give him the word, or he'd break down a door for you if you wanted him to. An' he can fetch and carry for me like a dog would. He'll come an' tell me when the cows come to the gate in the evenings at milkin' time. Now where can you find another goat that'll do them things for ye?'

'I'm sure you won't find another like Beauty,' said Susan tactfully. 'Look Brenno, leave it with myself and James and we'll try and think of something. Meantime why don't we all go down to Ned Clancy's and buy Beauty a good big can of stout and yourself a couple of glasses of whatever you fancy?'

James gave a resigned sigh – any plans he might have had for the rest of their evening were obviously not going to come to fruition. Still, there was a small consolation to be gained by the look on Ned's face when the three of them turned up at the pub, and Ned with gritted teeth was obliged to serve the two cans of stout to Brenno's pet in the new lounge in front of all the clientele, simply because Brenno was keeping better company than he was accustomed to, and Ned could not risk offending these two important visitors who were also picking up the drinks tab and paying it in Yankee dollars. As for Brenno, his heart swelled with triumph when James requested that Beauty's pint of stout be served in a bowl so that the goat could get at it more comfortably, and Ned had to go into the back and return with one of his own domestic utensils, the bar not being given to having pudding bowls among its glass collection.

They were joined during the evening by Stupendo's Publicity Executive, Marvin Heimer, whose enthusiasm for a successful outcome to his efforts at publicising the movie were causing him to work a sixteen hour day, much to the amazement of the good folk of Knockpeddar, for whom a sixteen hour week was almost pushing it a little at the best times.

'Any bit of news we could use?' he greeted them, automatically fumbling a biro from his breast pocket and a notebook from his briefcase, without which no one had even seen him in public. Already there were rumours emanating from his lodgings that he slept with it under his head in place of a pillow, which was an unjust lie, since Marvin settled for stashing his case *under* his pillow to be sure it was always safe and secure. He was to be found daily scouring the highways and byways of the village environs in search of little items of news which like a good P.R. man, he could convert into entertaining news stories which would keep the public interest alive in the Stupendo film until the unit returned to America. After that the bigger fictions aimed at the international media, such as rows among the cast, divorces, romances, dalliances and so on, could be dreamed up between editing, final printing and première date to send the whole production off in strength if not in good taste. Marvin was not having a very productive time – two early illegitimate pregnancies directly attributed to members of the camera crew for which the studio was already negotiating payments, two minor thefts of coils of electrical wire, and one case of gastroenteritis contracted after one of the property department was ill-advised enough to try a bowl of the pub soup, were hardly world shattering news items. True, Dawn's accident and the discovery of Allo O'Brien as a potential movie star had kept his achievement schedule up to date so far, but Marvin was beginning to feel somewhat desperate for news, now that the movie was so well underway.

'Have you done anything about the ghost at the Grange?' asked James. 'Maybe someone has already seen it walking around the corridors.' Marvin made copious notes as James told him the history of the Grange's Grey Lady.

'There's Holy Well in the woods and an ancient Sweat House,' said Susan helpfully, 'perhaps you could make something out of those . . . And the Canon tells me there's a giant's gravestone up in the old cemetery. He says the story goes that a younger brother of Finn McCool is buried there and the gravestone is eight feet long. And maybe there's a wishing stone around somewhere that you could take Dawn along to and have her photographed making a wish.'

'And we all know what her dearest wish is at the moment,' said James, as he caught sight of Allo O'Brien downing a quick pint at the bar counter before he slipped into the back lounge to catch up on the nightly television programme. Allo was followed by half a dozen of his friends and as the door closed behind them the last man turned, jerked his head at Ned, held up seven fingers and made a large circular movement in the air with his right forefinger before disappearing into the apperture.

Ned moved in behind the bar, where he busied himself loading a tray with seven pint glasses brimming with a fill of Ireland's national brew. Marvin emptied his glass discontentedly. 'Jeeze, this is the worst one-horse burg I've ever been in. There isn't a thing stirrin' in the place and no TV.'

'Well,' said Brenno eagerly. 'There's me goat here . . .'

James rapidly cut in before Marvin's interest in the goat was aroused – much as he wanted to help Brenno, he knew that if Marvin were to write a single line about the odoriferous goat, Oscar and Dawn would hang him out to dry and then pound his dessicated corpse into the ground. 'You know Marvin,' he said, 'you ought to spend more time in here because the local pub is the place it all happens at in village life. You get all the gossip going round, everybody drops by at some stage of the day to pass the time, and the publican is the real listening post for news in any Irish pub. He knows everything that goes on.'

Marvin listened with respect – after all, wasn't James a native Irishman and a second generation Knockpeddarite as well, and wasn't he the Film Advisor? His advice was worth accepting. Marvin was not given to frequenting hostelries due to the unfortunate fact that he was a teetotaller, thanks to being reared by an overpowering mother who flatly refused to have even root beer in the house. Marvin never drank anything stronger than a sasparilla and it was a liquid which was unknown in Knockpeddar if not throughout the pubs of Ireland. He was making do since his arrival with glasses of a nauseous raspberry cordial which gave him pink teeth and indigestion.

'I think you ought to make a friend of Ned,' said James earnestly, 'and forget about hanging round in the bushes hoping to get a scoop should Dawn go astray with Allo O'Brien any evening.' Marvin blushed. He didn't think anyone had been aware of his nightly sojourn behind Dawn's dressing room. It was as much a labour of love as a professional vigil, because Marvin cherished a hopeless passion for Miss O'Day who, so far, had been completely charming to him because he was busily trying to publicise her, and was prepared to take any instruction she cared to hand out, as long as he was allowed into her presence. Marvin didn't trust Allo one little bit, and he was aware that Dawn was more than willing to dally with Allo well into the reaches of the Irish evenings. Marvin knew that such dalliances would come to no good conclusion if that smart-assed Irishman were not kept under constant observation. So every night he hid in the bushes, ready to leap out like a hunting hound to keep that Irish stag at bay.

However he could see his job was on the line and his schedule would certainly have to be altered to fit in a couple of daily visits to Ned.

'Buy Ned a pint or two and chat him up,' advised James. 'You never know what he'll tell you when he's had a few drinks.' This confirmed Marvin's worst fears that, as his mother constantly pointed out, drink was a key that unlocked the tightest mouth to give the unscupulous humans (especially young women, she reminded him) total power over the unwise imbiber. (Three days of the raspberry cordial in copious quantity while he chatted up Ned, and Marvin in desperation and total discomfort moved onto Irish whiskey and from there on never looked back, remaining in a happy alcoholic haze until the day he died. He ultimately married an Italian girl who was the only offspring of a wealthy vineyard owner, and he subsequently fathered seven daughters in between drinks.)

'You know, there's something mysterious about this bar anyhow,' said James confidentially 'I'll bet there's a good story hiding here somewhere if you can get hold of it.'

Marvin perked up like a squirrel which has just seen a cache of nuts in November. 'What sort of story do you think it is?' he asked breathlessly.

'Well, it's either illegal, illicit, immoral or fat-making,' said James jokingly, trying to catch Ned's attention for a batch of refills.

Marvin ran a restless eye around the dim reaches of the lounge. The buzz of conversation had reduced somewhat since they had arrived, and many of the groups of male pint drinkers were no longer to be seen clustered around the counter. Even as he glanced around, the small door in the corner of the snug which bore a hand-printed notice saying 'Do Not Enter' opened a fraction, and a couple of locals pulled aside the heavy baize curtain and slid out, after cautious glances through the slit before they emerged. They moved like shadows to the side door of the pub and disappeared from Marvin's immediate view. 'Jeeze, they must be easily embarrassed down here if they act like that coming out of the john,' he said idly.

James choked slightly. 'That's not the john, Marvin,' he said when he had recovered his breath. 'The john is out in the yard. That area is strictly for the locals and isn't for the likes of you and me.' He winked at Susan and Marvin hurriedly put on his horn-rimmed spectacles so that he could see properly, replacing the sun-glasses he felt were part of the image of a whiz-kid P.R. executive.

Marvin suddenly had more important things to think about – he had just seen Dawn drive by in the Earl's car, an old but still roadworthy Rolls of ancient vintage, and he wondered where the star of Stupendo Films was off to. He noticed she was wearing a white lacy blouse and a tiara from the property department and his Lordship was sitting close beside her, engaged in earnest conversation with Miss O'Day, while Riordan, in his capacity as chauffeur, was driving the Rolls at a sedate pace down the main street out of town.

Susan watched him with some sympathy. 'Don't worry,' she consoled. 'Dawn will be as safe as a house with his Lordship and wherever he is taking her there won't be a news story in it, so you may as well relax.'

'Mebbe,' said Marvin uneasily. 'But Miss O'Day is easily led and who knows what a guff slinger like him could hand out that might make her say somethin' she shouldn't, and that chauffeur sittin' there listenin' to every word could make a stack sellin' the story to the noosepapers.'

'Marvin,' said Susan reprovingly, 'you mustn't be so suspicious of everyone. Riordan is a trusted employee of the Earl's – he does everything for him and there is no way at all he could be persuaded to sell a story to the press just to make a few bucks when it involves his own employer. You must trust people more, Marvin. Not everyone you meet is out to stab you in the professional back.'

'Anyway,' cut in James, crossing his fingers, 'the people down here are as innocent as a babe unborn, Marvin. They really don't know which way it is from Sunday. I mean, look at the place, there isn't a cinema, there is only one pub, there isn't a drug store and even the Earl hasn't a TV set. I ask you, have you seen a single television since you came here?'

Marvin shook his head. Come to think of it, he had noticed there wasn't a single television aerial in sight and now that he thought of it, the vocal group in the village didn't sing any pop, rock and roll or jazz numbers – only Irish ballads, all of which sounded the same to his uninitiated ears. (And there Marvin underrated himself, since the group had only two ballads off by heart, 'Danny Boy' and 'Eileen Aroon', both of which sounded exactly alike as sung by the group and played by Marita and her bodghran and Breeda on the Earl's little harp.) And the snug where they sat, he observed, displayed only ancient calendars and mirrors advertising alcoholic drinks from firms which were long extinct. No place on the shelves was there a box beaming out pictures which would remind him of home.

'You mean they don't even know what a TV looks like?' he asked incredulously.

'That's right,' said James mendaciously. 'They don't get it down here Marve, so don't bother asking about it because they wouldn't know what you were talking about.' James made a mental apology to the natives of Knockpeddar, whom he had found were smarter critics about the standards of the programmes on the goggle box than any professional critic he had met in America.

'Can you beat that!' said Marvin with considerable awe. 'What do they do with their spare time then?'

James chuckled. 'Well, there's the open air dancing and story telling of course, and there's the pub and the church. And I hear they're rather good at making their own music in the evenings!' Miss King sniggered into her drink and promptly removed herself to the yard, where in highly liberated fashion all customers had a communal share in Ned's toilet facilities, without any gender segregation other than a burlap curtain that divided the urinal from the seatless bowl. But then the experienced females of Knockpeddar never ventured into the area should they find themselves in need of cloakroom facilities – they were handy enough to their homes to run down the street and back to the pub within minutes, and those who lived farther out were always welcome to knock on any domestic door in the vicinity of the hostelry.

Miss King returned to the lounge looking somewhat shattered, and later Miss Dunphy wised her up about the system in operation so that she never made the same mistake again.

Marvin looked around the lounge with renewed interest. It seemed incredible that these grown people had never even seen a television, not to speak of owning one. He almost felt embarrassed for them, as if they had a slight handicap which in kindness he should avoid staring at. Marvin had never known a life which did not include almost constant exposure to the flickering world of soap opera, old movies, quiz shows and chat shows – his mother spent most of her day watching television and every room in their house had a set in it, so that one never got away from the programmes. Because Mrs Heimer had each set tuned into a different channel, Marvin managed over a period to view a surprising number of television programmes in bits and pieces. He found it hard to recall sitting down to watch a complete show and he rarely saw a movie through from beginning to end. The continual background noise of canned laughter, speeding cars and conversation, however, had become such an integral part of his home life that he couldn't come to terms at all with the wave of rural silence which descended on his domestic quarters each evening. In two days he had developed a nervous twitch, manifested by a continuous sharp turn of his head from side to side as if he were engaged in a permanent reconnaissance of his location (which he was). In a week Marvin was talking to himself at a steady rate just to kill the silence in his room, but within another five days his hearing sharpened no end and suddenly Marvin found he could pick up conversations clear across a room, through closed doors and even when people were conversing in quite low tones. Even as he sat in the snug he could catch a number of juicy bits of local gossip which, though they were of no use to him for the movie publicity, were nevertheless quite titillating to a good Jewish boy who had always been given to believe that Ireland was a place full of saints and scholars. At least Marvin discovered one thing that had puzzled him – within half an hour or so he knew exactly what several of the population of Knockpeddar did with their nights, and much of their days as well, and not all of it of a musical nature either. And he noticed that his newly acute sense of hearing regularly picked up what sounded like cars backfiring, unless he was hearing the sound of gunfire fairly close to the pub, yet he never saw any local people either carrying a weapon or producing the results of an evening's sporting activities by way of a brace of birds. He couldn't make out the situation other than to decide that all the Irish were slightly mad anyhow.

Marvin decided to stay a while when James and Susan took Brenno and Beauty back to their farm, Brenno now being somewhat under the influence, and the goat had developed a side stagger thanks to James having stood both of them two extra rounds of stout which Beauty was not accustomed to having. As he sat nursing his raspberry cordial, Marvin observed a steady traffic in and out of the small door in the corner of the lounge, and as it opened he could see that the inside had an additional hanging curtain of some dark thick fabric on the inside, which acted as a sort of soundproofing. If it wasn't a john he asked himself, then just what was behind that door? He noticed that no females appeared to go in, and at regular intervals Ned would slide over with a tray of drinks, knock carefully and pass the tray to a disembodied hand which emerged through the opening and grabbed the tray. They must have a strip club in there, he told himself, and then immediately dismissed the notion. Maybe it was a masonic lodge, he hazarded, but then as soon as he remembered Canon Hackett he also dismissed that idea rapidly. Some sort of religious group perhaps – nah, he said, those religious nuts wouldn't down the liquor with such regularity and rapidity as that lot behind the door manage to do. It must be something else – maybe a poker game? Yeah, Marvin decided – that must be it.

Ned was busy serving and had no time to dally with anyone who was only buying raspberry cordial, so Marvin saw he would have to wait until another time to question the publican about his back room. Meanwhile there was another lone drinker standing beside the bar, his glance buried deep in a creamy-necked pint of the black stuff. Marvin decided to ask him if he knew what was going on. He trotted up with outstretched hand, a wide American smile on his face.

He had to introduce himself twice before the local raised a dour countenance from the contemplation of his pint to look from Marvin's outstretched hand to his well-dentured grin, both of which were immediately totally bypassed for some object which seemed to site itself twelve inches to the left of Marvin's ear.

'Can I buy you a drink?' Marvin asked rather self-consciously retrieving his mitt from its floating position in mid-air, and relocating it in his jacket pocket.

'No ya can't,' replied the local, turning his shoulder and re-casting his eyes towards his pint. 'I have me own.'

Marvin felt this additional bit of information was meant to leave the door of hospitality a little ajar for a future invitation, so he beckoned Ned and with the air of a man opening up new frontiers Marvin ordered a ginger ale and took up a stance beside the dour drinker at the bar.

'If you're sellin' anythin' I'm not buyin',' began the local, who was known in Knockpeddar by the name of 'Ducks' Dunne, due to the somewhat unfortunate shape of his mouth and the even tighter rein he kept on his conversation especially with strangers like Marvin.

'I'm not selling a thing . . . in fact maybe I might even be giving something away,' hinted Marvin, carefully taking out his wallet to pay for his ginger ale and allowing Ducks to observe that the same wallet was well stacked with folding money. Ducks was unimpressed. He had done an instant expert count of what the wallet held and saw that what he carried in his own back pocket was about double the total of what the wallet contained. He did not want company while he had his pint – this was his hour for working out what trebles and cross doubles he would be placing on the morrow by way of augmenting his income, and he resented any interruption of his business operations.

'I'm the Public Relations Executive with the movie unit,' said Marvin chattily, sipping his ginger ale.

'Huh,' said Ducks, removing his racing sheet from his coat pocket and fishing a pencil from under his cap.

'This is a real dandy little spot,' said Marvin. 'Guess it's the "Little Bit of Heaven" the song mentions?'

Ducks stared at him in silence, not bothering to produce even his customary 'huh' before he pointedly opened his paper, folding and refolding it until he had the section he needed made into a neat rectangle.

'It's sure peaceful,' continued Marvin. 'There seems to be a real quiet way of life around here.' If Marvin hoped for contradiction he was in for a disappointment. Ducks continued to ignore him as he slowly put the odd tick against the names of his selection, before taking a slow but deep swallow of his pint.

'Guess guys like me could find it all a bit slow – bein' used to things goin' a bit faster back in the States,' probed Marvin delicately as he made gallant efforts to cope with the ginger ale bubbles which were tickling his nose.

'I like an odd card game myself ... or a flutter on the track ... an' I sure do enjoy the occasional gamble on the tables or on the slot machines.' Marvin felt he had covered pretty well any game of chance which might be taking place behind that door, and it was only left for Ducks to suggest that if Marvin was interested in losing his money then he could assist him with an introduction to the world of wagers through the door in the snug. But Ducks proffered no comment. In desperation Marvin dropped his tactful approach. 'They got a heavy game goin' on in there?' he asked, jerking his chin toward the door.

For the first time a wintry smile passed over Duck's features. He folded his paper, returned it to his pocket and replaced the pencil behind his car beneath his cap. Then he drained the last of his pint. 'That's not a game, it's a wake,' he said dourly, and turned away, clumping out of the lounge in a manner that suggested to Marvin it would be better if he did not follow Ducks hoping for further revelations.

'A wake?' Marvin said to himself. 'Wonder who the stiff is that they're giving him such a send off?' He would have questioned Ned further but the lounge was jumping with its nightly customers all shouting for drinks at the same time, so Marvin decided to leave things until morning, when Ned would be harnessed to the sink washing up the night's glassware and consequently a captive informant when he came into the pub for a morning draught of that perfectly appalling cordial.

Chapter Nineteen

There was no doubt that the entire village was feeling the effects of the new wealth brought by Stupendo Films Inc. Money was flowing through in a steady stream and the locals, denied many of the ordinary little labour-saving gadgets and luxuries they read about in their newspapers or heard about on their radios in the commercial breaks, were proving difficult to restrain from going berserk with their cash. The women wanted washing machines, fridges, driers and electric beaters. Their husbands had their eyes on electric machines that would leave them free to congregate more often in Ned's, and it took a deal or persuasion from James to prevent them from taking delivery of all their dream items at once.

'Wait until the unit has returned to the States – then you can buy what you want,' he pleaded at one of the regular gatherings in the village hall. 'You know if Oscar realises this is not the simple Irish village he thinks it is, he might pull the whole film unit out and leave you high and dry. 'He's as happy as a baby so far – no union troubles, no strikes, hardly a wet day to hold up the shooting and now Dawn is back in action after her little accident – don't rock the boat.'

And in truth Oscar was a very happy man. Miss Corcoran was coming along nicely he felt – any day now Oscar believed he would get to first base and in the meantime he had never enjoyed a pursuit more, since Carmel knew just when to slow down and let him catch up with her, so to speak. On top of all this he liked staying with the Earl, and Miss O'Day was generally in better humour on this film than she had ever been. Oscar saw less of her than usual which suited him fine and Dawn was busy laying her own romantic groundwork with the Earl, which kept her from being bored. For when Miss O'Day was bored, Oscar recalled with a shudder, her immediate company paid a ghastly price. Oscar's conversations with the dinner guest interested in film investment were also progressing, and he was pretty sure his new 'Angel' would come across before Mr Lipperstein returned to America. Oscar was planning on making a movie which he hoped would set new horizons in the kind of titillation that made heavy dollar signs at the box office, and he had Miss Corcoran in mind for the leading role – with her looks and the talent which kept a man as experienced as Oscar in the chase with such single-mindedness, he believed that she had something special to give the silver screen. Just what it was he would shortly find out – he hoped. Strangely enough too he found the limitations of the Knockpeddar telephone system quite acceptable. If something went wrong back home he couldn't be so easily reached, and so the studio bosses ended up sorting it all out themselves after a few abortive attempts to talk to him long distance. If he had a problem at his end he only had to wait a day and it seemed to get straightened out in some indefinable fashion. And because Mr Lipperstein really believed that the village was one of the great Gaelic primitives he was learning to take his time Irish fashion, even if he would never totally convert to all Knockpeddar's little ways.

He was finding however that the film was unlikely to come in on budget – somehow, the smallest request in Knockpeddar seemed to present problems which could only be resolved when a sizeable number of dollars was available. Farmers got a bit stroppy over rights of way, cart tracks, laneways; pigs and chickens being used in the movies got all sorts of rare diseases, only curable by expensive administrations of medications which Oscar couldn't even pronounce. And when the donkey fell sick its owner had to bring a faith healer from thirty miles away to get it back on its feet again, and of course Oscar had to meet the bill, which cemented his belief that the best racket of all to get involved in was religion. Furthermore, the running costs for the farmyard manure to keep the newly-built wharf and wall looking as if they had been in situ since the time of St Patrick's arrival was one of the heaviest outlays on the costing sheet. It seemed that no matter what the Property people did the manure got washed away every evening, because by morning the whole business of pasting it back on the walls had to be gone through afresh, and not only were the farmers in the delivery business continually raising their rates, but the workmen were demanding what they were pleased to term 'Smell Money'. The small boys of the village made nightly forays down to the river with sticks which they wielded in concerted effort, making enough wave and wash to swill the manure loose within minutes, and the farmers were more than willing to make a small contribution for their efforts out of their own profits.

The food being provided at the mobile canteen by the ladies of the village was quite superb and Oscar was extremely pleased with it. Which was not the case where Mr Fonsie O'Malley's building supplies were concerned. Even Oscar could see that Mr O'Malley was salting the constructing mine, so to speak. He had engaged himself in several arguments with Fonsie, until he found that production could be held up in a most irritating fashion when supplies of essential items like balsa wood, scaffolding, platform sections and so on went mysteriously on the short supply list, and Fonsie would say plaintively that his own work-force had to take the materials off to a building site he was committed to, whenever Oscar made sounds about hiring costs.

Fonsie was having his own problems – once his Dublin lady love heard there was a film unit in the village she wanted, right or wrong, to come down so that Fonsie could get her a part. It was taking all sorts of little gifts to keep her in a state of even minimum contentment, and Fonsie had to raise the Happy Money somewhere. He felt that since the film company was indirectly responsible for his present extra-marital strike, they should go some way towards meeting the cost of the oil for his troubled waters.

Even the Grange was feeling the warm wind of prosperity blowing over its newly cut lawns. Riordan, with a little help from a couple of local lads, had worked wonders with the place. The windows were freshly puttied and painted, the lily pond was again the justly famous feature it had once been in the books about historic houses, and whenever his Lordship worked out the eventual wear and tear costings in his little black book, he and Riordan agreed that the total would more than cover the installation of a decent central heating system throughout the Grange. Only on one subject however did the Earl and his butler disagree. That was the whole business of Miss Dawn O'Day and her suitability for the position of the second Countess of Grange Pedder.

Riordan was dead against it. Not that he couldn't see the financial advantages which would accrue, once Miss O'Day was taken to wife by the Earl, but he felt that his Lordship might come to regret the price he would inevitably have to pay, once the novelty wore off and Dawn found that country life was a lot less romantic than the British movies she was acquainted with would have the public believe. He visualised the Grange constantly filled with her transatlantic friends, with whom he knew the Earl would have absolutely nothing in common. He could see Miss O'Day hiring a Yankee interior decorator to transform the old-world charm of the Grange into a plastic abomination, all done out in white leatherette transparent plexi-glass and avant-garde lamp-shades. And the thought of addressing Miss O'Day as her Ladyship really stuck in his craw. Worst of all was the vision of a permanent association with her white poodle.

But none of these things could he express to his master – it was not his place and Riordan was strong on the fitness of things, no matter how intimate the relationship between servant and master might be. And his Lordship could not explain to his butler that he was quite aware of the pitfalls, but if Miss O'Day cared to spend some months on her native country without him this would not exactly break his heart, since he was a man fond of his own privacy – a fact which his first wife discovered rather late, and by then she had no reserves other than the willing chauffeur with which to fill the companionship gap between herself and her husband. What Miss O'Day might do while she was out of the country was her own affair, as long as the neighbours did not hear about it, he reasoned, with what must be acknowledged was considerable tolerance.

So as the car sedately took them out of Knockpeddar to a small but excellent restaurant where his Lordship had arranged an intimate dinner for the two of them, the Earl was contentedly reviewing his plans for the evening. Some excellent poached salmon, really well cooked veal, milk-fed on the best Irish milk of course, a good wine, followed at the meal's end by a couple of double strength Gaelic coffees, and he felt Miss O'Day would find it hard to resist whatever the Goddess of Romance might care to send. He stole a glance at her as she sat back in the Rolls, her eyes lowered so that he could observe the silken thickness of her lashes, which years of faithful nourishment with olive oil had helped to grow to quite a surprising length. Miss O'Day was wearing her

Irish crochet blouse and a soft swirly pure silk chiffon skirt, and no bra. She wasn't wearing much else either, other than a rather fetching gold varnish on her toe and finger nails. Just so that his Lordship might get an idea of how she might look in the family jewels, Dawn had borrowed a little tiara from Props and matched it with a bracelet of her own which was definitely not paste – and God knows she had worked hard enough to get that bit of ice from the particular skinflint who had donated it, she told herself. She left the blouse buttons undone as far down the front as she dared, and she knew, by the odd discreet glance that his Lordship kept passing over her as he looked out of the car window, that the accessibility of the remaining buttons did not escape him.

This was going to be her night, she promised herself. A smart girl, used to handling the best of Hollywood's grope and grab merchants, ought to be able to bring this sire of gentility to heel without too much trouble. Somehow, after this dinner, she should be able to manoeuvre him into a situation from which he would not really want to escape, and hopefully he would be agreeable to sinking down twice in the sea of her charms before she pulled him to safety by way of a well-thrown matrimonial rope, before he knew he was being hauled in. A couple of glasses of the best bubbly, she decided, would put him sufficiently off-balance for her to do her stuff.

'What a comfortable automobile,' she said, sweeping her lashes up to glance at the Earl with an air of total enthusiasm. 'Isn't it big inside too? Of course, we don't have anything as well preserved as this back home. It's all Caddies and Mercs at the studios.' Dawn stifled a small cry as the Rolls went round a corner and a sharp object stuck into the base of her spine. Feeling behind her, she unearthed a shooting stick.

'Oh dear,' said his Lordship apologetically, 'so that's where that stick went to. I've been searching for it for a month or more. Actually I haven't had the car out since before you came. It was – well – laid up for a while with some little mechanical problem. But Riordan has it in working order again, so there is no danger at all it will break down on us during the journey.' He was most anxious that Miss O'Day would not think he was being obvious – anyway he hated doing his courtship in the back of a car, even a Rolls. The morning-room at the Grange was much more comfortable. Miss

O'Day rubbed her back as well as she could. The point of the shooting stick had really dug into her and she was sure she would have a sizeable bruise by the morning. She bruised easily.

'You sure have a lovely country over here,' Dawn continued, 'I'm getting to kinda like the way of life here – nice and easy, an' so safe . . . maybe I oughta think about buyin' a little place here.' She hoped she wasn't rushing ahead too quickly, but a quick glance at the Earl reassured her – he was surreptitiously looking at the outline of her thigh through the flimsy skirt of her dress, its line unbroken by things as unnecessary as pantie edges or stocking tops, and almost absent-mindedly Dawn recrossed her legs, allowing the folds of her dress to get trapped between her slender thighs, adding to his Lordship's ill-concealed excitement.

Riordan hadn't missed a thing either, and he speeded up the Rolls with a jerk which did not exactly achieve what he had hoped for – the removal of Dawn from the seat to the floor. Instead thc Earl, caught off-balance as he leaned forward toward Miss O'Day, careered straight into her lap which, while it pleased them both quite a bit, effectively left Miss O'Day unable to utter another word, until the Rolls turned up a laneway leading into a long curving drive, at the end of which stood a low rectangular building, whose red curtained windows were illuminated by flickering candles in silver candelabra. The converted barn, for that is what it was, backed on to a silvery river which provided the salmon that the Earl and his companion were about to ingest. The foyer had a small bar decorated in tree bark while the rafters were hung with old farm implements, copper measures and dairy utensils. Dawn thought the décor was quite the cutest thing she had ever seen. The proprietor welcomed them himself, displaying a flattering respect for his Lordship which impressed Dawn in no small way. The Earl introduced her and from there on the evening could not have been more perfect. Guests suddenly appeared in the bar from the dining-room, and Miss O'Day had a lovely time signing autographs and displaying her charisma as well as her famous Frivvle.

The proprietor fixed them a couple of whiskey stingers on the house, that nearly took the roof of her mouth, and by the time they went into dinner Dawn loved the entire Irish world. The chilled wine was just right, the Gaelic coffees were far superior to any champagne she might have drunk had the choice of liquids been left to her, and when they finally left the restaurant and were picked up in the Rolls by Riordan to be taken home again, her state was not only langourous but also distinctly amorous. If this was gracious living, she felt, then she was all for country life.

She teetered out of the back of the Rolls, leaning heavily on the solicitous arm of his Lordship. They entered the Grange together while Riordan went to put the Rolls away, and almost as one they found their steps moving in unison toward Miss O'Day's suite.

Dawn was now beginning to feel the effects of the shooting stick in her buttock – in fact every step she took was an agony, but she valiantly persisted until they were both safe inside the door of her sitting room which she carefully closed behind them.

'Why dontcha pour us a couple of drinks while I change into somethin' more comfortable?' she murmured in time-honoured fashion, limping her way across to the bedroom.

'Have you hurt yourself my dear?' asked his Lordship with concern as he observed the effort it was taking her to traverse the distance from door to door.

'I think I gotta bruise from that shooting stick,' Dawn explained, massaging her exquisite rump for once without any notion of arousing her companion. It was a notion which failed entirely, since even the lions couchant on the de Lucey escutcheon would have become lions rampant within seconds, had they been privileged, as the Lord of the manor now was, to watch Miss O'Day's delicate hand massage her rear with devoted care. The Earl with a considerable effort re-sited his eyes on the facing wall, which was a bit unfortunate too, because it held the door to Miss O'Day's bedroom, which allowed him to have an unexpected look at the large four-poster bed with its lilac silken hangings in which, de Lucey history had it, the first Elizabeth was said to have rested herself when the particular piece of furniture had its home in one of the Great English Houses of the de Lucey ancestors. What with the close proximity of the four-poster, and the heady effect of Miss O'Day's posterior, his Lordship poured himself a double brandy by mistake and tossed it down his suddenly dry throat, before he realised what he was doing. Since the brew was Riordan's Revenge, due to the fact that it was on the drinks table in Miss O'Day's suite and not in his Lordship's own quarters, the immediate effect was to almost pulverise the unfortunate man's muscular co-ordination.

Fighting for breath on every count he sat down on the chaise-longue, collapsing back among the heap of downy cushions it held, with a feeling that his final moments in the world had suddenly come. He closed his eyes and it only seemed a second before he found himself being shaken into wakefulness by Miss O'Day, who had not only found an exotically comfortable lace négligée but had also managed to glamorise herself with a complete fresh make-up, her sexiest perfume and a re-style of her coiffure, so that her blonde hair now floated quite ethereally around her cheeks and took years off her age.

'Charlie,' she said plaintively. 'You gotta put some salve on my bum bruise – I can't reach it myself.' She handed him a large jar of cream and unselfconsciously turned from him, flipping up her négligée so that her famous bottom was revealed in all its cream splendour. Right across one rounded haunch was a deep purple weal which reminded his Lordship of a dollop of bramble jelly in a saucer of clotted cream.

In a welter of confusion the Earl scooped a fingerful of the soothing ointment from the jar and closing his eyes tightly, he placed the salve in the direction of the bruise, fervently hoping it would hit the right spot. As she felt the cool comfort of the salve Miss O'Day gave a little moan of pleasurable relief. It was too much for his Lordship who, dropping the jar of salve, clasped Miss O'Day to his chest and bore her back onto the chaise-longue where she settled with considerable satisfaction. Who knows what might have transpired, had not Riordan gone and spoiled it all by knocking on Miss O'Day's sitting room door.

'I would like to remind madam that she has an early morning call on the film set at six thirty tomorrow,' Riordan said softly through the door.

'Aw shit!' Miss O'Day said disgustedly, surfacing from what was turning into a promisingly torrid embrace.

'Quite madam. I will bring madam coffee and orange juice at five forty-five precisely in the morning,' replied the butler, removing himself downstairs again, once he heard the springs of the chaise-longue creak loudly enough to indicate that his Lordship was about to dispatch himself back to his own room.

Dawn was livid as she slammed the sitting room door closed behind the Earl. She swore that just as soon as she took over the domestic arrangements in Grange Peddar that two-faced uppity schmuck would be sent packing, and she would find a butler who would know his place. All efforts at charming Riordan over on to her side were finished, she told herself. From now on it was going to be war, and Dawn O'Day would certainly win. After all given the choice, what guy, titled or not, would settle for a fifty year old butler when he could avail himself of a glamorous twenty-nine (well thirty-two) year old sex symbol instead? Guess who would keep the manorial bed warmer, she mused with justification. However as she continued to think over the evening she decided perhaps that Riordan had, in fact, done her a favour after all. Let his Lordship long a little, she told herself. When the time came to move in he would be that much more willing, not to say eager. But next time, she said with gritted teeth, Riordan wasn't going to interfere. If she had to lock him in his own kitchen she would do so. Then in the small watches of the night a beautiful plan hit her, and when she worked it all out Dawn went to sleep with a beautific smile on her lips and contentment of disposition, which lasted right through the following day's filming.

Of course her feeling of well-being was assisted by Allo O'Brien, with whom Dawn had a most satisfying love scene to play. She made sure it took them all morning to complete.

Mr Benny Crisp, the Second Director, was delighted with his leading lady. 'Dawn baby,' he said at the end of the morning's shoot, 'you've never given it out so good – this guy O'Brien must really turn you on. Unless it's somethin' else?'

'Why Benny, how seldom of you to say so,' replied Miss O'Day with acid charm. 'But Allo O'Brien had absolutely nothing to do with it. I am deeply motivated by this wonderful story and for the first time I can relate to the plot and show my true talent. One gets so artistically frustrated with mediocre scripts even if they do make millions at the box office!' And turning from an open-mouthed Benny, Dawn swept to the side of the set with outstretched hands to greet the Earl of Grange Peddar who had come to collect her for lunch. His Lordship was definitely impressed by her words, she could tell by the almost reverential way he gave her an old-fashioned bow before he placed an absent-minded pat on her posterior.

'I hope the salve worked well for you?' he whispered with a boyish grin and Dawn squeezed his hand.

'You've got the real healing touch, Charlie,' she murmured. 'Maybe I should let you repeat the treatment tonight sometime.' The Earl's heart fluttered in anticipation, only to be quietened when Miss O'Day made a little moue of dismay. 'Ah heck Charlie, I don't think I'm gonna be free tonight – I gotta put in some time with my voice coach on my lines for tomorrow's shooting.' Which was absolutely untrue, since Miss O'Day had already learned her lines and actually did not have her coach with her in Knockpeddar, but Dawn wanted to put her marvellous plan into operation and she needed to be quite sober to do it, so she preferred to keep a low profile while she worked out the details.

She summoned Marvin to her dressing room in the late afternoon. Before he arrived Dawn set the scene – she peeled down to her lace bra and panties, slipped on a deep blue satin négligée which picked up the exact blue of her eyes, and as Marvin opened the door in response to her invitation to enter she was engaged in donning one of her long black nylon stockings, smoothing and settling the sheerness in a way that Mother Heimer would have instantly recognised as being the method of a female about to encourage behaviour unbefitting to a good Jewish boy. Marvin's Adam's apple threatened to choke him, as his eye followed the stocking seam until it disappeared beneath the edge of Dawn's scarlet knickers.

'Oh, come on in Marve,' said Miss O'Day carelessly, as she attended to the second stocking at a leisurely pace. 'Help yourself to a drink ... oh, sorry, I forgot you don't touch liquor ... never mind, pour me one.'

Marvin did so, clattering the glass and bottle in his highly nervous state and managing to spill a fair share of the gin and tonic that she asked for in his haste to answer her request. Dawn took a long swallow and put down the tumbler on her dressing table. Then she sat down in her dressing chair, crossing her splendid legs and causing Marvin to come out in a sudden sweat across his upper lip.

'Marvie, have you done a story yet about that ghost in the Grange?'

Marvin shook his head.

'Good,' said Miss O'Day, 'because I thought up a much better way to handle it than merely saying the house is haunted. I think we could make a real good number out of it with a little planning.' She recrossed her legs and took another sip from her drink, leaning over towards Marvin as she did so, so that her négligée fell slightly open at bosom level, displaying the microscopic bits of lace and ribbon she was wearing beneath and giving Marvin distinct shortness of breath. '*We* are going to stage our own haunting, and what's more we're going to get pictures of it for the noospapers,' said Miss O'Day.

'But ... but ... h-how are we going to do that?' asked Marvin. 'Very few have ever seen the Grey Lady. According to the Earl she only haunts the family or the family servants and not too often at that. And according to what I read about hauntings ghosts don't come out in photographs, seeing as how they don't actually have bodies.'

'Well, this ghost is gonna have a body,' declared Miss O'Day, 'and what's more, our publicity photographer, Harry, will take pictures of her.'

Marvin still didn't get it.

'Look,' said Dawn impatiently. 'We're going to stage the whole thing without a word to anybody, see? That Grey Lady wears a grey dress an' a sort of cowl thing over her head that covers her like a cloak. The Props department can come up with that sort of costume like a flash, and all you have to do is to walk down the corridor outside my room, wave that cloak thing about a little and then hightail it off in the general direction of the tower and get the hell back to your apartment before anyone spots you. Harry will be posted down the corridor with his camera, and I'll give him enough time before I start yelling to get a couple of vague shots of you – no one will recognise you with that cowl thing over your face.'

She sat back in satisfaction to see what effect her idea would have on Marvin. What she had left out was that once she started yelling and running down the corridor her feet would not stop until they landed her inside the Earl's rooms, where she would obtain a refuge in his manly arms – she hoped – which would not be interrupted, since she was planning the appearance of Grey

Lady to coincide with Riordan's night off. Once there she would guarantee that she wouldn't emerge again without a proper commitment from his Lordship.

Marvin gasped like a beached fish and until he got his breath back again he kept shaking his head from side to side until his spectacles fell off his nose.

'Miss Dawn, you simply can't ask me to dress up as a female ghost,' he protested nervously. 'I'd only make a mess of it. Gee, when I was in school I was the guy who always fell over the spear, or was late making an entrance with the rest of the crowd. I couldn't even get the gum to stick on my chin under the false beard!'

'Well,' said Dawn with a wave of her hand, 'you won't be wearing a beard or carrying a spear this time Marvie ... all you have to do is make like a ghost walking down a corridor. You'll be terrific, I just know you will, Marvie ... do it for me. I could be so very grateful because it's kinda important to me ...' Dawn pouted her lips and fluttered her lashes at the unfortunate Marvin and as a final inducement she leaned toward him once more and put her hand gently to his cheek, stroking the lobe of his ear with her little finger until he quivered like a plate of Jello.

'Think of the marvellous story you'll get outta all this ... I bet Oscar will sign you up for his next three movies on the results of the sort of coverage you'll get.' Marvin gave in, and for half an hour Miss O'Day showed him how to walk in a full length gown with his face half-covered by a floating scarf from her collection of accessories. Marvin got rather a thrill out of it all – after all, he reminded himself, as he minced up and down the dressing room, how many guys could say they got into Dawn O'Day's négligée, even if it was only doing duty as a ghostly gown. He began to enjoy the whole thing and was quite prepared to utter ghostly cries, were it not for the fact that Miss O'Day reminded him that Grey Lady was a happy spirit and as such wouldn't be caught dead groaning, moaning or wringing her hands.

'All you gotta do, Marvin, is drift down the corridor and then shove off and tell Harry to do the same, pronto. Don't bother about what I do – I'm an actress so I will play the scene through. But I don't want some smart-ass running into you in the Grange – you have no reason to be there and the folks round here aren't dumb. They might catch on when the noospapers run the story.'

'When are we going to stage this, Miss Dawn?' Marvin asked as he folded up Dawn's négligée and placed it tidily on a chair.

'The sooner the better,' replied Miss O'Day. 'Why not tomorrow night – then you'll make the weekend noospapers.'

She had happened to overhear Riordan inform Susan that he would be late home because he was driving into Cork to visit a colleague whose employers had arrived at their summer residence for the season.

'You go and fix things up with Harry and remember – eleven o'clock tomorrow night you start walkin', OK? And pick up the costume from Props first thing tomorrow mornin''.

Dawn gave careful thought to what she herself would wear for her big scene, because that was how she saw the haunting. She was quite looking forward to the affair – it was ages since she had had a part which allowed her to give a decent scream, she recalled, and nothing was more satisfying than a good loud yell, particularly when so much rested on its results.

She decided on a pale silk caftan trimmed with a ruffle of baby blue satin ribbon – men, she knew, couldn't resist blue, particularly on a blonde, and the caftan would float beautifully around her when she burst into his Lordship's rooms!

Chapter Twenty

The following night was brightened by a full moon which caused many of Knockpeddar's young lovers to wander in the vicinity of Friars' Walk and created somewhat of a problem for Marvin, who had a difficult job avoiding the recumbent couples as he made his way around to the back of the Grange into the rose patio, where Dawn had left the French windows open so that he could get into the house. Once inside Marvin donned the loose grey garment he had borrowed from the Property Department and adjusted the cowled cloak over his head. Immediately he began to perspire copiously, because he had left on his three-piece suit underneath the heavy serge of the costume. His spectacles steamed up so much that he realised he would not be able to see at all if he wore them, although he wouldn't be in a much better situation without them, Marvin being somewhat myopic. There was a sound behind him, and Harry the photographer slipped in through the French windows complete with camera and equipment. When he surveyed Marvin he sniggered.

'Jeeze, you look like a cross between that movie about the English king with all the wives, and de Mille's one about the Bible,' he whispered. 'That dame sure has you by the shorts to get you into that outfit!'

Marvin hitched up his robe – unfortunately he had not been able to fit it before he 'borrowed' it, since the Props department were not actually aware that he was availing himself of one of their costumes, due to turn up later in the final scenes of the movie when Dawn would be brought to the churchyard after her movie demise, followed by a procession of monks. Marvin had grabbed the nearest robe to the door and fled, and it was made for a somewhat taller person, like a six footer, rather than for his five feet four inch figure. Still, he told himself, the cloak would cover it all up, always provided it did not fall apart before he got out of the Grange. For Dawn was no seamstress, and in making the cloak and cowl Marvin had to resort to stapling the fabric together with the stapling machine from his office desk. However he hoped at a distance no one would guess it had started out as a horse blanket and was the only piece of grey fabric he could lay hands on at short notice.

The morning-room clock chimed the quarter before eleven and Marvin hastily put on his cloak, pulling the cowl well down over his forehead, which immediately blocked his entire view of where he was going; he promptly fell over a footstool, which knocked over a Benares table laden with items of brassware, collected with more enthusiasm than good taste by the late Countess while on a visit to India. Both men froze and somewhere close by a door opened. They quickly stepped outside the open window once more out of sight, and the light went on in the morning-room as his Lordship's head peered around the half-opened door preceded by a large blackthorn stick. With great pretence of mind Marvin mewed in what he hoped was a fair imitation of Riordan's cat, and the Earl expelled what was obviously a slightly apprehensive breath, switched off the light again and went away.

Harry moved back into the room. 'Never mind, Marve. If you lose your job in publicity you'll always be able to move over to the Disney studios as an animal imitator,' he said, picking up his pack which fortunately he had placed behind the couch and out of sight before the Earl had arrived. 'Come on, let's go, chop-chop, before someone else turns up and for Christ's sake don't fall over anything else on the way.'

They moved silently up the wide stairway on to the landing, carefully following Miss O'Day's directions. Past the first door under which a light gleamed – that was Susan's office, while Miss O'Day's suite was at the lower end – past the bathrooms, a couple of empty bedrooms and a boxroom. Harry moved in there and deposited his equipment on the floor, keeping the door ajar so that he could get a quick shot of Marvin and Dawn as they went by. He estimated that no more than ten seconds would elapse before Dawn's shriek would bring Miss King from her office at a gallop and God knew who else from the other parts of the house, so he was on a pretty tight schedule. Harry judiciously decided that he would only photograph the apparition from the rear, and Miss O'Day was to turn three-quarters profile so that he could get her well-practised expression of terror as she raced down the corridor en route to his Lordship's pad, though Harry was unaware of her destination.

They heard the tower clock chime the hour and Marvin moved into action. Miss O'Day put a cautious head around the door, Marvin gave her the thumbs up sign and, pulling the cowl well over his face, he carefully shuffled down the polished floor and Harry went into operation with the camera once Marvin passed the boxroom door. Miss O'Day was about to do her thing when Miss King's door suddenly opened. From the room emerged James followed by Miss King. Everyone stood stock still.

'Marvin!' hissed Miss King. 'What on earth are you doing here at this time of night and in those silly clothes too?'

Poor Marvin remained without a word while Harry slid unnoticed back into the boxroom. But James, ever quick on the uptake, saw that something was definitely afoot. Without a word he pushed Miss King back into her room and followed her like a flash, firmly slamming the door behind them. Marvin almost fainted with relief, and totteringly he moved off down the corridor, to be followed by Miss O'Day, who within seconds dutifully gave vent to her famous shrieks of fear. She fled still shrieking down the corridor in the direction of the Earl's rooms, while Harry stuck his camera out once more and grabbed the necessary photos, before Dawn disappeared in a positive cascade of ever-rising cries out of sight round the corner of the landing. Marvin thankfully gathered the folds of his robe around his knees and fled down the stairs, closely followed by Harry with his cameras. A few minutes later James stuck a cautious head out of Susan's office and Miss King followed him into the corridor.

'What was all that about?' she enquired.

'Whatever was going on I'll give you two guesses where Dawn is now to be found should anyone be foolish enough to go looking for her,' said James with a grin.

Susan looked at the hooded figure standing against the oak panelled wall near Miss O'Day's door. 'Marvin,' she said gently – 'is this a spoof between yourself and Dawn?' The figure did not reply but lifted a hand which later, Miss King was to recall, wore a large ring with a stone she recognised on reflection as being a ruby, and quite suddenly it faded into the woodwork without a sound.

Susan gulped and clung to James's arm. 'Did you see what I just saw?' she asked shakily.

James nodded. 'I guess we've both just been favoured by a sighting of Grey Lady – the real one,' he told her.

'Well, it sure wasn't what Dawn thinks she saw,' stammered Susan. 'I know that first figure was Marvin – I recognised him under that cowl, quite apart from the fact that when we came out into the corridor he got such a fright that he came out with "Oi veh," before he remembered he was supposed to be a ghost!'

James laughed. 'Well, let's go along with it anyhow. I think Dawn was staging something for his Lordship's benefit, just what I daren't imagine, but I guarantee that by now if she isn't sobbing "I will" then he's asking *her* "Will I". By tomorrow morning she'll be choosing a new knuckleduster for her engagement ring finger.'

James was not too far wrong. Miss O'Day had raced like a homing pigeon to his Lordship's study, to be met by the Earl at the door to which he had rushed when he heard Dawn's shrieks clear through the house.

'My dear, whatever is the matter, have you met with another accident?' he asked, taking hold of the star around her upper arms so that when she stopped her lovely face was very close to his. Dawn trembled her lower lip in a most fetching manner and actually managed to squeeze out a couple of tiny tears from her widened blue eyes.

'Oh, Charlie, I've had such a scare – I saw Grey Lady – she was outside my door when I came out into the passageway to go to the bathroom.' She sobbed, dabbing her eye with a wisp of cambric and lace, careful not to smudge her eye-shadow which she had spent so long applying.

'But my dear, I told you there is no need to be afraid of Grey Lady ... why, we all regard her as one of the family you know, and I explained she is a happy spirit with only goodwill toward everyone,' said his Lordship, stroking Miss O'Day's shoulder and moving his touch gently until his fingers managed to reach her neck and cheek.

'Oh Charlie ... I know all that! But I got so scared – when I opened my door, there she was – grey dress and that funny cloak thing with a hood over her face –' Dawn stole a quick look at his Lordship – it was the daily local girl who had described the Grange Peddar ghost to her and she hoped his Lordship would recall that he had never mentioned what the Grey Lady wore when she went haunting. That way Dawn's claim to seeing an apparition would be more readily believed.

She unobtrusively moved the Earl backwards until they were both well inside the study door and then she closed it with a flick of her foot.

'I really need a little brandy after all that,' she said in her weakest tones and the Earl rushed to pour her a glass of his choicest vintage. She sat on the couch and put her best trick into operation as he was fixing her drink.

When she was only a small girl Dawn discovered that if she held her breath and clasped her nostrils for a few seconds, she would not only turn wan and pale, but develop rapid palpitations, and if she persisted for another ten seconds she could make herself faint for a moment. It was a very useful move on occasions such as not having to explain at school why she had no homework done, or later on she used it on a few occasions to get rid of a too-presumptuous admirer. It had also got her own way over several movie contracts until Oscar got wise to it. Now, she felt, it was time to use the trick again, which she did. As his Lordship put down her glass on an adjacent table beside her Dawn gave a little sigh and keeled gently over.

'Oh dear me, dear me!' cried his Lordship in panic, one hand fanning Miss O'Day with a magazine, while the other hovered uncertain as to whether the ribbons round her thoat should be undone. He lifted her carefully and placed her on the big cushioned settee. As he did so Dawn opened her eyes again and put her arms around his neck, letting her face turn up to him in the best Hollywood tradition.

The Earl could not resist the closeness of that soft mouth. Miss O'Day felt like a fluffy kitten in his arms and her perfume quite scattered his senses. He kissed her softly and then when he got an answering pressure he repeated it more firmly. Dawn clasped him to her bosom, manoeuvred him in some miraculous manner so that they were suddenly both on the deep settee together, and after that nothing and no one could interrupt the satisfactory completion of Miss O'Day's campaign to become part of the respectable gentry of Ireland.

A little later she sat holding his hand and blushing prettily, in what could only be described as a Victorian virginal manner, which, when you knew Miss O'Day's track record, was a considerable theatrical achievement worthy of at least an Emmy award.

'Oh Charlie,' she murmured, 'I hope you won't think less of me ... I just couldn't help myself ... I do love you so.'

His Lordship was still in a happy haze of wonderment that he had managed to overcome his reservations about having it at home rather than away, so to speak. 'Dawn my darling, I think you are quite wonderful and I too care for you very much indeed,' he replied, kissing her fingers in a rather charming way that aroused Miss O'Day to new stirrings of desire, which rather surprised her. This guy wasn't half bad, she told herself – a bit out of proper practice but she could have quite a time getting him back into top gear!

There was a knock on the study door, and James came in accompanied by Susan. They had judiciously waited long enough for Dawn to get what they sincerely hoped would be to first base before they interrupted the pair.

'Dawn,' said Susan full of excitement, 'I saw Grey Lady too ... she disappeared into the wood panelling outside your door. We've been looking round the area since to see if there was a secret panel or something, just in case someone was playing a trick on you.' She looked meaningly at Miss O'Day, who stared her out firmly. 'But there isn't a thing except solid wall there, so you really do have a ghost in the Grange, your Lordship,' she told the Earl.

'Whaddya mean, you saw the ghost too?' Dawn asked in puzzlement, looking from James to Susan. She thought for a moment that they were endeavouring to throw a spanner into her plans until she saw they were actually on her side.

'Well, after you came down the passageway and over to this wing, when we came out into the corridor there was this cowled figure standing outside your door, and suddenly she waved a hand at us and disappeared into the woodwork,' Susan told her and Dawn paled once more, this time for real.

'I ain't sleepin' in that apartment again,' she said. 'That ghost might come in my room and scare the hell outta me again.'

'I just cannot understand what brought Grey Lady over to your side of the house at all,' the Earl said in puzzlement. 'She normally haunts the tower wing. You know, I think she came over to take a look at you for herself, my dear, and perhaps wish you good fortune for the film.' His Lordship smiled at Miss O'Day and pressed her hand. Dawn pursed her lips and blew him a kiss and Susan and James nodded at each other and quietly went away, leaving the lovers alone together.

It did not take much persuasion on Dawn's part for the Earl to give her his bedroom for the night, though to her disappointment he moved next door into his dressing room, so that he would not have to make to many explanations to Riordan next morning. Dawn had spent considerable time thinking about Marvin, and she decided he must have doubled back for some reason and waited outside her door for her to return. At coffee break during the morning's shooting Marvin came along to her dressing room. He looked as if he was about to go down with flu – he shook slightly all over and a heavy perspiration bedewed his forehead. In his hand he clutched a large manilla envelope and had obviously come direct from the photographic studio to show Miss O'Day the results of Harry's assignment of the previous night.

Eagerly Dawn grabbed the pictures. There were four prints – a front view of Marvin with down-bent head, well covered by the cowl, a close-up of Miss O'Day with her look of shock, a third showing her looking over her shoulder as a cloaked figure followed her down the passageway. And then there was the fourth photograph – there was Miss O'Day, her back to the camera, being followed by one cowled figure which she recognised as Marvin by reason that, blown up, one could see several of the staples in his horse blanket, but coming toward her in the photo there was the outline of another cowled figure with a hand clasping the hood close up under the chin, wearing a ring with a large oval stone set into it! There was no mistake – Harry had caught two ghosts in the picture.

'Jesus!' breathed Miss O'Day – 'Susan was right. There really is a ghost in this joint.'

'That's what I wanted to tell you, Miss Dawn,' said Marvin.

'That's not me with the ring on – I don't own a ring like that but I'll tell you where you can see the original of it – in one of those old paintings in the hallway. There's a good looking dame in a crinoline with a basket of flowers on her arm, and she's wearing that very ring on her left hand.'

'Who's the picture of?' Miss O'Day asked with bated breath.

'Well,' said Marvin. 'Underneath the painting on a brass plaque it says, "Her Grace, Duchess Caroline de Lucey" and the date says "born 1700, died 1738."'

'Ya mean that ring is well over a couple of hundred years old?' said Miss O'Day incredulously. It seemed unbelievable that anything could be more than a twelvemonth old without wearing out, as far as she was concerned, by which it can be understood that Miss O'Day was not exactly into antiques.

Marvin was still examining the photograph and his hand was still trembling slightly. 'Do you realise how close that thing was to me?' he asked nervously, 'and I didn't even see it go by me!'

'Hell, it passed me too and I didn't spot a thing either,' replied Miss O'Day. 'But I'll tell you one thing Marvin, that photo and negative has got to go. If anyone see it they'll realise we set the whole thing up and Oscar won't like it one little bit. So you go and tell Harry to burn the negative and print and forget he ever saw it.'

Obediently Marvin trotted off and Dawn went back on the set, where she had quite an exhausting afternoon trying to keep Miss Dunphy from upstaging her in their scene together and failing rather badly, since no one had told her that Miss Dunphy was an experienced drama festival contestant of many years' standing, and what she didn't know about holding her own against all-comers Dawn could balance on the top of a lipstick.

However good things were ahead for Miss O'Day after all. When she returned to the Grange in the evening there was an extravagant bouquet of roses and carnations awaiting her in her suite, with an accompanying note from his Lordship. The flowers, the note advised her, were a token of his deep affection and came with a request for permission to stop by before dinner to talk with her. And his Lordship hoped she would partake of the meal with him or, if not, then perhaps share a glass of champagne at least.

'This is it,' she told herself exultantly. 'I've cracked it!'

The Earl had given hard consideration through the preceding hours about whether or not he should remarry, and if so, could he survive being married to Miss O'Day when it all came down to the nitty-gritty. Then he thought of what it would mean to have the Grange and the estate operating properly once again. He thought of the rather pleasant social life that capital injection could provide at the Grange, and he even dared to consider that with sufficient cash flow he might, like Fonsie, be able to maintain a little pied d'amour up in Dublin should the pressure in Knockpeddar grow a little too intense at any stage. And after all, Dawn was really a stunner, he reminded himself, and a lady with experience of all the things the late Countess dismissed as 'not quite nice' during their brief and totally unsatisfactory matrimonial union.

Dawn was waiting for him, dressed in creamy cotton with ruffles at the neckline and pretty rouleau bows fastening the dress down the bodice. She looked innocent, untouched and very youthful, and his Lordship got rather a guilty feeling when his mind flashed back to the night before and he felt like a benign rapist. They sat close together on the antique love-seat. Dawn settled the folds of her dress around her knees, while she allowed a tremulous smile to flutter around her mouth.

'Charles, you haven't come to ask me to leave the house, have you?' Dawn believed in taking the fight straight into the opponent's corner. 'I know you may think you must, but I was completely swept off my feet by my feelings for you.' She took a quick look away and then back again, just in case she had overdone it this time. But the Earl was looking at her with love and concern – at least she felt it was love and concern – and he broke into her excuses.

'Dawn my dearest,' he said, clasping her hands in his own with fervour, 'if anyone is to blame for anything it must be me, since I was – er-the-er major player in the -er-activities,' and he actually blushed, Dawn observed with interest, as he skirted around his seduction. She decided to take another small chance.

'I don't know what Mr Lipperstein may say if anyone tells him I spent the night in your rooms – he will never believe that we didn't spend the whole time together,' she whispered, lowering her eyes. 'Oscar is such a prude, you see . . .' her voice trailed off, and his Lordship availed himself of the opportunity immediately.

'He will have no cause to point the finger of scorn at you, my darling,' he said with the sort of air that must have sent his ancestors out to many a battle. 'I hope he will not make so bold as to suggest that my future wife is entitled to anything but the highest respect.' He looked at Miss O'Day to observe her reaction and Dawn with a surge of triumph played her part like the trooper she was. She did her breath-holding bit so that she went an interesting shade of pale, fluttered her lashes and trembled her lower lip again, and then whispered the words she knew the Earl being somewhat old-fashioned would expect to hear.

'Why – this is so sudden – I don't know what to say . . . Charles, my dear. I am so honoured.'

'Then the answer is yes, my dearest?' asked his Lordship, dutifully feeding Miss O'Day the line he knew she wanted to follow through.

'Of course, Charlie darling . . . whenever you wish.'

'Ah,' replied his Lordship, 'you have made me the happiest man in the world. Let's go down and tell the others our good news, and then when we've had a little celebratory champagne perhaps you would like to choose one of the family rings to wear. There is rather a nice diamond cluster with sapphires, which is said to have belonged to Mary Queen of Scots.'

'Marvellous,' said Miss O'Day, without too much enthusiasm. She didn't want a second-hand ring from some Mary or other, she told herself, but it would do until she could get Charlie to a good jewellers.

Chapter Twenty-One

After the excitement of Dawn's engagement, which Oscar insisted on keeping quiet until the film was completed when the announcement would, he felt, give the movie a new run of publicity both in Ireland and back home in the States, Marvin spent a good deal of his time down in Clancy's, as advised by James.

The morning procession of the female population of Knockpeddar en route through the lounge to the corner door Marvin ignored, since he knew what they were up to, and had in fact been invited to give them a lecture on media communication. But the evening trek of Knockpeddar's menfolk was a different ball game.

For three frustrating nights Marvin stood at the bar as close to the doorway as he could decently place himself without risking continual collision with the locals who came and went through it so surreptitiously.

In between building up his taste buds with Ned's best whiskey Marvin bought copious drinks for everyone who would stand and talk to him, but the moment he brought up the subject of the world behind the small door the recipient would look into the dark reaches of his Guinness, drain the glass and drift away, usually through the same doorway.

And it was all too speedily done for Marvin to get a good look at what lay behind the heavy burlap curtain when someone pushed it aside to duck in beneath it. And he never saw a local carry as much as a pellet gun through the doorway – the locals, he decided, were not into active sports – all their strength appeared to be needed to lift their elbows and the attached pints of stout at the end of their arms that they wrestled with in Clancy's each night. Indeed there were times when Marvin wondered if the whiskey wasn't getting to him, because when he mentioned the gunshot/backfiring everyone looked at him in amazement. None of the locals seemed to hear the noise other than himself.

Nevertheless, Marvin knew in his bones there was a good story behind that door and he was determined to get it. He had managed to develop a tenuous friendship with Ned, largely because he was spending a fair share of company dollars and made a point of never questioning the rate of exchange which rose and rose every day that dawned. Marvin also began to stay behind after closing time to help Ned with the cleaning up, and because his mother had taught him well the bar had never looked so tidy and the glasses were actually beginning to develop a shine. On the third night, when the last customer had departed and Ned had finally got the door locked and bolted, Marvin suggested they had a quiet drink before beginning the nightly washing up.

'I'll pay,' he said and Ned rapidly poured out a couple of doubles. The double promptly went to Marvin's head. After all, it was on top of the four singles he had consumed throughout the evening and Marvin was still unused to the properties of Irish whiskey and Irish measures. He threw a fifty dollar bill onto the counter. 'Let's drink the worth of that,' he said, and Ned's tired eyes brightened like a lighthouse beam. If there was one thing Ned appreciated more than a good glass of whiskey, it was a good glass of whiskey which someone else was paying for. He broke open a new bottle, rinsed out a couple of glasses and they sat down companionably by the bar.

For the next two hours Marvin replenished Ned's glass at a fast rate, carefully avoiding any mention of the activities behind the doorway in the corner. They talked of drink, money, women, subjects on which he found Ned to be remarkably well informed. They talked of blue movies, film scandals and girlie magazines, on which he found Ned most desirous to be informed, until he thought it was high time he brought up the subject he wanted to know about.

Ned shook his head carefully so as not to make himself too dizzy. 'There's nothing in there, not a thing,' he said owlishly. 'Shure an' what could there anyhow?'

'That's what I want to know,' replied Marvin, refilling Ned's glass once more. 'Why are all those guys sliding in there and what's going on? Come on Ned, you can tell me.'

Ned began to look a little hounded. He buried his nose in the brimming glass, draining it in one swallow. Marvin stoppered the bottle and pushed it down the counter. Ned eyed it, feeling a draught of loneliness as it dawned on him that Marvin was about to shut off the source of free whiskey before the bottle was emptied, and Ned didn't like waste.

'What do they do in there?' Marvin persisted.

'Is it a poker game?'

'It's not that,' said Ned unhappily, moving to the row of bottles where he poured himself a quick whiskey and even more reluctantly passing a small measure over the counter to Marvin.

'If this was the States I'd think you were running a betting shop in there or perhaps a cat house,' Marvin observed, slowly moving his bottle back up the counter. Ned giggled.

'Well, puttin' on a bet is a way of life in Ireland so it's no big deal, an' as regards the other, we don't believe in buyin' a cow when the milk's goin' for free,' he said, reaching towards Marvin's bottle with an absent-minded air, only to be beaten to it by the Publicity man who eased it just out of his reach.

'Maybe I'd better ask your clergyman, Hackett, is that his name, what's going on in there then,' said Marvin. 'After all, I've always found that the clerics hear everything that happens in their parish.'

'Oh Jesus, don't do that at all,' said Ned in panic. 'The Canon is a real innocent and he'd not be able to help you at all. Shure no one ever tells him anything that goes on in the district.'

'Well then,' continued Marvin firmly. 'Either you tell me or I go to his Reverence for the information. And if it's all that hush hush, mebbe he wouldn't approve of whatever monkey business you're all up to.'

Poor Ned was in a quandary. If he told Marvin the locals would kill him, and if he didn't the Canon would surely come down on him as only Canon Hackett could. In desperation he looked for escape and his eye caught sight of a discarded copy of a tabloid well-known for its extreme political views. 'Well now, I couldn't tell you about it before,' he said in a whisper. 'You know about the troubles we have here in Ireland?' Marvin nodded.

'Well,' said Ned, leaning confidentially over the bar and sliding his hand once more towards Marvin's bottle, this time successfully, since Marvin was too engrossed in the conversation to notice. 'We have a small battalion here in Knockpeddar that's in trainin' for the time we'll be called to help our brothers in the North, an' we do have regular meetin's in the room there and talks

– ye know the way, just to keep the boys interested, like.' He took a covert glance at Marvin to see how he was reacting, and poured both of them a refill. Marvin was enchanted.

'Gee, fancy!' he breathed. 'And all these guys going in and out of the joint are kinda – guerrillas in that IRA of yours?'

'Shure they are,' said Ned expansively. 'An' what's more, they drill and do rifle practice an' all that every week or so.' He tossed off his drink and sat down suddenly on the stool behind the bar. His legs were feeling unaccountably weak and he was not quite sure if it was the long dry season he had gone through without a good drinking session, or the heady feeling of success at finding something to tell Marvin that would satisfy him and keep him from the real truth. He was astounded at his own inventiveness, Ned not being overburdened with an active imagination. With a feeling of supreme power he went on to greater flights.

'And them fellas that come down to talk to the lads, they're the head buck cats of the organisation – we wouldn't settle for less here in Knockpeddar. I'm tellin' you, if the police in Dublin could get their hands on some of the big nobs that go in that room at times they'd all be up for promotion in the Force.'

Marvin sucked in his breath. 'And the backfiring?' he asked.

'Target Practice,' said Ned.

'What a story!' he said. 'Why, this will hit every noospaper from here to the States and back!'

'Now wait a minute,' protested Ned. 'You can't give that to the papers good, bad or indifferent. Do you want all the lads in the village to be put in jail – it's agin the law to belong to the Rebels, don't you know? Shure the women would come and get you if you sent out a word of all this.'

Marvin looked totally crestfallen. 'But think of the marvellous publicity it would make for the movie,' he said plaintively. 'The whole world would know about the movie once they read the story and Oscar would surely book me for his next epic at about three times what he pays me now.'

'Aye,' said Ned with a copious yawn, 'but if you get all the fellas put in jail he won't have any wan to act in his pictures for him and that won't do you much good then, will it?'

Marvin had to agree, since he could see that Ned had a point.

'Now remember, you can't say a word about what I told you,'

said Ned, 'An' above all, don't tell the Canon. He's very anti-IRA.'

Marvin nodded. Ned was right of course – a movie without people to appear in it was back at the script stage, and everything had gone so well that Oscar was coming in under time which was keeping him in a decent humour, and he was infinitely less insulting to Marvin than he had been on any previous jobs the Publicity man had handled. All the same, the story was much too good to waste and somehow Marvin felt he had to do something about it.

Then he had an inspiration. He could still send it out if he put an embargo on it, dating its publication to coincide with the departure of the movie unit back to the States. This would mean that the American newsmen would be lined up at the airport when they would arrive back in America and everyone would be able to give interviews on the spot. Oscar would just love the whole idea, and the functioning of the movie would not be interfered with in any way. If the villagers got a little hassle from the city fuzz, Marvin decided virtuously, they would just have to put up with it. After all, he told himself, they should not get involved with outlaw organisations in the first place. Anyway, he would be long gone before the huzaka hit the fan.

When he had finished writing the story, Marvin thought it was the best thing he had ever done. In fact he toyed with the idea of leaving the publicity business completely and trying his luck at newspaper reporting instead. He gave long thought to the headline on his copy, finally coming up with 'Gaelic Village Hotbed for Terrorists – Gunmen Bone Up in Bar before Battle for Pat's Pad,' and the story with suitable sub-headings ran to three pages, at the end of which Marvin was careful to append that the permitted date for the publication was not before one week from receipt of copy, by which time he knew the unit would be well on its way back to Hollywood.

He didn't even trust the post office with his bundle of envelopes but drove into Cork city himself to send the lot out express post to their varied destinations. Then he sat back well content. And so it might have remained for a week, had it not been that the Irish news editors had grown cautious about copy concerning terrorist activities. On top of which they wanted to avoid walking into contraventions of the Offences against the State Act, and embargo or no embargo most of them decided to do a little advance checking with their local friendly police contacts before the embargo date was up. And while one such check might be dismissed as imagination on the part of some local freelance reporter, when the more serious newspapers telephoned for corroboration that such a guerilla cell did exist in a largely unknown Irish hamlet, then the boys in blue decided they were definitely onto something. It only took a couple of top level meetings before a detachment of the country's finest policemen climbed into a discreet covered van and a couple of fast black cars to make the journey from Dublin to the outer reaches of Kerry.

For the second time in a few weeks the long black cars swept down the valley into the village which was quiet in the setting sun. The ducks were still immaculately white on the pond, and plastic flowers in the iron pots were as bright as ever, thanks to their daily dip in a well-known whiter-than-white detergent along with the household tea-cloths, and even the pig had got quite used to his playpen and actually honked to be put into it whenever he wanted to snooze.

The first limousine made an incredible swerve as it sped its way down the village street to come to an abrupt stop outside Ned's bar.

'Holy God, will you look at that paintwork?' said the driver in awe – 'I feel like a caterpillar stuck in the middle of a head of cabbage!'

His companions emerged somewhat warily onto the pavement to be joined by the occupants of the second limousine. The entire group made a concerted rush for Ned's toilet (it had been a long haul from their last stopping place) and the sanitary arrangements did not exactly endear the publican to the city men.

They sat in one of the corner booths while the driver made what he hoped were casual enquiries after one Marvin Heimer. Ned sent one of the local children in search of the Publicity man and the officers sipped pints of Guinness and endeavoured to get their collective teeth into some of Ned's sandwiches while they waited for Marvin to appear. Meanwhile they kept a constant watch on the small door with its 'No Entry' sign, and Ned in turn kept a sharp eye on the strangers. He couldn't make out exactly what they might want, though he sussed them for policemen immediately. Maybe they were being lent by the governent to the film unit for parts in the movie, he thought, but a straight enquiry on the subject brought forth no more than a stern stare and a statement that the officers were down on official business.

Ned began to sweat slightly. In his cellar he was holding around forty gallons of Pat Brodie's best poteen, maturing slowly for the coming Christmas trade among local emigrants returning in the New Year to places like Canada, America and Australia, where decent Irish home-distilled whiskey was rarer than hens' teeth. If the boys in blue were down in their official capacity who knows where they might decide to probe, should their business include a search warrant.

He was about to sidle into the back of his premises with a view to making a fast removal of the jars of poteen through the kitchen and into the depths of Knockpeddar woods, where many a consignment had rested in the past in times of official harassment, when the officer in charge came to the counter, and in soft tones that scared the hell out of Ned advised him to stay within sight until told to move.

Marvin arrived at a gallop. He had been told no more than the fact that there were some people down from the city who wanted a word with him, but with all an amateur's innocence Marvin never for a moment connected them with his journalistic revelations.

He immediately took them to be a group of tourists waiting to be shown how the great American movie is made, so he bounced forward with wide smile and outstretched hand at the ready. 'Hi there, I'm Marvin Heimer. What can I do for you fellas?' he burbled. 'If you would like the guided tour over the movie lot we can arrange that without any hassle, and I know our top star Miss Dawn O'Day would be happy to sign autographs and let you have some really great pictures. We might even persuade her to have a photo taken with you guys, and think what a picture that will make to take back to your offices when your vacation is over?'

The policemen looked at him in silence. Marvin began to sense that all was not as he believed. These guys weren't the least bit impressed by his offer – in fact they couldn't raise a grin among the lot of them.

'Mr Heimer, these are the Gardai, the Irish police force, like,' Ned whispered. 'I don't know what they want but they asked for you.'

'So?' said Marvin carelessly. 'They're cops, so what? I haven't done anything against the law since I've been in Ireland, unless I violated a speed limit while I was in Cork that I don't know about.' He smiled again at the policemen, and sat down at their table on a chair that mysteriously appeared in front of him when the lead copper guided him by the arm to where the other officers were seated.

'We want to know about this IRA story you wrote the newspapers about,' said the leading policeman, a thin-mouthed six footer with thinning hair and experienced grey eyes.

Marvin sat up. 'Who told you about that?' he asked accusingly. 'There was a special embargo on the release date for that story. Now who blew it on me?' He began to feel very hardly done by and his indignation grew as he realised that the timing was going to be shot to hell by some big mouth, who had to go sounding off to the city fuzz. Then as he sat there, looking at the hard and unsmiling faces before him, the enormity of what just might happen if things got out of hand, and Oscar got called in, began to occur to him and he started to perspire. There was a strangled moan from behind the bar, and the policeman glanced sharply over at the trembling Ned, who promptly grabbed a bar cloth and almost rubbed through the counter top in his efforts to appear not to be listening.

At that moment six of Knockpeddar's male citizens drifted in to the bar, gave the high sign to Ned and slid through the doorway. At that the police officers perked up considerably and a couple half rose from their chairs, only to be halted by their superior who tersely told them the time was not yet ripe to investigate. Ned set up a tray of large whiskeys on the house in desperation and Marvin suddenly wanted to go to the men's room.

In the village the bush telegraph was working at full spate, and every mobile Knockpeddarite hurried over to Ned's to protect the population from whatever they needed to be protected from. As usual Brenno was one of the last to hear about the arrival of the boys in blue, and it was a passing child who told him that there was an official raid on Ned's with forty policemen hauling contraband poteen from the cellar, wagon-loads of tobacco from the attic, not to mention bundles of counterfeit banknotes from under Ned's bed. It all interested Brenno greatly, and he quickly slipped the chain on Beauty and tied a couple of potato sacks on his pet's back, so that if there was any real loot being liberated they could bring back a modicum of it to thwart the Law, for whom every God-fearing Knockpeddarite had the most total contempt.

James and Susan were caught up in the excitement by accident, for they had been strolling hand in hand in Knockpeddar woods, and Susan had an armful of rhododendron sprays to prove it, Knockpeddar's silvan glades being justly famous for the profusion of rhododendron bushes which grew wild there. They had decided to amble down to Clancy's for a drink or two, and a chat with whoever might be holding up the bar that evening. They ran into Brenno, who was standing outside the door holding his goat by the collar, while he observed with some disappointment the lack of exterior activity around the public house, where he had been sure he would find bottles and boxes lying on the roadway just waiting to be deftly removed by a man and a goat to a secure hiding place.

'Arra, that fella Ned Clancy is probably up for after-hours drinkin' again,' said Brenno in disgust. James spotted Marvin looking haunted among the policemen. He hurried inside just as things were beginning to hot up a little around the vicinity of the door. Several hefty locals were standing in somewhat belligerent attitudes defying the minions of the law to break through them, and already heated voices were raised in altercation and even as James approached a deal of pushing and shoving began. Susan watched from the street doorway, nervous that James might get thumped in his role as peacemaker.

'We've got to do something before a fight breaks out,' she cried to Brenno, who was now occupied with restraining Beauty as his pet was pawing the ground in a highly excited manner. The voices from within got louder and more argumentative, and Susan feared even more for her beloved.

'Brenno, can't we stop it? In another minute someone will throw a punch and those policemen will arrest the lot of them,' Susan said, near to tears. Brenno would have enjoyed a real good knock down and drag out which, he could see, was about to erupt in the pub at any moment, but he couldn't bear to see Susan weep, so he bent down, and slipped his pet's chain and whispered into Beauty's ear.

The result was quite incredible, as Susan told James later. The goat's eyes turned bright red, he bared his teeth and ground his horns into the wooden surround of the pub door and drummed his hind legs in a most alarming fashion. Then he took off like an express train, straight into the lounge. With a single toss of his horns he upended the table around which the officers had been seated, scattering glasses, bags of crisps, and sandwich remains into the air. He butted the head officer accurately at the base of the spine, sending him head first through the counter partition to land up with his head in the slops bucket at the other side of the boarding. Two policemen were pitched among the seating, while the crowd protecting the doorway in the snug went every which way to get clear of Beauty, whose prowess was only too well known. Beauty finally caught up with the car driver and headed him through the plate glass window out into the street where he landed on top of the car bonnet.

After that Beauty trotted calmly back to his owner who rechained him, and both sat on a bench outside the pub flanked by two somewhat bruised and very irate officers of the law who kept a civil distance between themselves and the goat. Susan hurried out to them.

'Brenno, that was quite something I know, but it was a bit drastic!' she said.

'Arra not at all, Miss,' said Brenno with some satisfaction. 'Shure it was the only way to keep them fellas from arrestin' Ned and everyone in the pub. If they closed up Clancy's where would we all go for a drink?' He gave her a child-like smile. 'Anyhow, your young man came out of it without as much as a scratch, now didn't he?'

The senior policeman gave a curt nod and his companions lined up behind him. Then they all burst through the door which up to now had remained firmly closed despite the confusion in the lounge. Pistols appeared like conjuror's rabbits in the hands of the officers, which rather disconcerted the eight pint drinkers who were seated around the big television set on which a forty year old western film was being unfolded. Only one viewer turned his head when the officers crashed through the doorway, and it was the mess his pint made when he dropped it in shock that aroused the attention of the other seven males.

There was no time taken for explanations – the stern faced policemen manhandled the men into the cars, and just as swiftly they collared the unfortunate Brenno, who was obliged to leave his beloved Beauty behind because under no circumstances would the officers allow the goat into the limousine. The cars wheeled out of the village as swiftly as they had sped in, and they left two officers in the village to ensure that Ned didn't emigrate before the rest of the official party returned to continue their investigations.

But unfortunately for poor Marvin's future with Stupendo Inc. the police had made no exceptions in their sweep-up of bodies. Oscar happened to be stashed in a discreet corner of the second snug off the main bar with Miss Carmel Corcoran enjoying a very quiet drink. They had been out for a short drive together and Carmel felt that it might be safer in the confines of Clancy's pub than parked up some laneway with Oscar, whose manual perambulations grew more ambitious every time he took Miss Corcoran out for a little socialising. One of the officers did a quick sortie through the public house and Oscar, with his obviously American pale blue sharkskin suit and dark glasses and his outsize cigar, was a natural for inclusion in the police swoop on the grounds that he might be one of the Irish Americans heavily into supplying illegal arms to the miscreants the police were sure they had just captured.

Hollywood's Most Adventurous Producer was therefore hustled from his seat, bundled into the van and removed unceremoniously to jail with the rest of the locals, where, after several hours of considerable discomfort, argument and vituperation, he was finally allowed to return to Knockpeddar, only because the sergeant in charge of the police station in Cork was a film buff who, when he heard Mr Lipperstein's name, sent for the director of the Cork Film Festival committe to come and identify Oscar, after which Mr Lipperstein was set free.

James and Susan drove Canon Hackett to the city the following morning where the Canon leaned on a few official contacts and got the innocent pint drinkers out of jail and back to the village. With Brenno he was not so lucky. Brenno had been charged with aggravated assault and battery, incitement of a vicious animal to riot, behaviour likely to lead to major breach of the peace, and a raft-load of other charges that grew like Topsy the more the senior policeman examined himself for new bruises.

The Canon was extremely angry over the entire business. 'I knew no good would come of this venture,' he said crossly. 'We should never have allowed this film company into the village. That young man in charge of publicity is entirely at fault for sending out such a base fabrication. I really think the entire business is most upsetting – what with our young men being taken like common criminals to prison and all the unwelcome notoriety which has put the most unworthy ideas into the minds of the entire village. Why, the children won't even take a message these days unless they get payment for it.'

But the Canon's temper was nothing to that of Mr Lipperstein. Someone had given the story of his arrest to the news agencies, and the newspapers were filled with unflattering photographs of him on his way out of the police station with wildly inaccurate accounts of the entire procedure. Even worse, the initial deception over the activities in Ned's lounge were also splashed all over the newspapers and, all in all, Oscar felt he had been made to look a complete schmuck. What the studio bosses would say he shuddered to think, but meantime convenient heads were rolling at a rate faster than the speed of the French tumbrils. Marvin was already packing his briefcase and suitcase and Oscar was insisting that there was no way the movie could now continue. The whole thing was cancelled, kaput, washed out. Oscar was still metaphorically bleeding from wounds inflicted upon him by Miss O'Day, who declared the gross deception had nullified her contract and she was therefore opting out as and from that very moment of all connection with Mr Lipperstein and his rotten movie. Which rather left Oscar precariously ensconsed on the timber, as it were, and in a mood evil enough to strike terror in the most virtuous of breasts. He ordered Susan to book the unit back to the States as quickly as the Knockpeddar communications system could be made to achieve his wishes, which gave Miss King some leeway until Oscar would cool down, or so she hoped.

She went into his suite where he was sitting looking rather like an overdone rice pudding in his white suit and black and white spotted tie. In her hand she was carrying a jumbo sized Gaelic coffee of which Oscar had become inordinately fond since his arrival in Ireland. Sourly he put his mutton-like paw around the glass and Susan waited until he had taken an initial satisfying sip.

'Oscar,' she began delicately. 'Don't you think it would be a mistake to pull out the unit and go home without doing what you came to do – make an Irish movie with Dawn O'Day?'

'Forget it, I ain't goin' to complete dis movie – anywhere it would be shown we'd end up lookin' bigger monkeys than the chimps in Bellevue, at least on that I can agree with O'Day. An' there's no way she'll complete the picture – ya heard her cancel her contract and I've never known her change her mind over a contract. An' for once I can't say I blame her.'

'Oh, I don't know, Oscar, I think everyone is just a little paranoid over what will only be a day's wonder, after all. I feel sure you could pull this one out of the fire and end up with a good movie if you put your mind to it.'

'Humph,' said Oscar. 'That's as may be, but even if I found a trick or two what do I do without a leadin' lady?'

'I wouldn't give up on Dawn, if I were you,' advised Susan. 'I'm prepared to bet she'll come round when she cools down. Another thing, Oscar,' continued Miss King slyly, 'are we going to give the know-alls the laugh on you by quitting now – wouldn't it be better if they were to see that you're bigger than the gossip, and that you always put the show first rather than running for cover when publicity takes a little tilt at your reputation.'

Oscar visibly straightened. 'Yeah, I was never the kind of guy that ran out on a show,' he said. 'I always looked after the gang workin' it, dinnen I?'

'Of course you did, Oscar,' said Susan soothingly, 'and isn't that why you're called Hollywood's Most Adventurous Producer?'

'But I tell you one thing,' said Oscar. 'Dere's no way this movie can wrap as it is – I'd never live it down, so we'll have to think of somethin' to do about it.'

Susan agreed. Even she could see that the long commercial memories back home would perpetuate Oscar's little embarrassment, not solely because that was how the cookie crumbled but also because Mr Lipperstein was not one of the industry's favourite sons.

'You could get a rewrite job done on what we already have, you know,' she suggested. 'The story is still the same simple appealing sort that the punters love. All you need is a new angle on the basics, you drop a few scenes here and there, add in a few new ones and you have your new movie, and once it's launched no one will remember that it started out as something else.'

'Yeah, dat sounds real simple, don' it?' said Oscar with some scorn. 'Where's the new angle to come from at this stage of things – Klatch rewrote the original script four times before we all settled. What can he come up with at this stage, even supposin' O'Day comes around and agrees to stay with the movie?'

Even as he spoke Susan was developing a marvellous idea. She felt a cosy glow of triumph come over her as the whole outline flashed before her.

'Oscar, leave it with me for this morning and don't worry about Dawn. We'll win the Academy Award yet, so just you have a little patience.' She actually patted the top of his head as she left and hurried off in search of Mr Klatch and James.

Chapter Twenty—Two

By mid afternoon the three of them had a fresh outline for Oscar. They trooped into his suite accompanied by Mr Crisp, Mr Wineberger and Mr Schlimminger, all of whom were prepared to coax or bully Oscar into acceptance of the new treatment. None of them really wanted to return home without at least having a try at digging themselves out of the unpalatable stew the luckless Marvin had cooked up for them. Apart from which they really liked Susan's new idea.

They gathered around the big old mahogany table and at a nod from Mr Klatch Susan outlined what she had now come up with.

'I've been doing some research about the old country customs since we've been here, Oscar,' she began brightly. 'It seems there is a marvellous Fair here in Ireland every August. It's called Puck Fair, and for three days in a village not a hundred miles from here the natives go on a spree, and beforehand they go up into the mountains and catch a big wild billy goat which they later hoist up onto a platform and they crown him as King of the fair. Then everyone gets plastered and has a great time.'

'So?' said Oscar without much interest.

'Well,' said Susan, 'if we used the whole background of the Fair we could build a romantic affair around the heroine falling for a handsome stranger whom she meets during the Festival, and have plenty of crowd scenes, torchlight processions, kind of Mardi Gras, you know.'

'We could use all the footage we already have, apart from the fisherman's bits,' suggested Mr Crisp.

'And we could turn the whole movie into a sort of fictional documentary cum love story; that way we could enter it for one of the cultural awards at Monte Carlo,' added Mr Wineberger.

'I could get real good effects for you if you wanted illuminations,' offered Mr Schlimminger helpfully.

Oscar thought about it and then he pushed back his chair. 'Ah, shit – for a minnit I thought der was sumptin' good in dis,' he said unhappily. 'August is three weeks away – I can't keep an entire unit sittin' on its asses for three weeks until the damn fair opens.'

'Why Oscar, we don't need to go to Puck Fair at all,' explained Susan with infinite charm. 'We can build our own set right here – one small village is pretty much like another when all is said and done, and you have your actors trained in already. Why move the unit to somewhere else?' She drew a final deep breath. 'We won't even have to waste time looking for a Puck goat either, since we have one right here in the village.'

Oscar leaped to his feet in an unaccustomed burst of energy. 'No!' he shouted, little specks of foam suddenly appearing around the corners of his mouth. 'I won't have that damn goat. Dat bum's lucky I didn't sue after that wild animal of his attacked me.'

'But Oscar, you won't have a single thing to do with Beauty,' explained Susan patiently. 'Don't you see, the goat will be tied up on a platform about thirty feet up in the air during the entire time you'll be hiring him, and if you're that worried you could have Brenno stashed up there with him.' She crossed her fingers in the hope that Brenno's devotion to his pet would not allow him to stay on the ground while his goat was harnessed up on the platform.

Oscar thought about it some more, and then he almost chuckled – at least he made like he was smothering a burst of flatulence, a noise which indicated that he was at least amused. 'Dis means that dose two yobs will be stuck up a pole all day an' half the night?' he enquired. 'Dat'll teach dose bastards!'

And immediately the group saw they had sold him the new movie outline. Mr Klatch gathered up his notepads and pencils and disappeared into the depths of Ned Clancy's where, after eight hours of concentrated work, aided by James and copious draughts of Ned's best porter, he managed to have the script completed by closing time.

The major snag to all the planning was the undeniable fact that Brenno was languishing in the jail in Cork city. Frantic telephone calls by James failed to arouse any agreement in the matter of his release by the police, until Miss Dunphy, an interested not to say concerned spectator of the telephone calls, in her capacity as public telephone switchboard operator, suggested that a little political muscle might be called for.

'Fonsie!' she advised quietly, and James made his way to Mr

O'Malley's house where Fonsie was grateful to be interrupted in the middle of a domestic argument with his lady wife.

'Women!' said Mr O'Malley, as he ushered James into his office. 'I declare to God they never know when to give a man a bit of peace, or a bit of anything much else either.'

It hadn't been a good couple of days for Fonsie. He had taken himself off to Dublin where he had been presented with a sizeable bill for a pretty little fur jacket by his actress friend, it being her birthday come November, and on his return he had had to face recriminations on his home ground, because Mrs Fonsie had been informed when she telephoned his government offices that he hadn't been in the place for two months. Fonsie was finding it hard to explain where he had hidden himself and why, and he had already been well and truly slated by a number of local voters for his absence from the village when the police arrived.

'Public life is a mug's game,' he said, closing the door. 'But what can you do when the people want you to represent them?'

James nodded. 'It's clear you are the most influential man in the area, Fonsie,' he said earnestly. 'Which is why I decided to come directly to you myself on our producer's behalf.'

Fonsie preened himelf – a big Yankee producer needing a favour from the local politician was sweet music to his ears. Who knew where the favour might lead to. 'You're havin' a bit of trouble – deliveries, unions or what ?' he asked.

'Neither,' replied James. 'We just have one of our future actors in a little jam – like he's in jail.'

'Ah,' said Fonsie. 'Got a little drunk in Cork, did he? The police there are very strict with strangers, but shure you can bail him out without any trouble once he sobers up.'

'It's not as simple as that,' said James. 'You see, he's in on a number of charges for things like assault, incitement and so on. But I'm sure you could help us with a word in the right ear.'

Fonsie looked at him. 'You wouldn't be takin' the mickey out of me now, would ye?' he asked, 'because I'm thinkin' that the person we're talkin' about is that Brenno O'Mahoney.'

'That's right Fonsie,' nodded James seriously. 'Mr Lipperstein needs him for the movie so we have to get him released. Otherwise Oscar will pull out the unit and there won't be another dollar for anyone.'

Fonsie looked horrified. 'Ohmigod,' he said, mopping the

sudden sweat that dewed his upper lip. 'That'll be entirely disastrous – shure we haven't milked – I mean – we haven't established a long-term liasion between our two communities of sufficient durability that we would put distance between you and us. As our Revered Leader might put it, were he discussing the situation at this point in time.'

James looked at him in considerable admiration. 'Fonsie,' he said, 'your Revered Leader would never have put it so succinctly – didn't I do the right thing coming over to ask for your assistance in this matter, which is, after all, relatively minor to someone of your expertise.'

Fonsie looked gratified. 'Now where exactly is Brenno being held and who's in charge of the case?' he said, pulling a sheet of paper towards him and taking out his gold fountain pen with the sort of flourish that had endeared him to the nuns of at least thirty convents in his electoral area, whose best parlours he had graced with his presence at regular intervals through the years they had been voting him back into his political seat. 'Sergeant O'Hare, is it? Well now, that's a bit of convenience. Isn't he a second cousin of the wife's, and even though it may well cost me a promotion for him to get him to spring Brenno, won't it be worth it in the end,' said Fonsie in satisfaction when James gave him the details.

And watching Fonsie in action when they finally drove back to the jail in Cork, James was almost tempted to recommend to Oscar that he should hire the politician and take him back to the States with the unit. Never, he told Susan, had he seen such a talent for manipulation, back-scratching, bribery, veiled blackmail and sheer flattery, as Fonsie produced. However it was most effective and Brenno was delivered into their charge with no more than a token payment from James of a bail bond for fifty pounds, to ensure that Brenno would eventually turn up at the court for his trial.

When James and Susan finally told him of their plans to turn Beauty into a film star, Brenno almost died from sheer ecstasy. 'Ye mean Beauty is goin' to be King Puck himself?' Brenno asked incredulously, looking from one to the other.

'Sure he is,' said James. 'We told you that somehow or other we'd get Beauty in the movies – now here is his chance to become famous!'

Brenno went back to his farm with an extra can of stout for his pet, and even though Beauty did not exactly appreciate his efforts Brenno gave him a bath in shampoo he had bought from Miss Dunphy, specially to make the goat's coat as shining and silky as the shampoo advertising promised. And when Beauty was finally laundered and dried Brenno brushed him, polished his horns with butter and even put a little boot polish on the goat's hoofs. When Brenno was finished Beauty looked quite magnificent, so Brenno installed him in his mother's old bedroom for the night, just in case the goat might get dirty again if he were left to his own devices in the barn.

They were all on the set bright and early next morning. High above on a platform Beauty was hoisted into place accompanied by Brenno, who settled down comfortably on the pile of straw on the platform with a gallon jar of the national brew thoughtfully provided by order of Mr Wineberger, who did not want Brenno climbing up and down during the filming breaks for sustenance over in the pub.

Beauty was already wearing the tinsel coronet with which, though she did not yet know about it, Miss O'Day was to crown the goat as King of the Festival when the Director shot the opening scene. The goat did not like the feel of the ornament over his horns, and he grew increasingly bad-tempered as he tossed his head, trying vainly to remove the object from over his ears.

Mr Crisp, the Director, was delighted – here was a somewhat new, strange and fierce animal with which he could titillate the American audiences and he spent a considerable amount of the morning shooting Beauty from every angle, getting in each eyeball roll, every bared tooth and every toss of Beauty's white forelock, while Brenno held his pet firmly by the chain and consoled him with regular saucers of black porter when camera breaks permitted. By lunch-time Beauty was tired after all the plunging about and also more than a little sozzled after the libations Brenno had administered to him. He settled down finally in the hay on the platform and fell asleep snoring loudly. Mr Crisp decided it would be a good time to have Miss O'Day do the crowning scene, since she was supposed to meet the handsome stranger after she had performed the goat's coronation bit and he was anxious to get the dicey part of Dawn's meeting with Beauty in the can as fast as possible.

Fervently Mr Crisp prayed that nothing would occur to cause Miss O'Day any little upset. Only his Lordship's intervention the night before had prevented the cancellation by Miss O'Day of her part in the movie, revamped or not. James and Susan had pointed out the consequences of a pull-out by the Stupendo star from the film, and the Earl was only too conscious what a personal loss to his rental business one way and another an exodus of film personnel would cause at this moment. Another week or two and the bed and board, the special utilities, not to mention the various charges for wear and tear, would not only add the new central heating plant but would also remodel the old-fashioned kitchens and re-roof the mews. So he exerted all his polished Irish charm and persuaded Dawn that her artistic future depended on sticking with her contract. She was now in her dressing caravan, blissfully unaware of what was ahead of her when she came on the set.

'Can you prop that animal up so that he looks as if he is awake?' Mr Crisp called up to Brenno. 'If so, we'll lower you both down.'

'Shure I can,' replied Brenno agreeably, 'but do you want me to wake up Beauty for ye? I'm sure I could get him to stand up by himself if I tried.'

'Jesus, don't even attempt it' replied Mr Crisp. 'The only way I'll be able to get Dawn within a mile of that thing is if he stays unconscious, and I'm not even sure that'll be successful either.'

Brenno and Beauty were lowered carefully down from the platform onto a low staging beneath the scaffolding. Beauty opened a sodden eye as the platform landed on the stage floor and then rolled over on his back resuming his snoring.

In vain Brenno attempted to get him into a position where his head was in an upright position for the crown to be replaced in situ, but Beauty was a drunken weight that defied all his efforts. Mr Crisp called for volunteers to help but there were no takers, even when he offered extra money for the assistance. Then he remembered something he had seen back home, and he ordered a sling to be constructed from a strip of webbing and some rope. This he got Brenno to pass under Beauty's stomach and then the sling was secured to a winch. A couple of heaves and the sleeping animal was hauled up on its four legs and before it could collapse again Brenno pushed a bale of straw on either side of his pet, sandwiching him securely so that he could not fall down. Mr

Crisp took the precaution of pushing a couple of his own personal sleeping pills into the goat's mouth in between snores, so that he would stay safely without waking until the crowning scene was shot and Miss O'Day was back again in her dressing-room.

When she came on set Dawn got her first look at the sleeping goat and immediately all hell broke loose. She absolutely refused to have anything to do with it, and declared that her contract did not include coming into close proximity with a dangerous animal. She stalked off the set and Mr Crisp sent for Oscar, who came at a gallop accompanied by Susan.

Oscar wanted no more hassle. He wanted his movie completed and he wanted the chance of a cultural spin-off, and the last thing he needed was a temperamental leading lady. But he failed to bully or bribe Miss O'Day from her avowed intention of stopping work as and from that very moment. Not even for his Lordship, she said, would she venture onto the set alongside that stinking heap of skin and hair.

Oscar went into a huddle with his trusted right-hand woman. 'Will I get dat Irish guy she had the hots for, and see if he could persuade her back on the set?' he asked.

Susan shook her head. 'He's lost his charm at the moment, now that she's got herself engaged to the Earl,' she told Mr Lipperstein.

'Well, what then?' Oscar asked, chewing his cigar to a mangled wreck.

Susan smiled at him. 'Leave it to me, Oscar, I think I just may know the right button to push.' She disappeared in the direction of Miss O'Day's dressing caravan, closing the door firmly behind her.

Once inside Susan wasted no time on the niceties with Dawn. 'Get your ass back on the set, Dawn, unless you want his Lordship to hear about certain ghostly appearances which were set up for specific reasons,' she said tersely. 'His Lordship is a little sensitive about being taken to the cleaners ever since his first wife played him for a sucker, so unless you want to give up your chances of becoming a real live Countess, I think you'd better get over your aversion to that goat. Otherwise James and I might be inclined to put a certain photograph where his Lordship would be most likely to see it!'

Dawn gritted her teeth until she almost ground down her

porcelain cappings, but she went back on the set, much to Mr Crisp's relief and Oscar's amazement. It was as well that Beauty was still out for the count because, Brenno told Susan later with some annoyance, that Miss O'Day had banged down the crown on his pet's head hard enough to spancel him. But because she was terrified she would have to do a retake Dawn reached new heights of histrionic abilities, and for the first time in her career a single take sufficed to wrap the scene up to everyone's satisfaction.

However among the extras of Knockpeddar the crowd scenes of the Puck Festival were what everyone was waiting for. They had been informed by now of the proposed script changes which were greeted with considerable jubilation by the entire village population, and the street was truly an amazing sight at eight o'clock next morning which was the day scheduled for the main shoot. If there was one thing Knockpeddar loved it was a party, particularly one that someone else was paying for, and the place was thick with people, at least half of whom were certainly conspicious by their absence on the studio payroll. But they were not overly concerned with the day's pay as much as with the day's drinking. The prospect of a free and uninterrupted procession of creamy-headed pints or amber measures of the hard stuff being doled out without anyone calling 'Time' was the closest thing most of them would ever come to a religious experience.

The addition of several false pub fronts down the street proved a little confusing for the arrivals who had not the original experience of being 'Took On' in the early weeks, and it took several hours before the crowding around the only authentic hostelry in the place, Ned Clancy's, was under control.

When Ned had seen the crowds he opened the pub to catch the early trade, but he simply could not keep up with the demand and finally James took pity on him and moved in behind the bar to give him a hand serving the thirsty hordes that milled around the counters.

'Jasus, I never seen the likes of this before,' said Ned helplessly. 'There's no way I'll have enough stock to keep goin' – we'll be drunk dry before teatime!'

'So why don't you trot off somewhere and collect fresh stock and I'll handle things here until you get back,' offered James and with relief Ned got out the battered van he owned and took himself off to replenish his dwindling shelves before opportunity turned the back of its head on him again.

Half an hour later the bar was out of the distilleries' best amber brew, and James went down to the cellar for replacement bottles, only to find there were none. Hurriedly he searched the shelves without any luck. Meanwhile frenzied rappings from upstairs suggested his customers were growing not only thirsty but irate, and it was then James spotted the jars of his Uncle Pat's poteen reposing in the darkest reaches of the bar cellar. With a prayer of gratitude he grabbed a couple of containers and hared it back upstairs. From then on it was noticeable that the merrymakers at the Festival were all shorts imbibers-Knockpeddar's locals got the bush telegraph working at full pelt, and James actually had to dispatch Susan out to his Uncle Pat for fresh supplies of the Brodie brew.

Mr Crisp kept this cameras rolling – he caught little artistic gems on film, like Paudie Quinn managing to spit twice his own championship length. He caught the electrifying sight of one local putting his waistcoat carefully on the bemused village pig before getting the animal up on its hind legs to dance, and he filmed the interesting pursuit of a short, plump young woman by two burly young men, who were chased in turn by a dangerous looking mongrel dog with yellow teeth and no tail. There was an exciting terrier race won by a black crossbred dog, which promptly bit the judge and got kicked for his temerity, causing a slight altercation between the bitten one and the dog's owner.

Outside Ned's, keeping close to the source of alcoholic supply, a card game was in progress and Mr Crisp zoomed in on the players. 'Say fella, can ya put down that ace of diamonds and make like you're winnin' a trick?' Benny called to one of the players, as he moved in for a close-up shot of the card game. There was an instant stony silence among the six men around the table.

'I thought ye said ye hadn't a trump . . . ye reneged, ye bugger.' shouted a ginger-haired man, throwing his hand of cards on the ground and pushing back his chair. Benny moved rapidly out of the way as the entire table of players erupted into the middle of the street, fists flying. With unholy joy the street got into the battle. They poured out of the pub and even came at a run from the laneways where they had been button counting with a fair percentage of the local female talent. Mr Crisp was in his artistic element. His cameras were everywhere he could send them, and he viewed the blood and gore with infinite delight, while he avoided the flying glasses and furniture with dexterity.

By this time the originators of the fight were safely ensconsed in Ned Clancy's bar with their arms around each other, each man clutching a large measure of Brodie's best poteen in a bloodstained hairy fist, while they reminisced together about previous bouts they had enjoyed in past times.

Mr Crisp only called a halt when he saw that the street battles were running out of steam through sheer exhaustion, and no one even noticed as the unit pulled out and put away the equipment until next call. Ned drove into the village, avoiding recumbent bodies scattered on the pathways and in the yard at the back of his pub. He staggered in through the back door with a crate of whiskey. Benny Crisp and Oscar were seated together, each with a glass of clear colourless liquid in front of them.

'I ain't never seen anythin' like that lot,' said Benny. 'Dey wuz inspired Oscar, inspired. We'll get an award for dis movie or my names's not Benny Crisspovich.'

He reached for his glass and took a deep and thirsty swallow of the contents. 'Kee-rist!' he gasped through watering eyes. 'If that's what dey drink no wonder dey get such a head of steam up. Dat stuff's pure dynamite, whatever it is!'

Oscar took a cautious sip. He swallowed, sipped again and then sat up. 'Benny,' he said with awe, 'whatever dis stuff is, I wanna know how dey produce it. It's better than mother's milk, an' if we could make it back home we'd ride the greatest gravy train of all time.'

Ned looked at the empty poteen containers standing on top of the servery counter. 'Sweet Mother of God,' he said, 'Who brought those up here?'

'I did,' replied James with satisfaction, as he collected another batch of empty tumblers from the bar tables. 'Ned, my Uncle Pat is lost as a farmer; he should be in the distillery business. We couldn't get it moving out fast enough . . . whatever its going to cost the company it's money well spent.' He lowered his voice. 'Even Oscar is downing the stuff – he's on his third glass of it already.'

Ned seized the last half-empty container and shoved it under the counter. 'My God above!' he said. 'If the police had come in the bar while you were handin' out that stuff I'd lose me licence for ever – we're not allowed to have it, let alone sell it over a bar counter.'

'Well they didn't, and everyone had a great booze-up and Benny Crisp is delighted with the day's shooting, so everything is just terrific,' said James unrepentantly. 'I'll tell you though,' he continued, as Ned heaved the containers down to the cellar again, 'Oscar will be looking for some of that to take home with him, so you could make a good profit on a few bottles.'

For a moment Ned was interested but then the thought of being caught put the idea of a temporary profit from his mind. Unless, of course, he could come up with a way of showing Oscar how to get it out of the country without being found out by officialdom.

Brenno and Beauty had quietly betaken themselves to the food wagon while the fight was in progress, Brenno reckoning that it would be Beauty's only chance of a good meal until night-time. Beauty had shown surprising preference for spaghetti bolognaise, when offered such diverse delights by his owner as hamburgers, scrambled eggs, lettuce, grilled bacon and sardines. They had the canteen to themselves, everyone having raced off to watch the outcome of the fight. Now, well satisfied with their meal, the pair arrived in Ned's, ready for a couple of pints of stout before making their way back to the farm.

Benny and Oscar, after their fifth drink of Brodie's best brew, were in love with the whole world. They greeted Brenno with delight. 'Have a drink, have two!' urged Mr Crisp as he staggered to the counter and brought back another round. Brenno took him up on his offer and a bowl of the black stuff was quickly placed before his pet, and Benny generously laced it with a dash of poteen.

Two rounds of the same mixture later Beauty weaved over to Mr Crisp and placed his head in Benny's lap, gazing soulfully up at him while he suddenly sat down on his haunches.

'Look,' said Mr Crisp, 'that goat loves me. He's like a pet dog. Now isn't that sumpthin'?' He patted Beauty lovingly between the horns, and to his infinite delight the goat licked him on the nose, before moving across to Oscar whom he suddenly began to nuzzle in a most libidinous manner. 'Oscar, I gotta marvellous idea,' said Benny, carefully rescuing Oscar's tie, which Beauty was endeavouring to remove from Mr Lipperstein's neck, in the mistaken idea that it was a length of spaghetti.

'Yeah?'

'Let's take this goat out to the States an' do a promotion tour with him for the movie. He'd go down a real bomb with the kids.'

Oscar considered it. He had a benevolently happy glow towards all of his fellow men and their pet goats. 'Why not?' he said, waving his empty glass at Mr Crisp who nodded at James for a refill.

'We might even get a whole spin-off business going,' mused Mr Crisp dreamily '– toy goats, printed tee-shirts, story books, a strip cartoon for syndication in the comic sections, breakfast cereal giveaways – Jeeze Oscar, we could be on to a real good thing!'

Brenno looked from one to the other of them – Beauty was going to be world famous, it was quite obvious, but taking his pet to America didn't appeal to him at all. 'Beauty wouldn't go anywhere without me, Mister – he gets lonesome for me,' Brenno said somewhat timidly.

Benny looked at him for the first time. 'Well, that goat needs a manager,' he said expansively, 'I guess you'll have to be it.'

Brenno looked frightened. 'Ah, shure I'd know nuttin' about managin' anythin'' he said. Then as James brought over the refilled glasses, Brenno saw the solution to his problem. 'But Mr Brodie here could be Beauty's manager, if he'd agree. I'd trust him to do the right thing by me goat, so I would.' And he smiled trustingly at James.

Beauty slurped up the last of his stout and then sat beside his master. Brenno put his arm around his pet.

James looked at the little man. 'Brenno,' he said gently, 'I couldn't look after Beauty the way you could. I'll manage the business side of things for both of you, but you really will have to come along with us and see that Beauty is properly cared for.'

Brenno took a delighted look at Ned who was leaning across the counter, listening unbelievingly to the conversation. 'See now, Ned Clancy,' he said triumphantly, 'and the lot of yiz said me goat was no use. But he's goin' to Amerikay and so am I. An' when we come back we'll expect to be drinkin' in the *front* lounge sittin' at a *table*!'

Having seen the rushes of 'Gaelic Affair', which Benny Crisp who invented it was convinced was the most subtle title of the year, the entire production team up to and including Oscar felt that they had a money spinner in the can at last – it only remained for it to be edited back in Hollywood, and already someone was working on the kind of musical background that non-Gaels were convinced was truly representative of the Irish ethos, especially if they happened to have served their musical apprenticeship in Brooklyn.

Mr Lipperstein was full of plans for a coast-to-coast promotion tour, especially since James had been wise enough to have had a cast-iron contract signed on Brenno's behalf before Oscar and Benny recovered from their night of poteen drinking.

Surprisingly enough they both came to next day around lunch-time without the smallest degree of a hangover, which prompted Oscar to take his big decision.

James and Susan drove out to say goodbye to James' Uncle Pat, whose excellent brew had done much to provide the successful outcome of the movie. They were surprised to find Mr Brodie busily packing not only the travelling trunks, but also his poteen equipment, which he was carefully dismantling and spreading unobtrusively amongst his luggage, his fishing gear, his disassembled bicycle and his old-fashioned wind-up gramophone.

'I was going to come in later and see you, me boy,' said his uncle as James climbed out of the automobile and opened the door for his lady love.

'What's going on Uncle Pat?' James asked, surveying the profusion of coils, bits and pieces, which no one but an Irishman would recognise as being the guts of a first class poteen worm.

'Well, I had a caller yesterday – no less than that Producer fella of yours – the one with a face like a bull with the Red Water,' said Pat, as they sat down in the big kitchen with a mug of strong tea apiece. 'He offered to set me up in the production business if I'd come with him to America. He offered a sixty-forty percentage as long as I give him all the free poteen he can drink. It seemed like a good deal, so I said I'd try it.'

'But I'm sure there are liquor laws to prevent you making poteen in the United States as well as here in Ireland,' said Susan.

'Not when I finish mixing it with a few other things,' said Mr Brodie with a wink. 'By the time I'm finished inventin' a new kind of drink, even the United States President will be askin' for it.'

'You mean you're actually going to do it all nice and legal?' asked James in some surprise.

'I might as well,' said his uncle. 'I'm getting too old to go on the run from the coppers. Anyway, I always wanted to try living in the States but your father beat me to it when he went, so I was the one who had to stay here with the parents.'

'Won't you miss Knockpeddar?' asked Susan.

'Well,' said Mr Brodie, looking into the middle distance, 'I thought I wouldn't miss it so much if I knew I had someone of the family living here so that I could come home on a visit every five years or so.'

James looked at him – hardly daring to believe what he was hearing. 'Me?' he asked.

'Who else?' replied his uncle. 'But there's a condition. This young woman will have to be part of the deal – otherwise you're daft enough to get caught making the poteen! Here,' he continued, 'have a swig of this batch until I tell you how to make it – my customers will expect you to produce as good a quality as I've got them used to, so you'd better learn fast.'

The Earl of Grange Peddar too was packing – wisely he had decided to accompany Miss O'Day back to America, where it was felt that his voice and presence would add some upper class tone to the movie promotion. Dawn felt the coast-to-coast trip would be an ideal way of getting a free honeymoon if they married with all the vulgar publicity the company could muster, and, as she told his Lordship, it would save them the considerable cost of putting on the nuptials themselves in Ireland. They could, she pointed out, have a really super gala celebration when they returned to Knockpeddar after the movie promotion was concluded. Meantime she would have an interior decorator flown from the States to do a little making over at the Grange. It all fulfilled Riordan's worst expectations, and he decided that the time had come to inform his Lordship that the future comfort of the de Lucey family could no longer be his responsibility.

Anyway, the way things were going with the commercial world of Knockpeddar, Riordan had been made an offer he didn't want to refuse – the job of Co-ordinator of Knockpeddar Enterprise Limited, a cooperative formed by the ladies of the village, whose ambitious plans needed the entrepreneurial abilities of his Lordship's butler to match the organisational talent of Miss Dunphy. For Allo O'Brien the world of movie fame ceased to attract, once he totalled up his earnings and found he could now buy the farm alongside his father's property. A fine, upstanding young man with land had unlimited areas of romantic satisfaction available to him without seeking it across the waters of the Atlantic.

As for Miss Carmel Corcoran, Oscar took a chance and signed her up on a six month contract, for which Miss Corcoran at last showed her gratitude in a practical fashion. Before they departed for the airport, after consultations with Ned Clancy, Carmel filled six mineral water bottles with the best poteen, labelled them 'Holy Water' and stashed them along with her prayer books and rosary beads, like the good religious Irish colleen that she was.

Canon Hackett watched the last of the limousines pull out of the village and heaved a sigh of relief. Perhaps Knockpeddar would now at last return to its original rural peacefulness, he told himself.

But as he stood there, bathed in the afternoon sun, down the road to his infinite dismay came the shambling figure of Mary Heffernan's transient from Galway.